Contents

Bloody Badajoz

Book 8 in the Napoleonic Horseman Series

By

Griff Hosker

Bloody Badajoz

Published by Sword Books Ltd 2020

Spain in 1812
Author's Map

Prologue

They say marry in haste and repent at leisure. I am not sure how true that saying is but I did marry in haste, however, that haste was forced upon me by the French Army and Emperor Napoleon Bonaparte. In truth, I never regretted for Emily was the love of my life and asking her to be my wife was the best decision I ever made. I would not have been able to come home and seal the knot but for the fact that I had been badly wounded at the battle of Fuente de Oñoro and given leave. There was an irony in that my regiment, the 11th, had arrived in Spain just as I had left. When I reached England, I could not have even dreamed that I would be able to make her my wife. However, fate intervened and I had been obliged to visit the home of the woman who would become my wife, Emily Smithson, for I had saved both her and her father's lives in Spain and, if I am to be true to myself, I had found myself smitten by Emily as soon as I met her. She was the widow of an officer killed at Roliça, Lieutenant de Lacey. When she had discovered the truth of her husband's death she had reverted to her maiden name because it had saved embarrassment from the officers who knew the truth. When Emily had left Spain, she had intimated to me that she had feelings for me and as a soldier who had never had time for such things it had triggered strange thoughts in my head. On the journey from Portugal, I had dwelt on her words and wondered if I should risk visiting her. The voyage home gave me chance to think and I decided to take the risk. When I reached King's Lynn in July I was, to say the least nervous for I was entering a world for which I was totally unprepared. I could face any number of enemies and hope to survive but one hint of rejection from the lady would be as a mortal wound to me. I was prepared for her to have had second thoughts and decide that to be widowed once was enough. If that was true then I would have gone to my club, recuperated and returned to the Peninsula and carried on being a soldier. To my surprise, both she and her father were delighted that I wished to marry her. Godfrey Smithson was an MP and a local landowner who wielded much power in the area. The banns were read, and we were wed within the month.

Sending Sergeant Sharp off to enjoy visiting the small town in which he had grown up and to visit the graves of his family, I had the briefest of honeymoons with Emily. We spent it in the family home at King's Lynn. Her father took himself off to visit friends in the north, at

Wynyard Hall, and we were left with a couple of servants and sunshine-filled days.

One day, a week after we had been married, we were walking across fields at the rear of the house. I suddenly laughed and Emily asked, "What is so funny, Robbie?"

"Nothing but I have to pinch myself." She knew my whole story for I had told her all before we were married. She had to know my past and the baggage I brought. I had not omitted anything, including the people I had killed. If she was going to marry me then she had to know the dark side of Robbie Matthews. "It is just that since I was barely a youth, I have had a sword in my hand, and I have been riding to war. Even when I stayed in Sicily with my Italian family, I was a fugitive. This is the first peace I have known… well, ever and I have to pinch myself so that I know it is not a dream."

"Robbie, your business in London does well and you are a rich man, and you can sell your commission and even if you were not my father is rich. You have a home, Bilson's Farm, and no one has yet lived in it, save your man, Jenkins! You need not fight, and no one could say that you have not done your duty. The last wound needed forty stitches and your body looks like poor tapestry work. Enough is enough and the next wound may be fatal. Leave the army." I was learning that Emily was not afraid of voicing her opinions.

I stopped and held both of her hands so that I could look into her eyes, "I know what you are saying but in your heart you are conflicted, for you know that I am needed to fight England's enemies and if I did as you said then the initial happiness would sour. I think that you know me. Do you honestly believe that I could let the Dunbars and Mountshafts of this world fight in my place? You saw how small flaws and weakness can result in not only tragedy but disaster. For good or ill, I am a good soldier, and, in the Peninsula, I can make a difference. Sir Arthur has good men advising him, but he needs my eyes and ears."

I saw tears in her eyes, "You are right in all you say for I have witnessed your skills at first hand and yet I would not lose you."

"You say that my body is a badly made tapestry and you are right, yet I have survived thus far and I honestly believe that I am destined to survive this war. If anything, I have more reason to live for I have you. Hitherto, I have rarely taken leaves. Now that will change. The army rarely fights in winter and I will ask Sir Arthur for time off. How does that suit?"

She reached up and kissed me, "Better than nothing!"

"And we will visit Bilson's Farm and you can inspect the house I have had built."

"Are you fit enough to ride?"

"I will have to be and this will be an easier test than the roads of Portugal and Spain. We do not have far to ride." I knew that I did not need to worry about Emily who was a good rider. Sharp had returned from his visit north and so the three of us rode to the farm I had bought and demolished. The last time I had seen it had been when there was one dwelling and that a small one used to house Jenkins. I knew, from Mr Hudson, that all the work had finished, and that Jenkins was managing my estate well. I also knew that Jenkins had married, and the house had servants. Emily would have ladies to look after her.

The farm was on the outskirts of London at Tottenham Court. It was not a large estate, but I am no farmer. We stopped to view it and I was impressed. I had seen the drawings; indeed, I had been party to drawing them up but now I saw them translated into a hall and stables. Emily shook her head, "And you would rather fight than live here? I love my father's home, but it is old. This is new! Come, I cannot wait to see inside."

I knew Jenkins was conflicted when we arrived. He was pleased to see me, but I knew that he and his wife, Annie, would have liked to prepare for us. I put the two of them at ease straight away, "What a fine job you have done for me. I thank you and this is Mrs Matthews, I have married, Rafe."

"That is good news sir, and will you be coming to live here?"

I looked at Emily, "I am still serving His Majesty and will be returning to Spain soon."

Emily laughed, "Do not worry, Mr Jenkins, my husband may be returning to fight Bonaparte, but I shall be moving down here! You are a goose, Robbie! I lived with my father because I was a widow but that is his home, and this shall be mine." She turned to Rafe and Annie. "I shall just need a week after the major leaves to sort out my affairs." She waved a hand around the entrance hall, "This is lovely but if it was furnished and decorated by my husband then there may need to be changes made!"

Annie Jenkins beamed, "You are right there my lady! It is what I have said since I came here! This was a house built and furnished by soldiers who are happy with a tent over their head so long as they are fed!"

As we toured the estate Sharp and I were reunited with Joe Fenwick who had been a sergeant in the 23rd Light Dragoons. He had lost his leg in Spain and I had given him a job on the estate. I knew, from Mr Hudson, that it was not charity and he was raising horses for me. He stumped over on his wooden leg, "Why Major, Sharpie! It is good to see you both."

"And you Joe. I see the loss of the leg has not impaired you."

"No sir, although my dancing has suffered!"

That made all of us laugh and, indeed, the three days we spent there were joyous. We renamed the farm one night as we ate in the hall. Now that I was married and might have children and heirs, we named it Matthews Farm. I thought to call it D'Alpini Manor but that seemed presumptuous and so the simpler, Matthews Farm became its name. We had to return to King's Lynn with Emily so that we could prepare for our journey to Portsmouth and then Lisbon. In the end, we had an extra week for Sir Godfrey used his influence to get us berths on a ship he owned which was able to travel from King's Lynn. The journey to Portsmouth and the longer sea voyage would have taken a week and so I enjoyed Emily and the peace of East Anglia for a little longer. The parting was tearful but there was joy there too. A man can fight for his country but fighting for his family is better and, for the first time since my father was executed by the revolution, I had a family and this one was one I cared about.

Part 1

Ciudad Rodrigo

Chapter 1

The voyage south was one of reflection for Alan and me. The farm we had left was now a home. I had not seen the building site since before I had left for Spain to help Sir Arthur build his defences at Torres Vedras. It was still far from complete but, thanks to my new wife, I was able to see it as it might be. As my sergeant and I watched England slip by, we spoke of living at my new home. Alan was quite honest with me, "When I went to the graveyard and saw all of the graves of my family I realised that I have to make a mark. I have money set by, and Mr Hudson manages it well for me. I shall buy something close by."

"You have no need, Alan, for Emily and I would be more than happy for you to live on the farm."

"But I want a home for the wife I have yet to meet, sir."

I laughed, "And the estate is more than big enough for you to have one built. Find yourself a woman and we will have Mrs Matthews design you a house. It seems that you and I do not have an eye for such things!" Emily had made it quite clear to me that some of the features I had come up with were far from satisfactory. The rest of the voyage was spent planning for a future which did not involve marching, fighting and fearing a knife in the night.

We reached Lisbon in August and spent four days there for I was briefed about the war. Despatches were waiting which I had to deliver to Viscount Wellington. The news I heard was mixed. We had gained Almeida without a fight and Marshal Beresford and his Portuguese Army had defeated Soult, but the first and second sieges of Badajoz had both ended in bloody and abject failure. The word around headquarters was that Viscount Wellington was less than happy with the way the sieges had been prosecuted. Perhaps it is selfish, but I knew that my old regiment, the 11th, would not have been involved in the disaster. Cavalry did not besiege! Colonel Fenton was a fine officer and the 11th were his family but he had not fought in either Spain or Portugal and neither had the regiment. I feared that like many other new regiments they would pay the price of coming up against Bonaparte's veterans. When you fought in the Peninsula you learned quickly or paid the price and died! I was not sure if I would be with them but so long as I was in the same army, I could offer advice.

Donna Maria, the widow whose life I had once saved, had been fond of me and in her will had left a small house in Lisbon to me. It had a stable and Paulo lived in the house and looked after our horses, Donna and Mary. I had used my contacts with the D'Alpini family and Mr Hudson to have Paulo also act as an agent for me. The profits from my business, importing wines, whilst not great, were enough to maintain the house, pay Paulo and provide a small profit. We found it easier to stay in the house rather than either at the embassy or headquarters.

We were about to leave for the British camp when a young lieutenant rode up to our accommodation, "Major Matthews, sir, I have been sent to ask you to come to the embassy. There is someone who wishes to speak with you."

I frowned for I had been there the previous day and I was now ready for the ride north.

"Sharp, have our gear put on a packhorse and I will get back as soon as I can." I mounted Donna and followed the young officer. "Who is it wishes to speak with me?"

"He is a Colonel, sir, but he doesn't wear a uniform." Even before the lieutenant told me the officer's identity, I recognised the description. "Colonel Selkirk is his name. A Scot, I believe."

My heart sank. The Colonel was Intelligence and often worked behind enemy lines. He was Sir Arthur's version of Joseph Fouché, Bonaparte's spymaster. Although Colonel Selkirk was responsible for my commission in the British Army, my encounters with him were something I dreaded for he used Sergeant Sharp and me as though we were disposable. For him, this was a great game he played with Bonaparte!

I knew the room he occupied for it was filled with his noxious cigar smoke. He beamed when I entered, "Matthews! I hear you were briefly a Lieutenant Colonel! Still, one day it might be permanent. And you have married! Was that wise, dear boy?"

My hackles were raised, and I replied stiffly, "What I do in the army is your concern, Colonel Selkirk, but my private life is just that, private! I shall continue to serve Sir Arthur as well as I have always done,"

He shrugged and smiled, "Your line of work, my boy, puts you closer to a bloody death than almost any other soldier I know but, as you say, it is your business. Just being polite. And a friendly word of warning. Sir Arthur now prefers the title, Viscount Wellington! No matter." He pulled over a map and gestured for me to sit next to him. I saw that it was a map of Spain and Portugal. "I would take this to Viscount Wellington myself but I am needed elsewhere." He leaned in, conspiratorially, "Firstly the Emperor has promoted Auguste Marmont to be Marshal and it is he who commands the Army of Portugal. This is his first command in Spain and before this he was Governor of Dalmatia. He has fought and defeated Austrians but I think that the Viscount will be too much of a match for him. I have heard that Boney is planning to make war on Russia! If he does, then it bodes well for us. I must head east. So, I wish you to brief Viscount Wellington. The map you may keep but the figures and all else must remain in your head." I nodded. "Viscount Wellington is in trouble! Soult has an army in the south of over ninety thousand men. Fortunately, only twenty-five thousand are available in the field for he has to hold many of the Spanish fortresses the French captured. Beresford can hold those but it means that the other armies can all concentrate on Viscount Wellington! Dorsenne has replaced Bessières in the north. There are ninety thousand men there. In the centre, Marmont has his army and King Joseph's. That is a further eighty-three thousand men. The Spanish in Catalonia and in the west are holding down a further ninety thousand men. If the French ever manage to combine their armies, then even Viscount Wellington might struggle."

"Is there any good news, sir?" I said, wryly.

"A glimmer. Ciudad Rodrigo has less than two thousand men in its walls but Badajoz, thanks to the two costly sieges, has now been reinforced and there are over five thousand men inside." He leaned back and lit another cigar. "You have those figures in your head?"

"Yes, sir. And any advice for Viscount Wellington?"

He burst out laughing and almost choked on his cigar, "You are a wit, Matthews! Do you think Viscount Wellington values the opinion of any other than himself? No, I have no advice and if it were me then I would simply sit behind the border and let the guerrillas bleed the French to death. We simply do not have enough men. His Majesty's Government sends men to the West Indies and the Low Countries where they are killed, not by human enemies but insects and disease and to make matters worse there is a movement to make war on America! One war at a time. Boney has bitten off more than he can chew if he thinks he can take Russia without haemorrhaging men!" He handed me the map, "Well, off you go and good luck! I shall have to buy myself a thick greatcoat and a fur hat, what?"

I left the embassy happier than when I had arrived for the Colonel had not sent me behind enemy lines and if he was in Russia then he would not be back for some time!

Sergeant Sharp and I headed north through a land we knew well. We had first come long before the disaster of Sir John Moore's fateful retreat and we had heled Viscount Wellington and Sir Richard Fletcher build the might defences of Torres Vedras. They had defeated Masséna and the Marshal had been sent home in disgrace. We stayed in Torres Vedras itself as we knew and liked the town. We had reached there in the early afternoon and were enjoying a late lunch when we saw and heard an altercation. Both of us could speak Portuguese although Alan still struggled with his pronunciation. I had no such problem but then again, I had grown up speaking both English and French! The noise was so great that all eyes were on the large, well-dressed man who was raising his stick to strike a small child of no more than five years of age. A woman, I took her to be the boy's mother, was trying to intervene and he backhanded her to the ground. Sharp and I jumped to our feet and, in one move I had the man's hand in mine. He was a big man, but he had run to fat.

"Hold!"

Sharp lifted the woman to her feet, and she held the sobbing child while my sergeant protected the two of them.

"Do you know who I am that you dare to put your hands on me?"

Alan and I were not wearing our uniforms and so he had no idea that we were soldiers. "All I know is that you are using a stick to beat a child and you have assaulted the child's mother. That is enough for me for in England we do not do such things!"

"She is my servant and the brat she drags around with her dropped the jug of wine he was carrying." I saw that the small child had been carrying a stone amphora and it was almost the same size as the child. "Now out of my way and let me continue to punish my servants."

I tore the carved stick from his hand and snapped it in two. "You will not touch them again!"

"I am the Marquis de Oviedo and I do not answer to you."

"And I am Major Matthews of the 11th Light Dragoons and I am here to say that you do." I turned to the woman, "Do you wish to leave the service of this...?" I left the sentence hang.

"Thank you, my lord, but I have to care for my son. I have endured such beatings before."

"I ask again, do you wish to stay with him?"

She shook her head, "But I have to."

"No, you do not! I have a house in Lisbon. You and your son can live there and serve me." The look on her face told me that she was delighted about that.

"You cannot! She is mine!"

"She is your slave? You bought her?"

"I pay her wages!"

"And now I do. Sharp, get a room for the two of them." I saw that our discussion had attracted the attention of some of the British soldiers who were travelling south. From their bandages, they had been wounded.

The man glared around and pointed a finger at me, "This is not over!" He thought to push over the woman and her child but had reckoned without Sharp. As the man barged towards them my sergeant deftly threw the man to the ground and the British soldiers all cheered. When he rose to his feet, he glared daggers at us but left the square.

I smiled at the woman and child. "Go with the sergeant, you will be safe."

I went back to the table to finish off my wine. The sergeant who was with the wounded men came over to me. He had his left arm in a sling, "Sergeant Hall of the 43rd, Major. I didn't catch a word of that but me and the lads are pleased with what you did. We have been here two days waiting for the wagons to take us to Lisbon and that big bugger, sorry sir, that man, treats all of his servants the same way."

"Well, not that one. I am sending her and the child to my house in Lisbon." An idea came to me. "Sergeant, I wonder if you could do me a favour. Would you take them with you tomorrow and give them protection? I will give you my address in Lisbon. It is not far from the harbour."

"Of course, sir, delighted." I took a couple of silver dollars from my purse. "No need for that, sir."

"There is for you may need food and one good turn deserves another."

He took the money and we made arrangements to meet tomorrow. Sharp returned and I could see the anger on his face. "It is not right, sir, Maria was married to a soldier. He was killed at Talavera. That…" I could see him struggling for words to describe the aristocrat who had abused the woman and her child, "took advantage of her. I got them a room and the manager said this Marquis is well known. He supplies the Portuguese Army and he lives here in Torres Vedras. He has a big house just across the square." He shook his head, " Maria and Juan need to be looked after. He is a canny bairn!"

I smiled, "They seem to have made an impression on you Sergeant."

"Aye, well, I don't like to see folks treated like that by those who think they are their betters. You would never do that, would you sir?"

I did not answer for I felt I did not need to. "She will be looked after. There are some wounded returning to Lisbon. They will escort them to my home there and I will ask Miguel to find her work. The only trouble is that they cannot go back to their home for clothes."

"From what she said to me they have little enough anyway. Don't you worry, Major, I will see that they get some clothes. I have a few coins."

Sergeant Sharp was changing. I wrote the letter to Miguel while Alan took the woman and her child to buy clothes and food. They were watched from the big house and I knew that the Marquis was planning something. There were fifteen wounded soldiers on the two wagons heading south and the woman and her child would be quite safe.

Maria kissed the back of my hand, "Thank you, milord, you are a saint."

"No, Maria, I am doing the right thing that is all."

I left Alan to say farewell and went to pay our bill. When I returned the wagons had gone and Sharp was watching the house of the Marquis. "You know, sir, I have a mind to march up to his house and give him a good hiding!"

Shaking my head, I said, "He has influence. He supplies the Portuguese Army. It would not end well for us. Let us get north as soon as we can."

We left the fortress town and headed north. We had many days of travel ahead of us, but we knew the route and would be able to have a roof over us each night. However, we were just eight miles from Torres Vedras when we both sensed we were being followed. It was Donna who alerted us when she became fidgety and restless. I looked at Alan who nodded. He sensed it too. We did not turn around for that would alert those following us. I knew that they would be using the trees which lined the road. We could have tried to lose them by riding hard but then they would merely have chased us. Instead, I would try to manufacture an ambush. The road climbed and fell, twisted and turned through the mountains which had thwarted the French. I had travelled on it a great deal with Sir Richard Fletcher and Sir Arthur. I was very familiar with it and when I spied a section where the road fell away sharply to the left and turned around a huge wall of rock, I knew I had somewhere we could use to ambush our followers. As soon as we turned and were hidden from view, I dismounted and dropped Donna's reins. I drew my two loaded pistols and primed them while Alan tethered the packhorse. Our followers would have to leave the woods and use the road. Alan had just primed them when six men rode around the corner. They were little more than bandits, although the remnants of a uniform showed that once they had been soldiers. The horses they rode were little more than donkeys. The men were armed with a variety of weapons, but I only saw two pistols and they were holstered.

"My friends, why do you follow us?"

"We are using the road! Just because you English built it does not mean that you own it!"

"No, but you were following us in the woods for you wished to be hidden. Did the Marquis send you?" His face gave me the answer. "Turn around now and stop following us. This is the only warning that you will get."

"You threaten us with a pair of pistols." He laughed and drew his own. He had yet to prime it! "You are right, the Marquis sent us for we are poor men and your horses, purses and weapons will help us to become richer."

"Drop the pistol or I will shoot you!"

Even as he was laughing, he was trying to prime it and a second bandit was drawing his pistol. I fired one pistol at the leader. I suppose I could have just tried to wound him but there were six of them and so I fired at his chest. As he was just ten feet from me, I could not miss, and he flew over the back of his saddle. That might have been the end of it had not two of them drawn their short swords to ride us down. My second pistol hit one in the heart and Sharp's two pistols emptied another two saddles. The last two turned and galloped away towards Torres Vedras. I went to examine the bodies. Three were dead already and the fourth was dying. We could do little for him.

Just then I heard hooves from the north and I began to reload my pistol. Alan said, "It is some Portuguese cavalry." I had forgotten that there were still forts manned by the Portuguese. A Lieutenant looked at the bodies. "You have an explanation?"

I nodded, "I am Major Matthews of the 11th Light Dragoons with despatches for Viscount Wellington. We were attacked by six men. Four lie here and the other two headed for Torres Vedras."

He nodded, "Bandits and, from their clothes, deserters. Would you like us to escort you north, Major?"

I shook my head, "We will be fine."

"Then I will catch the other two and dispose of these bodies."

The rest of our journey was, thankfully, without incident.

The two sieges at Badajoz had ended in failure and so Viscount Wellington had his headquarters at the smaller border town of

Fuenteguinaldo which was close to Ciudad Rodrigo. The army was camped outside the fortress and the town. Sharp and I were well known, and we were cheerily greeted by familiar faces as we rode through the tented town. We made our way to the Headquarters building. Sir Arthur was using a two-storied house with a walled garden at the front. A Foot Guards sentry was on duty and he did not recognise me. The '**Squire's sons**' as they were known were all arrogant, even the ordinary line and this one was no exception. He did not know me, and it was obvious that he would not let me in easily. Inwardly I sighed for I did not need this.

"Major Matthews with a message for Viscount Wellington."

"Have you a pass, sir?" There was the slightest hesitation before he said 'sir' but the tone was insolent.

Next to me, Sergeant Sharp growled, "Keep a civil tongue in your head or you risk losing teeth."

I said, reasonably, "The Private is just doing his duty, I hope, I would hate to think he was deliberately obstructing a senior officer."

The Foot Guard kept an impassive face, "Sorry, sir, but unless you have a pass you shall not enter."

I was not willing to argue and so I simply said, "Who is the Sergeant of the Guard?" I raised my voice slightly so that the men in the guard room would hear.

Sure enough, a sergeant and a corporal came out. He glared at the private, "Yes sir, how may I help?"

"Major Mathews of the 11th Light Dragoons and aide to Viscount Wellington. I have ridden from Lisbon to deliver a report to the General but apparently your chap here needs a pass before he will allow me to enter."

"He is just doing his duty, sir, but…"

Just then a window above our heads opened and Viscount Wellington shouted down, "Sergeant, stop being such a Tom Fool and let in my aide… and his sergeant! God save me from stiff-necked guardsmen!"

The window closed and the red-faced sergeant said, "If you would follow the corporal, sir, and I will have a word here with Private Woods."

"Of course."

The news we had heard as we had ridden through the camp told me why the General was in such a foul mood. He had failed twice to take Badajoz and it had been reinforced so that he still had two fortresses to reduce. That would not sit well with Viscount Wellington; he did not lose. I recognised Captain Dunbar and General Craufurd. There was also a Lieutenant Colonel I vaguely recognised.

I had fought alongside General Craufurd and we did not always see eye to eye, but we respected each other. He gave me a sly smile, "That's the trouble with the Guards, they think they are better than anyone else. Of course, in the case of a cavalryman, they are right."

I smiled back, "As I recall General, it was cavalry who saved your bacon on the Coa!" I knew it to be so as I had led the cavalry!

The smile left his face as I knew it would and Captain Dunbar did his best to hide the smile. Viscount Wellington had no time for such banter. "Enough of that. You have news from Lisbon?" That was the General's way, no small talk about my wound, England, my marriage, he cut to the chase immediately.

"Colonel Sinclair briefed me, sir." I gave him my report and Sharp held open the map so that I could point out where the French Corps and Divisions were to be found.

He smacked the map angrily, "And now Badajoz has been reinforced! Dammit!"

"The Colonel also said that Bonaparte was considering attacking Russia."

"Is he, by God? Now that is good news. Russia has a poor army, but the land will chew him up and spit him out and, more importantly, it will starve Spain of reinforcements." He stared at the map as though some answer would manifest itself. A smile appeared on his face and that did not bode well for me. He stared at me and then said, "Gentlemen, I would like a word alone with the Major. Sharp, you will be bivouacked with the 11th, cut along there with the Major's gear eh?"

"Sir!"

General Craufurd was not happy but he had little choice.

When we were alone Viscount Wellington said, "I hear you married. Was it that girl who you showed around, the daughter of the M.P.?"

"Yes, sir."

He grinned, "You sly dog! That guarantees you a fine life after the army. I didn't think you had it in you." I did not answer him for he was wrong, but you did not say that to Viscount Wellington. "And the wound?"

"Healed, sir."

The pleasantries over, he said, "Now then, as I recall you and your fellow called in at Badajoz after Talavera."

"I went there, sir, but it was some time ago and in British hands then. It may have changed."

"Exactly and that is why I want you to get inside again and spy out their defences."

Colonel Sinclair was not risking my life, but Viscount Wellington was, "That will be difficult, sir, you have just failed in a siege and they will check everyone who enters."

"Normally, I would agree with you, but you seem to have the knack of getting into impossible places and, more importantly, getting out. This is a perfect time. We failed a couple of months ago and they will not expect it. If you enter from the Spanish side, you can pretend to be a Frenchmen. You have done it before, Matthews."

"Yes sir, and almost been caught each time I have done so!"

He leaned back and folded his hands together with interlaced fingers. He put them behind his head and said, "Major Matthews, it is an order. When you return, I may allow you to rejoin your regiment, but I want to know what Badajoz is like." I nodded, "And Ciudad Rodrigo!"

I did not believe that I would escape without injury from one fortress and so two made little difference. I nodded.

He almost leapt forward and clapped me about the shoulders, "Good fellow and you will return, of that I am certain. There is something about you; perhaps you are just lucky."

I stood to leave.

"And you have just four weeks for both missions. The Badajoz one is the more important but as Ciudad is just a few miles away you might as well assess their defences first. If you can, then report back here but, otherwise, go directly to Badajoz. I don't want to try to teach an old dog new tricks Matthews, but if you could stay behind enemy lines then it will make your story more plausible."

He was, of course, right but as I had not even concocted a story yet, the point was moot. When I left the building, I was saluted by a still red-faced Private Wood. I returned his salute and gave him an icy stare. He would admit me a little quicker the next time. Donna was waiting for me where Sharp had tied her, and I mounted. As Viscount Wellington had not said to leave immediately, I would take the opportunity of acclimatising myself to Portugal and it would be good to speak to Colonel Fenton, Major Hyde-White, Sergeant Major Jones and the rest of the regiment. I would not give Private Woods the satisfaction of feigning ignorance when I asked him where the 11th were camped, instead, I used my instincts. We had not passed cavalry camps and so they had to be ahead of me. The Coa effectively marked the border and the horses would need water so I followed my nose. As I rode, I began to devise a plan.

When I had scouted out Masséna's army I had played the part of a merchant. That disguise would not work a second time for whilst

Masséna had been replaced there would be officers who remembered me as we had shared the same hotel, albeit briefly. The idea, when it came, was radical and incredibly dangerous but it was brazen enough to work and relied on the suspicions and rivalries Bonaparte had allowed to fester within his leaders. France had over three hundred thousand men in Spain and yet the leaders could not work together. Each was not only trying to outdo his rivals but also keep information from each other and that was a weakness. I would try to exploit it.

I turned my thoughts to the regiment. They had not been in the Peninsula thus far and perhaps that was a good thing. The leaders of the cavalry now knew their business and I had fought alongside the other hussars and light dragoons and knew their worth. I might be able to offer them some advice. When I had joined the regiment the de Vere brothers had been in the process of taking it over. I had been a fly in the ointment. I had almost been court-martialled but the two brothers had left the regiment and it had become a happier place. I knew that age, death and promotion would have changed it since I had last served with them, but I hoped there were enough familiar faces from the old days to make me welcome. I knew that Jack Jones, the Sergeant Major, was still with the regiment and he was like a rock. The Colonel, I knew, was too old to be leading the regiment into battle but he was a sort of lucky charm. The 11th were his.

I recognised the regimental standard and rode towards it. I recognised one of my old troop sergeants, Tommy Grant. I saw that he was now Quartermaster Grant, a promotion for he was an officer! He grinned and saluted when he saw me, "Good afternoon, sir. Good to see you. I saw Sharpie and he told me you were back. Are you back permanently, sir?"

"Perhaps. How is everyone?"

His face darkened, "Have you not heard sir, Old Colonel Fenton has had to be invalided back to England, sir? We have no Colonel at the moment." He then went on to tell of the disaster at Elvas when the 11th, along with a recently arrived regiment of German hussars had been on piquet duty. The Quartermaster was honest with me and told me that all had been ill-prepared and some of General Latour-Maubourg's Troopers had managed to catch them unawares. Colonel Fenton, brave to the end, had been seriously wounded. His life as a warrior was over!

"So Major Hyde-White is in command?"

Shaking his head, he said, "No, sir, he was wounded when we served in Ireland. We were ambushed by some agitators. He retired and we have a new gentleman, Major Wilkinson," lowering his voice he said, "He was a Captain in the Foot Guards, sir, and bought the commission." I knew there was more to it than that but the Quartermaster would not be indiscreet. I was an officer and he had recently been a non-commissioned officer and was now promoted. Jack Jones might tell me more, but Quartermaster Grant would hold his tongue.

I nodded, "I will be back briefly, Quartermaster, but I shall need to leave some gear here: my Baker and the like. I take it you can look after it for me?"

He nodded, "It will be as safe as in the bank of England, sir." He saluted, "And it is good to have you back sir. The regiment needs you!"

I dismounted and walked Donna over to the horse lines. Sergeant Sharp must have been watching for me, as he strode over, "I will take Donna, sir." He pointed to a tent, "The large one is yours, sir. I am billeted with Jack Jones and Tommy Grant." He lowered his voice, "All is not well, sir," and tapping his nose he strode off.

Forewarned I went to my quarters. Sharp had laid out my uniform. I had not worn the dress uniform of the 11th for some time. If we dined formally then I would not look out of place. I took off the coat I used on the road. It was an anonymous blue one such as Viscount Wellington wore and had no marks of rank upon it. I put my hat on the bed and washed my face in the water obligingly left by Sharp. I had a couple of clean shirts; Emily had ensured that I had enough new clothes and I felt smarter. I put on a clean frock coat rather than the dress uniform. I had not brought my Tarleton helmet and, indeed, had not even worn it for some time. The result was that when I left the tent, I did not look like an officer of the 11th and that, in hindsight, was a mistake.

When I left the tent, Sharp had not returned from the horse lines and so I asked a passing trooper where the Headquarter's tent was. He pointed me to a large marquee, and I headed for it. I could hear a raised voice inside as I approached, and I did not recognise it. The other, I did, it was Sergeant Major Jones, "But, sir, the Quartermaster has not received any of the new shakoes so he can't issue them yet."

The other voice was a bullying voice and it brought back memories of officers with whom I had served before who used such a tone. It was not a commanding voice, it was merely threatening. "Sergeant Major Jones, until a new Colonel arrives then I command! I do not care how Grant does it, but I want the first regiment to have the new shako to be this one!"

"But…"

I strode into the tent, smiling, "Sorry, am I interrupting?"

The Major, I later learned his name was Wilkinson, whipped his head around, "Of course you are! Who the devil are you and what are doing here?" I took in that his uniform looked as though it had been cleaned just moments earlier. His waxed moustache had been neatly trimmed and had flamboyant curls at the end. He obviously put appearances before functionality.

I knew how to deal with bullies and I spoke reasonably and calmly, "I am Major Robert Matthews, Major, and I am an officer of the 11th," I paused just long enough for Major Wilkinson to start to open his mouth and added, "at the moment I am seconded to the staff of Viscount Wellington but he asked that I be accommodated with my old regiment." I looked pointedly at him, "And that is what I am doing here, Major, reporting to Regimental Sergeant Major Jones."

The Major's eyes narrowed, "Ah, I see. Where is your uniform?"

Smiling I said, "As an aide to Viscount Wellington, this is my uniform." Ignoring the Major, I turned to the Sergeant Major, "I was sorry to hear about the Colonel and even sorrier to have missed him. How is he?"

"Not good, sir. He should have retired years ago like Major Hyde-White and at his age any wound is serious." His eyes flicked to the Major. "The good news, sir, is that it is his nephew, Colonel Cummings, who is to take over the regiment. He was the colonel in command of the depot squadrons. He is on his way from England with replacements."

Major Wilkinson's voice had a sneering quality which I did not like for I had heard it many times before, "But for now, I command. You say you are to be accommodated with us, Major?"

I nodded, "Yes, but I shall only be here for a day or so."

The silence told me that the Major expected elaboration, but I merely stood there, and he broke first, "Right, well I shall see you at dinner, that is if you have a dress uniform. If not," he gave me a silky smile, "then you will have to dine with the other ranks. I intend the regiment to have higher standards now that I will be running it! Just because they served in Ireland does not mean they have to dress and behave like peasants!" He turned on his heel and strode out.

I waited until he had gone. I saw Jack's hand hovering close to his pipe, "Smoke if you like, Jones."

He nodded gratefully, "The major is a by the book sort of officer." He nodded to his pipe as he began to fill it, "It keeps away the flies, sir."

I took the spare seat, "What is his story, Sarn't Major?" This would not be gossip for we were old friends.

"He was a captain in the Foot Guards, sir. He sold his commission and was able to buy this one. It is a shame as the Colonel was all set to

18

promote Captain Stafford. He joined the 23rd instead and Captain Lutyens joined us." He saw my inclined head, "Captain Lutyens is a good 'un sir."

"Thank God for that. And the adjutant?"

He smiled, "Captain Platt, sir."

That made sense for the Captain did not enjoy the life of a horseman, but he liked regular food and drink. "And the rest?"

"Pretty much the same as when you were here. Will you be rejoining us, sir?"

"Eventually but first I go behind the lines." He nodded. "Keep that to yourself. As far as the Major is concerned, I am engaged on Viscount Wellington's service."

Jack tapped his nose, "Say no more, sir."

"I know the sergeants are good ones. Tell them that the cavalry over here know their business. They have Chasseurs and Dragoons. The Dragoons know how to use their muskets. Do the lads still keep up the practice with the carbines?"

"Some do and some don't."

"Then I had better try to use my influence to persuade the other officers to do so. Are Captains Austen and Hargreaves still with the regiment?"

"Yes, sir."

"Well that is a start and we can only hope that the new colonel gets here quickly. I am not sure that a Guards Officer knows much about cavalry apart from knowing how to ride a horse!"

I left the tent and went to my own. As I had expected, Sharp was there already and he was cleaning my travelling clothes and boots. "Well, Alan, is it good to be back?"

He shook his head, "It would be but for the new Major, sir." Alan was always honest and open with me. "He is a martinet and it is all about clean uniforms, smart horses and the right salute. The lads are not happy, but they were cheered by your return, sir."

I nodded and sat on the camp stool, "It will not last." I told him about our mission and my plan. To be fair to Sergeant Sharp he did not look surprised and he merely nodded as I told him all. "See Jack and get some paper, the best he has, some ink and some sealing wax."

"I'll see to it now."

"And I will have a little wander and see the officers and NCO's."

Jack's assessment of the new officer, Captain Lutyens, seemed accurate and he had heard of me. That helped. He was with Hargreaves and Austen and so I told them what we would be facing. "The use of the carbine and being able to adapt to ground which can go from gully to hill in a heartbeat is more important than wearing the right headgear."

Captain Austen laughed, "You heard then, sir?"

"I did, Percy, but we have a new Colonel coming."

Captain Lutyens shook his head, "We have a couple of months yet, sir."

That explained why Colonel Selkirk had not mentioned it. As I made my way back to my tent, I spoke with Sergeant Emerson and Sergeant Seymour. They were both reliable and had both been promoted to Troop Sergeant. Sharp had done as I asked and, after closing my tent flap and lighting the oil lamp I set to work forging the document which, I hoped, would get us into Ciudad Rodrigo. I used my father's old signet ring to seal the document, but I adapted the wax while it was still molten to look like an imperial eagle. It might not pass close scrutiny, but it would pass a cursory inspection.

Austen came and coughed outside the tent, "Sir, just a warning, it is almost time for dinner and the Major does not allow anyone who is late to dine!"

"Thanks, Percy." Luckily all was laid out and I knew how to dress quickly. "Sharp, hide this document and then get yourself some food. I was going to leave the day after tomorrow, but we might as well strike sooner rather than later. If I stay here, I can see that I might cause more problems for the regiment."

As I walked to the Officer's Mess, I knew that I was procrastinating. The new colonel would not be here any time soon and I knew that we would be called into action. I would not allow the Major to hurt the regiment. I barely made the Officers' Mess in time. I saw the wry grin on Sergeant Major Jones' face as I slipped beneath the descending flap. I also saw the look of disappointment on the face of Major Wilkinson. I saw an infantry uniform next to him and wondered at that. Percy had left a place between him and Brian Hargreaves. We were four places from the Major and that suited me. I scurried to my seat and stood, as were all of the others. Before me was a glass of wine.

The Major looked down the line to ensure we were all in position and then, raising his glass said, "King George, England, Viscount Wellington and the 11th! He downed it in one as we all did. "Gentlemen, you may sit."

I turned to Captain Hargreaves, "A little formal, eh?"

"You don't know the half of it, sir. You know how hard it is to keep things clean here at the best of times, but the Major seems to think that appearances are all."

I nodded, "I will have a word with Viscount Wellington." In truth, I did not think he would be concerned in the least, but I would do what I could for the regiment. I owed it to Colonel Fenton. Just then the infantry officer said, loud enough for the whole mess to hear, "Lieutenant Colonel Matthews! I thought it was you. Captain Gilbert of the 24th, I fought in your brigade at Fuentes de Oñoro."

I vaguely recognised him but the fighting had been desperate in the narrow streets of the village, "Good to see you, Captain, but I was just a brevet Lieutenant Colonel. Back to plain Major now."

He turned to Major Wilkinson, "Damn me, Roger, but this chap led us to clear the village. It was a proud day for our regiment and, I believe, won us the battle!"

I shook my head, "You will learn, Captain, that one action rarely results in a victory. When Viscount Wellington wins it is because the men he leads know how to fight and they are, by and large, well-led."

It was the wrong thing to say for the Major took it as an insult and the men who had known me took it as a criticism of him. However, it had shown the Major that, technically, I outranked him and could turn up to dinner dressed any way I wished. Major Wilkinson quickly engaged his friend in conversation and the officers around me bombarded me with questions about the battle. I knew that I had been lucky in that I had been with the infantry when they had cleared the village and with the cavalry when we had defeated the French horse. That I had been wounded and close to death was not mentioned. My omission was not an attempt to garner glory but rather so as not to make them fear the enemy in battle. A man who worried about wounds was hell-bent on acquiring at least one.

By the time the port came, there was plenty available to us, the officers around me were a little worse for wear and their lips became looser. "By Gad, sir, I wish you were back with us! You have more experience than any officer in the regiment!"

"Peace, Brian, for the Major might hear, and it does not do to upset such men. Bide your time and before you know it the new Colonel will he here and all of this will seem like some sort of bad dream. Between you and me it is getting close to the end of the fighting season. I have been here for three years or more and the land changes when autumn comes. Watch out for your horses and keep them free from disease, injuries and malnutrition. The last is the biggest killer."

They nodded sagely but I could tell none of them had thought that far ahead. Percy asked, "Will we be expected to join in the attack on Ciudad when it comes? The Colonel kept us out of the attack on Badajoz, but we were in reserve."

21

I shook my head, "Cavalrymen do not attack walls but when we do begin the siege expect to be in the saddle from dawn until dusk in case the French try to relieve it."

I left with the three captains. The Major stood to speak with me. He had not drunk as much as some of the others, "If you returned to the regiment then you would outrank me!"

I nodded, "I suppose so, but the running of the regiment is the work of a colonel. It is only useful if a soldier seeks to be the leader of a regiment and I do not."

He genuinely looked surprised, "Really? I shall end this war a Brigadier General at the very least and then... who knows!"

It was as though I was dismissed, and he sat down once more. Captain Gilbert had fallen asleep!

Sharp was still awake and seated outside my tent where he had lit a fire. It was more to keep away the insects than for warmth although he was smoking a pipe. "How was dinner, sir?"

"Interesting. And did you learn anything new?"

"Nothing that you hadn't already discovered." He chuckled, "I had it confirmed that every man in the regiment wants you back as their Major, sir."

"Let us get this mad adventure out of the way first. Is everything ready for the morrow?"

"Yes, sir. Quartermaster Grant will send two of his clerks for our spare gear. He found some spare baker ammunition which he will keep with the guns. There are oats and he has some captured French powder and balls."

"Good. And we have nothing on us to mark us as English?"

"No sir, the marks on the horses have been doctored to look like the French ones and all my gear is French."

The two of us were like magpies after a battle and we took from the dead. I had been scorned by some officers and called a grave robber but then they did not have to masquerade as a Frenchman.

"You had better pretend that you are a nasty, anti-social character and speak as little as possible. I am not sure your accent would hold up. Besides, it might help the characters we are going to play. React when people speak to you to show you understand them but leave the speaking to me."

Chapter 2

I did not worry that the whole allied camp was awake and that we were seen heading from the camp. I had no intention of riding directly to Ciudad Rodrigo. I planned to head due east and cross the River Agueda well upstream from Ciudad Rodrigo. It would mean spending a night in the highlands to the east of the fortress but it would also mean that we would be approaching from the right direction as far as the French were concerned and they would be less suspicious of two riders coming from either Salamanca or Madrid. Marshal Marmont was at Salamanca and while we risked French patrols, if we could not outwit them then we could outrun them for our horses were in the best condition. Their time grazing while we had been in England had given them both a new lease of life and they were both keen to gallop. We were in as much danger from our own cavalry vedettes whom Viscount Wellington had thrown around the fortress. We both carried a brace of pistols in our belts and another brace in saddle holsters. I had my French heavy cavalry sword and Sharp had a Chasseur's sword. In my boots, I had two daggers: the stiletto I had taken from an Italian bandit some years ago and a longer broader knife which was more robust than the assassin's blade. We soon left civilisation for the war had devastated this land and farmers had either been killed or fled to join the guerrillas. We rode, largely in silence for neither of us needed to make small talk. The silences were comfortable.

The camp we made was a cold one as we were in enemy territory, but a fire was unnecessary as the nights were warm, it was late August. It is a strange thing, but it does not take long for an old soldier to reacquaint himself with life on the road. You choose the place you will sleep carefully and if there are patches of long grass you use them. Of course, you forego that comfort if your horses need to eat. We were lucky and we found a dell which had not been grazed by sheep. That was probably because the farmers had been driven off and foragers from both armies had taken the sheep. We had passed a stream and so the horses had drunk well, and our canteens were still full. We ate the bread and ham we had brought and just lay down to sleep. Our silence, when we camped, was vital for sound travelled at night and whichever language we used, we risked an enemy hearing. The quiet was better. Nor did we keep watch for we needed the sleep, besides, Donna was a good horse and she was alert. If any came near to us, she would whinny, and her noise would awaken the two of us in an instant. When we awoke it was always a relief to find out that we had been undisturbed.

We rose before dawn and were riding along the small road to the main road which led to Ciudad. There were English vedettes camped nearby but I hoped by rising early we would avoid them, and we almost did. I had spied the fortress town ahead and we were riding along the Salamanca road when the carbines cracked behind us. Whoever had fired the guns had made a mistake for the English troopers had been too far away. If they had used a Baker carbine or rifle, then they might have stood a chance, but the balls struck the road a good twenty yards behind us telling me that they had been fired at extreme range. We did not look back and just dug in our heels for if their carbines could not reach us then we had a good lead and I knew that our horses would be better than theirs. I heard hooves on the road, but they seemed to be some way back, even so, I lay flat along Donna's back to make as small a target as possible although I doubted that the English troopers who raced after us would be able to hit us.

Ahead of us, in the garrisoned Convent of San Francisco, I heard the drum sounding for the French to man the walls. I had been to the fortress before the battle of Talavera and then the convent had not been fortified. One of the strengths of our enemy was that they knew how to defend. The road ran along the side of the convent and then swept along a small stream before turning around to the River Agueda where there was a bridge and the only gate into the town. As we passed the convent I looked across to the town and fortress walls and saw sandbags and cannons. They would not waste cannonballs to fire at the horsemen but infantrymen were lining up and preparing to fire. We were ignored. Our scrutiny would come later. Now that we were safe from our countrymen I sat up and looked around. The French had made changes to their defences and I saw, to my right, just two hundred and fifty yards from the convent a new fort on the slopes of the Great Teson. This was a piece of high ground which overlooked the town. I made a mental note of it although the cavalry vedettes who had been watching the town should have reported it.

As we neared the town, I saw that the French had fortified the Convent of Santa Cruz and that meant they had the north-west of the town protected too. I observed that they had a *fausse braie* or earth bank which now protected the ditch before the walls. French soldiers must have toiled to throw up the huge earth mound. When we attacked, the artillery would have to waste shot and shell to destroy it before they could begin work on the base of the walls. Destroying the walls of a fort was a long process. I saw the walls manned; they had been alerted by the shots. There would be a reception committee waiting for us. We had slowed our horses once we had neared the convent and were walking them as we approached the gate and the bridge. Viscount Wellington already knew that an attack across the river was suicidal. He would have to attack from the same direction we had taken and take the defending forts first. The gates were open when we reached the bridge but there were levelled muskets and a Captain waiting for us.

"Stop and identify yourselves!"

I reached down and took out the forged document which I had prepared. I had also prepared a rank which would make the officer respectful. I used a snarling tone. When I had been a trooper in the Chasseurs, I had heard many arrogant officers use such a tone. "I am here on Imperial business. My name is Colonel Fouquet and I am from the Ministry of Police!" I did not relinquish my hold on the document and the captain had to hold the bottom to read it. I doubted that he had ever seen an imperial seal, nor would he recognise the signature of Joseph Fouché. I had seen both. My forgery would not fool anyone who had seen such a document, but I gambled that Napoleon's spy catcher would not have sent many letters in this part of the world for the guerrillas tended to eliminate his messengers.

I saw the captain recognise the name and he stiffened and saluted, "I will have someone escort you to the castle and General Barrié."

I allowed myself a thin and silky smile, "Thank you, Captain. Your cooperation is appreciated, and I will tell Paris of your help."

All the time we had been speaking Sharp had just glowered at the French. I saw them move well away from him as we entered. Of course, getting in did not guarantee getting out and we had far sterner tests ahead of us.

The sergeant who walked next to me had been standing next to the captain and while I was not certain he could read would have recognised the seal. "Sergeant, I am here to discover if this fortress can hold out against the English. Your moustache speaks of experience. Before I speak to the General what is your opinion? And before you answer know that I was a sergeant once and I have dragged myself up to my elevated position. I know that not all officers are like the Emperor. When I served with him in Italy and Egypt, we saw incompetence. You may speak freely."

The sergeant looked up and, as we were close to the entrance to the castle, we stopped. Remarkably the sergeant, who must have been a recruit back then, said, "I recognise you, sir, you were a Chasseur à Cheval in the Consular Guard, sir! You rode a big black beast of a horse!"

I smiled as I answered but, in truth, I was worried. If this man recognised me then there might be others inside who did too, "That is right and you have a good memory! Then you know I am close to the Emperor."

He nodded and, in that instant, changed for he saw me as someone completely trustworthy. That I had been lucky was clear. He could have been one of those who knew I had deserted and then my war would have been over but sometimes the Fates conspire with us and not against us. He lowered his voice, "The General is not a popular man, sir. That is not always a bad thing but in General Barrié's case, it is. He does nothing to rid us of the English patrols and seems content to just squat in the castle. I have never seen him walk the walls. When we were in Egypt the Emperor knew us all!"

I nodded, "Thank you. It is good to know that the Emperor still has loyal men such as you. We can take it from here."

"I will take you to the officer of the day, first, Colonel, for the General is fussy about such things." I saw him roll his eyes.

I knew that the word would soon spread, and the Sergeant's confirmation of my identity would make life much easier. We had to dismount to enter the gate and we walked in behind the sergeant. I allowed him to get ahead of us and he stopped at a wooden sentry box where he spoke to another sergeant. When the duty sergeant looked at me, I knew that my story had been repeated.

"If you would wait here sir, Sergeant Leroux will fetch the Lieutenant." He saluted and I saluted back. I felt a twinge of guilt for I was deceiving someone who had been a former comrade and he trusted me. Such was my life now and I had chosen my country.

The Lieutenant, his name was Debussy, had been informed of my identity and he could not do enough for me. He had some of his men take our bags while three others took our horses. "Be careful with my horse! I will have the backs of all of you laid open if she is not happy when I leave!"

The Lieutenant was too petrified to even speak as he led me through labyrinthine passages to the room where General Barrié conducted his business. Someone must have raced ahead of us for when we arrived, I saw the General with his senior officers waiting for me. Even though he outranked me he looked nervous.

"I am honoured that the Emperor has sent you here, Colonel. Is this in response to the letters I have been sending to him?"

"I am here, General, because the Emperor needs to know that this fortress will be held. It is vital to his plans to re-take Portugal. I will be here for one day and I do not have time for pleasantries. My assistant will take notes while you show me your defences. I have much to do before I return to Paris."

"If you do not mind me asking, Colonel, what about the guerrillas? Are they not a risk?"

I smiled, "Only if I allow them to be. I was sent because I am able to survive no matter who are my enemies. Do not worry about me, General. Now, your defences?"

It was the middle of the afternoon by the time we had finished our tour. I learned that there were almost four thousand men in the fortress and that was more than Viscount Wellington expected. The General was exhausted when we had finished, and we returned to his office. His officers, too, were also suffering for they were anxious to know what my report would say. I smiled as I sipped the wine the General had provided from his personal cellar.

"Well, General Barrié, you seem to have the situation in hand and…"

We were interrupted by Colonel St. Cloud bursting in. He proffered a piece of paper, "I apologise for the interruption, General, Colonel, but this is intolerable. A rider has come from Talavera. King Joseph demands that my regiment and two others be sent to Talavera to reinforce him. It will leave us with less than two thousand men!"

The news was a godsend, but I kept an impassive face as General Barrié exploded, "This is a scandal!" He turned to me, "Do you see, Colonel, what I have to put up with? My messengers have their throats cut. I am surrounded by the English and now the Emperor's brother takes away more than half of my garrison! Marshal Marmont has the entire stock of siege weapons here in Ciudad Rodrigo. That is a rich prize for the English! What am I to do?"

I sipped more of the wine and then said, smoothly, "It is, as you say, intolerable but it is an order and you must obey. However, if you put your objections in writing, then tomorrow, when I leave, I shall ride to King Joseph and deliver it, personally. I shall add my own support and, perhaps, not only will you receive your men back, but I may be able to get you some additional troops. I can be very persuasive." I put as much latent threat into my voice as I could. The men in the room thought I came from Joseph Fouché and that I was one of his secret police. They beamed.

"Thank you, Colonel. Colonel St Cloud you had better prepare the men to leave. By the time they reach Talavera they may have to return here!"

We were wined and dined like a pair of kings. No one thought to questions Sharp's silence and I was grateful for his gritty features. They did not invite conversation. With the General's letter added to my forgery I now had a choice of documents! When we parted from the general at the bridge, I said, "I will not risk the English vedettes. The messenger from Talavera will have alerted them. I will cross the Agueda lower down."

The General nodded, "I can see why you are given such important jobs Colonel, thank you."

I had no intention of riding to Talavera. I would change my plans and ride back to Viscount Wellington before I headed to Badajoz. The information I had in my possession needed to be acted upon and quickly!

We had to pass the English picket lines just two miles from the fortress. This time I was recognized as it was the 14th Light Dragoons and I had served with them. We galloped into the camp in the late afternoon. The Foot Guard on duty was not Private Wood and I was admitted directly. I guessed the sergeant had spoken about me. The General was in conference and it was Captain Dunbar who came to speak with me. I had not made notes in the fortress and so, while we waited, I dictated my report to him and I drew my own map.

"The crucial information, Captain, is that they are stripping the garrison of men and the French have stored their entire arsenal of siege weapons there."

The Captain might be young, but he saw immediately that the paltry guns which were now labouring from the abortive siege of Badajoz could be augmented if we took Ciudad. "I will tell the general directly. Will you wait?"

I shook my head, "I want to get to Badajoz as soon as I can and that is some distance away."

We went to the kitchens downstairs and I used my authority to have us fed with hot food and ale. It was the least that the General could do for us and we were on the road after a stop of just one hour! My life was anything but glorious.

The road we took was through the wild and inhospitable lands between Spain and Portugal. Even in peacetime, it had been a lonely place but now, after years of war, it was desolate and abandoned. There were guerrillas and patrols both allied and French. We would have two nights where we camped and ate cold rations with no fire. The first night's camp was just twenty-five miles from the main encampment we had just left. It meant we arrived just as the sun set and we had little time to inspect the site. However, we were close enough to the southernmost Portuguese camps for me to feel relatively safe and to even risk conversation with Sharp.

I know that Viscount Wellington and many other officers thought that I was supremely confident. I was not and as we drank a little water to wash down the bread and cheese, I wracked my brains to come up with another plan to get into Badajoz. This was where Sergeant Sharp proved his worth. He had the ability to bring any problem down to its simplest level. He saw my frowns and knew what it meant. When he spoke, it was in French for that was how he improved language skills. It meant he had to use simple words and that often helped. "Come on then, sir, spit it out. What is troubling you? What is there that will not work!" He used the French phrase, '*ne marche pas*' but I grasped his question.

"How do we get into Badajoz without alerting the garrison?" The simple language I was forced to use helped me for that was the only problem we really had to face and everything else would follow on from that.

Sharp held up his fingers as he gave me his thoughts, "One, use the letter from Fouché. It worked once. Two, we use the letter from General Barrié. We can say we couldn't get through the English lines. Three, use a combination of both."

I confess that I had not thought of using both and I reflected on his choices. Had we had a fire my thoughts would have worked quicker as I found that staring into flickering flames helped me to think. If I produced the forgery first, then it might be examined closely whereas if I showed General Barrié's letter backed up by the forgery then we might get by. I would have to come up with a story as to why I was behind the English lines and then it came to me. We could pretend to be French versions of ourselves, spies. I explained it to him, and he agreed. As his superior officer, I did not need his agreement but as he had suggested it and as his life would be in danger too, I thought it incumbent on me to do so. He then asked me about the man who had recognised me.

"Sir, what if, next time, it is someone who knows you deserted who recognises you?"

"Simple, I will become loud and tell them they are wrong. I will use the forged letter."

We both knew it was not as simple as that. I had been recognised once before and we had had to flee when we had scouted Talavera. It was a risk and every time I went behind the lines then that risk increased.

When we were just ten miles from Badajoz, we stopped to view it. I knew from Viscount Wellington that Marshal Beresford had his Anglo Portuguese army to the south-east of the town. Elvas was in Portuguese hands and guarded the north-west. It meant we would not have to negotiate allied patrols. To give legitimacy to our story we had to arrive from the north-west. We would have to negotiate the fort at the bridgehead as well as Fort San Cristóbal. Having been recently attacked by the British these men might be more curious than those at Ciudad Rodrigo. Once again, we would be living on my wits!

They were light infantry who were guarding San Cristóbal and as we attempted to pass the gates we were hailed from the ramparts. I saw that we had nowhere to run for the river was close to us on our left and muskets were aimed at us.

"I am Captain Villain of the 28th Leger, what is your business here?"

The captain was young, and I used my sinister voice, "I am Colonel Fouquet and I have been sent from Paris to study the defences of the border fortresses. I have urgent business with General Phillipon." I flourished the forgery. "I also have news of Ciudad Rodrigo which necessitates action. Minister Fouché does not appreciate his officers being delayed."

That worked, "I shall send a sous-lieutenant to facilitate your passage into the town."

The young officer walked with us to the small detachment manning the small artillery piece at the bridgehead. We were allowed across quickly although I saw that we were scrutinised. Few liked the secret police! This time it was harder to get into the fortress. The fact that we had been escorted across the bridge meant that we had no guns pointing at us but there were enough soldiers to restrain us if that had been necessary.

"Yes, sir?"

The Major who stopped us did not know my title but obviously erred on the side of caution. I merely repeated what I had said to Captain Villain, "I am Colonel Fouquet and I have been sent from Paris to study the defences of the border fortresses. I have urgent business with General Phillipon."

He nodded, "Follow the corporal to the castle and someone will take care of your horses, but no one approaches the General with loaded weapons."

I laughed, "Major, you show me a fool who rides with a loaded and primed weapon and I will show you a man who has not long to live." I took out two of my pistols and shook them. No balls fell out.

He smiled and shrugged, "They are the orders Colonel!"

I was not sure how long we would have in this fortress for security seemed much tighter than at Ciudad Rodrigo. As we headed up to the castle, I had a bad feeling for I vaguely remembered a French soldier called Phillipon. The man had been a Sergeant Major in Italy. I could not remember meeting him, but the name was familiar. However, if I could not recall his face the odds were that he would not recall mine or it could be a coincidence, and this might be another Phillipon. As soon as we were brought into his presence, I knew that there was no coincidence and it was the same Sergeant Major. He had been a legend and all the sergeants had admired him. Worse, he had been in Egypt and his senior position meant that he would have known of my duel and desertion. I forced myself to stay calm and to brazen it out.

"I understand you have news from Ciudad Rodrigo, Colonel Fouquet?"

"Yes, General Phillipon." I handed him the letter from General Barrié reserving the forgery for later.

He read it and shook his head. He turned to Colonel Lamare, his engineering officer and handed him the letter, "Look at this! Why do those who are not soldiers interfere in military matters? It is fortunate that we were reinforced after the last attack and that Madrid sees this route as the one the allies would use!" While his engineer read the letter, he turned back to me. "And what brings one of Fouché's spies here to Badajoz?"

"The Minister is concerned that the British and the Portuguese may break through and he wishes to have a report on the defences."

I saw and heard the old sergeant major in the General's next words. I almost snapped to attention, "Minister Fouché should worry more about his own position than mine. He has upset the Emperor too many times and I know that I have the Emperor's complete trust. We have withstood two sieges and we will survive another!" He stood and I saw that he was angry. His engineer handed me back the letter and I wondered if I had made a mistake with this disguise. It was not working as well as it had in Ciudad. "Come!" He strode from the room and Sharp and I followed along with his engineer. General Phillipon spoke as he walked, "Colonel Lamare has worked tirelessly as have every man in the garrison! The breaches made by Beresford have not only been repaired they have been improved." We had reached the castle parapet and he pointed down to where some French Engineers and line infantry were adding stones to the top of the wall which ran around Badajoz. "Look there, Colonel Fouquet, we have dammed the stream so that there is a lake there now. It is not deep, but any attacker would have to wade through that and it would slow them down." He pointed to the recently erected defences before the walls, "See how the Colonel has placed ravelins in front of the glacis to protect it. We have the river protected by one fort, the south by a second and Fort San Roque on the other side of the River Rivellas is a third. Then we have Fort Picurina further south. With the manpower available to us we have done all that we can! If Minister Fouché wishes to strengthen us, then have him command King Joseph to send a couple of regiments from guarding him in Madrid. Here they could fight for France!"

It was as though a gale had blown across the Spanish plain. I was bereft of words. I caught the hint of a smile from Colonel Lamare.

I nodded, "Then I will do so and when I deliver General Barrié's letter to King Joseph I will support your request, sir."

The General smiled and, putting his arm around me, led me back inside, "Forgive me my outburst but I tire of those in Paris who do not know this land. They do not understand the guerrillas and they have not fought this allied army which, I have to say, is the equal of the French. I can speak to you for any man who can cross the Spanish plain and survive the guerrillas is a soldier!" He suddenly looked at me and there was a hint of nervousness in his face, "I am not disloyal you understand?"

It was then I made my mistake. If I was who I said I was then I would have used a threatening tone, but I liked General Phillipon. He reminded me of many of the soldiers alongside whom I had fought, and I said, "Of course, sir and I will honour your trust in me."

He stopped and his eyes narrowed, "How did an officer like you end up working for Fouché? That you are a brave man is clear for you have managed to evade the guerrillas and you carry yourself like a soldier and not a spy!"

"I was promoted, sir, and a man does not refuse promotion."

He nodded, "I can see that, and you look like the sort of man the Emperor would promote." He stared at me. "I know your face. Did we fight together, a long time ago, perhaps?"

"We may have done, sir, but I cannot remember. I was in the cavalry and not the infantry." That was my second mistake for he had not told me the arm in which he had fought.

He smiled, "My memory does strange things! You will dine with us this night."

All I wanted to do was to get out as fast as I could but that would merely alarm the General. "Of course, General Phillipon, but I must leave early. These hot Spanish days can hurt a horse."

He laughed, "And that shows that you are a cavalryman." He looked at my sword, "Cuirassier?"

"No sir, Light Cavalry, Hussar."

"Ah, the glory boys. And in which battles did you fight, Colonel?"

I was saved from answering when an aide came in, "General, there is a Portuguese patrol close by Fort Panderleras."

He nodded, "We will continue this discussion at dinner. Colonel Lamare could you find some quarters for our guests?"

"Of course, sir."

As the Colonel led us down a corridor he said, "He is right of course. Minister Fouché usually uses sly little men who do not like to fight to do his work. You are the first we have seen for this is Spain and men, such as yourself, who ride alone do not last long." He glanced at Sharp, "Your silent friend is a good soldier also?"

I nodded, "Alain was my sergeant and we keep each other safe."

He opened a door to reveal a small room with two cots. "This is your room. It is basic but then this is the border. I will have water and towels sent." He went to the door and turned, "A word of advice, Colonel, leave the Police and rejoin a regiment. That is where all true soldiers should be and not skulking around trying to find out secrets from soldiers who are just serving France!"

Again, I should have said something, but I had dug a hole for myself and no matter what I did I would be compounding it. I remained silent. What was obvious to me, as we washed ourselves and tried to smarten up our clothes, was that I would not be able to examine the defences in detail, but I had learned enough to give Viscount Wellington a decent report. If he thought his two sieges had weakened the fortress, he was wrong. Thanks to Colonel Lamare they had strengthened it. I had wondered if the flooded inundation was the result of weather, but I could now see that it was deliberate. While I dressed, I worked out the possible places that Viscount Wellington could attack, and it became clear that the best place would have to be at Fort Picurina which occupied the high ground. His batteries would need to batter down the walls and that would mean an attack through the water. It was a brilliant defence which Lamare had devised for no one could move quickly through the water and even with fewer defenders then the French would be able to decimate men crossing it.

There was a knock on the door and a sous-lieutenant said, "You are invited to dine, sir."

We followed him and I saw that it was a semi-formal affair and every officer the rank of Captain and above were there. This would be an ordeal. I was seated next to the general and on my right was General Veiland who, I learned while we ate, acted as General Phillipon's Quartermaster and ensured that every man was where he should be and had all the equipment necessary. Such men were vital.

I did not remind the general of his question and was actually grateful when General Veiland asked me about Paris. I shook my head, "I am sorry, sir, I have not had the pleasure of Paris for many years. As General Phillipon observed I am a soldier and I am used to assessing defences. I worked in Italy for a while but since the English have cleared Portugal the Emperor is concerned about Spain."

General Phillipon wiped his mouth with his napkin, "But not enough to come here himself and defeat this Wellesley once and for all."

I saw a way to extract myself from the hole I had dug for myself. Thanks to Colonel Selkirk I had knowledge about Bonaparte which he would not. I leaned forward conspiratorially, "He is concerned about the defence of Spain for he believes he has good leaders like yourself and he is heading for Russia! His Empire will soon be much larger!"

I said it with the pride the character I played would have. It proved to be a masterstroke for the officers around the table then began a heated discussion about the merits of such an invasion. Some thought that they would walk all over the Russians and be in Moscow within weeks.

General Phillipon contributed little to the discussion but instead, turned to me, "Were you not in the Consular Guard in Egypt?"

I gambled on the integrity of this soldier whom I still admired even though he was an enemy. "Yes, sir, I was!"

He beamed, "Good, I remember you. You were known for your bravery and you rode a huge black beast of a horse." I nodded. He frowned, "Was there not some scandal which saw you leave the Guard?" Before I could answer he continued, "Of course, it was a long time ago and the Emperor left but..."

"Yes sir, I did leave. It was a matter of honour."

He laughed and shook his head, "You cavalrymen and your honour. In the infantry, we would have gone behind the barracks and only one of us would have returned." He waved a hand at the others in the heated debate. "What do you think of the Emperor's decision to attack Russia?"

"I think, General Phillipon, that Spain is a smaller version of Russia. I do not think we have conquered the Spanish and Spain. How could we do that with Russia? I agree with you. The Emperor should come back and finish what he started before he begins another war!"

He nodded, "We are both old soldiers. There are not many like us left; we fought in Italy, Switzerland and Egypt. Colonel Lamare is right, Fouquet, leave the police and come back to the army!"

When we closed the door on our chamber, I breathed a sigh of relief but I did not sleep well as I hated deceiving someone who had been a brother in arms at one time. My guilt was exacerbated when we left the next day for both the Colonel and the General gave us pleasant goodbyes. The life of a spy was a hard one!

Chapter 3

We reached Headquarters without incident although we had had to avoid many French patrols and that showed me just how many cavalry they had. I had no doubt that my papers would allow us to pass through them, but I did not want General Phillipon and General Barrié to have any suspicions about the Colonel Fouquet who had inspected their defences. I hoped that my disappearance and the non-arrival of the letter would be put down to guerrillas. The result of hiding from the patrols was that we reached Viscount Wellington a day later than I had expected and Captain Dunbar greeted us with an anxious look upon his face.

"Viscount Wellington feared the worst and that you had been captured!"

I shook my head, "No, but the roads to the south of us are filled with French cavalry patrols."

As he led me upstairs to the room Viscount Wellington used, the aide nodded, "His lordship has noticed increased French activity too. He will tell you himself, but he fears that Marshal Marmont may come to the aid of Ciudad Rodrigo before we can begin our assault. The guns are still some way away!"

I knew the problem. Siege guns needed teams of oxen to pull them and the irony was that if and when Ciudad Rodrigo was reduced then the siege train would have to move all the way back south to Badajoz!

Viscount Wellington was alone when I was escorted into his presence; it was his preferred state. He looked up and said, "What kept you?" Then without waiting for an answer, he said, "Dunbar, fetch us some food and drink and pen and paper. This may take some time."

"Sir."

"French cavalry patrols, sir."

"What?"

"The reason for the delay. I did not want my cover story to be ruined by being seen."

"Aah. Well, you have done exactly what I have asked thus far. We will wait until Dunbar returns before I go into details, but did you manage to access Badajoz?"

"Yes, sir!"

"Thank God. Now, as for these cavalry patrols, they are a nuisance and we need to be more aggressive. Until I need you again, I intend to return you to the 11th. I think you would be more use there until the new colonel arrives." He gave me a wry smile, "I hear that you do not get along with Major Wilkinson."

I shrugged, "I have met worse."

"And served under better, I know. You will deal with it, I have no doubt." He tapped the map before him. "We may have to pull in our patrols and vedettes from the far side of Ciudad Rodrigo and I fear that Marmont is probing us. I have decided on a strategy to counter and discourage this. Major General Anson will take six squadrons of light cavalry and six light companies. He will patrol to the west of Ciudad Rodrigo. Major General Picton will have a larger force to the south-west of Ciudad Rodrigo and that force will include your regiment and the King's German Legion Hussars. Major General Alten will command the cavalry and there will be six battalions of foot. You will have an encampment close to Ciudad Rodrigo. I do not want Marmont to know what we intend. Your initial intelligence was good, but I wish to ask more pertinent questions than Captain Dunbar managed."

The Captain had just re-entered, and his colouring face told me that he had heard. Viscount Wellington had not a sensitive bone in his body.

"Right Captain Dunbar, make a note of all the information which the Major supplies."

"Sir."

It was an interrogation worthy of Fouché's Secret Police! When I had told him all about both fortresses, he seemed pleased. "From what you have told me, Matthews, then I should attack Ciudad sooner rather than later." He held up the letter from the French General. "This General Barrié will assume the letter has reached Madrid and will be watching for reinforcements. What we need to do is to keep Marmont busy and when the siege guns finally reach us, we will attack."

Captain Dunbar looked up, "Even in winter, sir?"

Viscount Wellington rolled his eyes, "Dunbar, this is not the north of Scotland! It may be cold, and it may be wet but as soon as we can then we will attack. We take the guns we capture as well as our original siege guns and we head for Badajoz. From what you say that will be a harder nut to crack but I will not fail a third time."

"To be fair, Viscount Wellington, Marshal Beresford failed the first time."

"Dunbar, it is I who commands this army and I take responsibility!" The Captain shrank back. "So, Matthews, Alten commands the light cavalry but you are to command the 11th. Is that clear?"

"Sir."

"Do you need it in writing?"

I smiled, "I don't think so, sir."

I could tell that I was dismissed, and I left. Sharp was outside with the horses. "Well, Sergeant Sharp, you had better dust off your uniform and see if the Quartermaster can find you a Tarleton helmet. We are rejoining the regiment until further notice."

He laughed, "I am guessing, sir, that Major Wilkinson will be less than pleased."

I nodded as I swung my leg over Donna's back, "Especially as Viscount Wellington has asked me to look after the regiment until Colonel Cummings arrives."

I recognised Major General Charles Baron Alten as we passed the encampment of the King's German Legion. Although we had never spoken, we had nodded to each other when there had been staff meetings and, bearing in mind that I would be working directly under him I reined in when I saw him speaking with some German officers.

I dismounted, "Major General Alten?"

"Yes." There was just the hint of an accent in his voice.

"I am Major Matthews and Viscount Wellington has just briefed me. As I am to command the 11th I thought I should say hello."

He smiled, "Of course, and I have heard of you and your exploits. I am just surprised that you have not yet been elevated. You were Lieutenant Colonel earlier this year, were you not?"

"Yes sir but, as you yourself know, such promotions are temporary."

"Quite. Well, I am happy that you are serving with me. You have experience and everyone tells me what a reasonable chap you are. You know that it is Sir Thomas Picton who leads us?" It was a leading question. Sir Thomas had a certain reputation for he had been convicted of torturing a woman in the West Indies when Governor there and he was unpopular with a certain type of officer for he had a foul mouth. He also refused to wear any kind of military uniform, but I respected him for he knew how to lead men and his language rarely offended me.

"I fought alongside Sir Thomas at Bussaco, I can cope with him. I suspect our job will be to keep the infantry safe."

He nodded, "Brigadier Anson has the better command!" I heard the envy in his voice.

"Yes, sir, but all that we need to do is to keep Marmont from relieving Ciudad Rodrigo before winter sets in." He nodded. "When do we leave?"

"You have five days. Will that be enough?"

"Of course, sir."

I could work with the Hanoverian and his Germans were good soldiers. I would rather have them at my back than some British regiments which were badly led and often acted as though on a fox hunt. The behaviour of certain regiments had almost led to disaster at Talavera.

When we neared the camp of the 11th I said, "When we get to the Headquarter's tent I shall dismount. You see to the horses and then go to the Quartermaster. Get what you need from him and ask him if he has a couple of Baker carbines. As much as I like the rifle it is too cumbersome to use from the back of a horse and make sure that the regiment has enough of everything. Let him know what we are going to be doing." Sergeant Sharp knew what I meant without me saying. Grant would be staying in the main camp along with the clerks, farriers and the surgeon. The veterinary surgeon was still on sick leave and he would not be with us either.

I saw that the troopers were all busy polishing weapons and boots. I sighed; Major Wilkinson had a mistaken idea of what campaigning was all about. I dismounted and headed for the large Headquarter's tent. Sergeant Major Jones and his clerks were all busy and I hated what I was going to have to do but it was necessary. I had to make it work otherwise we would not be ready for the mission.

The Sergeant Major beamed when he saw me, "Glad to see that you are back, sir. Sorry, I can't stop to chat, but Major Wilkinson has asked us to update all of the records for the officers and troopers, sir. He wants to reorganize."

I put my hand on the papers he was studying, "Forget that, Sergeant Major. All of you, stop what you are doing. We have more important things to be getting on with. This regiment is going into action."

Jack looked nervously at the tent flap as though he expected Major Wilkinson to manifest himself like an apparition. "But sir, Major Wilkinson?"

"Sergeant Major, Viscount Wellington has put me in temporary command of the regiment."

Jack beamed and then a frown filled his face, "Does he know, sir?"

I smiled, "Not yet and I shall inform him myself. I want an officer's call in an hour. We will hold it in the officer's mess. Who is the regimental bugler these days?"

"It is still Corporal Dunne sir, try and take that bugle away from him if you dare!" He laughed.

"Then send him to me. We will be leaving the main camp in five days. I would like you to make a list of those who will be remaining here for the temporary encampment will be just that."

"Right sir." He turned to his clerks. "You heard the Major, now snap to it."

Major Wilkinson's tent was almost as large as the Headquarter's tent. I saw that he had surrounded himself with the younger officers who had recently joined, and I now understood his attempt to reorganize, He would marginalize the more senior officers and build up his own cadre of young officers loyal to him. He would reward them with temporary promotions and more favourable duties. I saw that his servant was polishing his spare boots and that was the measure of the man. I was aware that I had not had time to change into my uniform and I knew that it was a mistake, but I ploughed on anyway. I was already tired from the mission behind the lines and I did not need confrontation.

"Major Wilkinson, if I might have a word?"

"Of course." He spread his arms inviting me to speak.

"In private, if you please."

"Oh come, Major, these are all officers of the 11th, whatever you say to me can be said in front of them."

I saw some of the young officers grin and knew that he had been speaking in a derogatory fashion about me. My tiredness made me ignore the inner voice which counselled caution and I said, "I have just come from Viscount Wellington and he has put me in temporary command of the regiment until the Colonel arrives. Further, we are commissioned to join Sir Thomas Picton in an action against the French and as it is in less than five days, I have asked for a meeting with all officers in one hour." I smiled, "As you have most of the young officers here then you have saved Sergeant Major Jones a major task."

He stood and his face was red and effused with anger. He turned to the young officers, "Go! Now!"

His servant must have been used to such outbursts for he joined the officers and hurried away leaving us alone. We were like the centre of a storm. The two of us stood in silence for a moment.

"I do not believe you! I only have your word for this! I am a former Guards officer and you are…"

"Be very careful in your choice of words, Major. I will excuse your anger for I know that you expected to command but I will not brook any insubordination. I am not accustomed to being called a liar. Would you care to apologise now?"

In answer, he turned and said, over his shoulder, "I will see Viscount Wellington and get this sorted out!"

I sighed, "Be at the meeting in one hour or there will be consequences!"

He turned and looked at me and the first hint of doubt crossed his face. This was a man who was used to getting his own way! I had no time for this, and I turned and headed for the Officers' Mess. It was mercifully empty save for the clerk who was laying a map and paper on the table. "Sarn't Major thought you might need these, sir."

"Thanks, and could you get a mess orderly to organise some wine and glasses. Put it on my mess bill."

"Sir!"

I began to make notes on the piece of paper I had been given. I was unused to speaking in public to a large number of officers and I knew that thanks to Major Wilkinson, some of those listening would be looking for mistakes. I needed the regiment to know exactly what it would be doing for the battlefield was not the place to learn lessons! Officers began to drift in, and I knew that Percy Austen and Brian Hargreaves would be amongst the first. They did not disappoint me although they did not say anything, and I barely glanced up. The mess orderly had put the wine and the glasses out. I said, "Help yourselves to the wine, it is on me!"

"Good fellow, sir!"

There was soon a buzz of conversation, but I kept writing. Sergeant Sharp ghosted next to me, "I wasn't sure if you wanted me here, sir."

I nodded and said quietly, "Secrete yourself at the rear and keep an eye on things, eh? You know the form."

"Yes, sir." Sharp would do what he did behind the enemy lines and become my eyes and ears.

Sergeant Major Jones and Dunne came in. "Sir?"

I looked up at them. "Sergeant Major, make notes for me, eh?"

"Sir." He sat next to me.

"Dunne, when I have finished my briefing, I want you to speak to Sergeant Sharp. When we go into action you and he will be my shadows, the two of you need to act as one," I smiled, "Sergeant Sharp knows me better than I know myself and, I daresay, can be more candid than some."

"Yes, sir and I know Sergeant Sharp! Good to have you back, sir, and don't you worry. I have a good horse!" He headed out of the tent. Non-commissioned officers and other ranks are never comfortable in a gathering of officers.

Sergeant Major Jones glanced at his watch and then up at the officers. He said, quietly, "All here sir, except for the Major." He took out and tapped his watch meaningfully.

"Then I had better begin. I said an hour and now the hour is up." I stood and saw a red-faced Major Wilkinson appear in the entrance to the tent. He was out of breath and all eyes swivelled to watch him. I spoke, "Gentlemen." Every eye turned back to me and the Major took a seat. "Viscount Wellington has asked me to take charge of the regiment until Colonel Cummings arrives from England. The senior officers, Major Wilkinson excluded, all beamed at the news. "The reason is a simple one. The regiment has been either in England or in Ireland and has no battle experience here in Spain." I knew that Major Wilkinson had no battle experience at all for he had always been based in England and it was ceremony that he understood. "I, on the other hand, have been fighting in Spain and Portugal for the past three years. I am not saying that I know it all but I know enough to stop us making the same mistakes I saw green regiments make at Talavera, Bussaco and Fuentes de Oñoro." It would do no harm to give the younger officers a list of my battle honours.

I held up a map and showed it to them all. "This, gentlemen, is a map of Ciudad Rodrigo and the surrounding area." I put it down. "When I have finished with the briefing you will study it and either copy it or memorise it for we need to know this land as well as our home in England. In less than five days we will be operating less than eight miles from the fortress. We, along with the Hussars of the King's German Legion, will be serving under Major General Alten and protecting the infantry of Sir Thomas Picton."

As I had expected there was a buzz of conversation. I suspect that had Major Wilkinson been briefing them then he would have demanded silence. I sipped some of the wine and then looked pointedly at the younger officers. They all stopped talking.

"As of now, we will act as though we are about to fight a battle. Here are my standing orders. Every officer and trooper will clean and practise with his carbine. There will be no exceptions!" There was shock on the faces of many of the officers before me. "All of you will clean and practise with your pistols. I have four and even that is not enough! Corporal Dunne will be riding close to me at all times and you will obey every command when you hear his bugle. I will not have officers leading their men off as though they are hunting foxes. Punishment will result from such action. Is that clear?"

A few of them nodded. "Gentlemen, I want to hear you! Is that clear?"

"Yes, sir!" I noticed that Major Wilkinson kept his mouth closed. I would need to speak with him again! I had hoped that his meeting with Viscount Wellington would have changed him. I was wrong.

"We will be taking just what we need for our patrols. Dress uniforms and spare equipment will remain here at the camp. Sergeant Major Jones and Quartermaster Grant will command the camp in my absence. For the next three days, we will practise riding in formation and firing carbines from the backs of our horses. I have a number of manoeuvres which you will all need to know. A key one is to fire our carbines as a troop. A Troop will fire first and then we will open ranks so that they can ride to the rear, reloading as they do so. B Troop will advance and fire and then retire. This way we can use every gun in the regiment and keep up a withering rate of fire. Believe me, it takes a brave man to ride into such a devasting and relentless lead storm. I am sorry that we do not have more time. Had I known that I was to be given command then for the last week or so you would have all been practising rather than wasting your time polishing boots!" That was a deliberate dig at Major Wilkinson and I saw him react. "We will begin at dawn and end at dusk. Each of you is responsible for your own troop! I will be watching, and I will let you know if you fall short of the mark. Now any questions?"

As I had expected it was Major Wilkinson who spoke, "Am I to understand, Major Matthews, that if the French cavalry attack us, we will not be counter charging but using our little pop guns to deter them?"

"Very perceptive, Major Wilkinson. You have listened and understood the meaning of my standing orders. Be under no illusions, gentlemen, the French cavalry we face are better than we are… at the moment. They have something we don't have, experience. They have to fight not only us but guerrillas. Their Dragoons are happy to dismount and use their muskets. Their Chasseurs know how to use their swords and they fight well with them. To give you a clear answer, Major Wilkinson, we will not be counter charging, at least not in the way you expect. Our job is to keep French cavalry away from the infantry and that is all!"

There were no further questions and so I left them to study the map I had left. As I had expected Major Wilkinson did not stay but left the tent and I followed him, "Major." He turned and glared at me, "I am not a fool, Major Wilkinson, so do not treat me like one. I know that you did not say yes sir when I asked you to and you have disobeyed one order already by not studying the map." He opened his mouth and I continued, "Let me be quite clear. You have purchased a promotion although for the life of me I cannot work out why you chose a cavalry regiment. I am guessing, although I do not know, that you hope for some glory, perhaps with a view to a career in Parliament after this is over." He was not a good actor and could not disguise his reaction and I had hit the mark. "Unless you agree now to obey my every order then you will remain here in camp and I shall take Sergeant Major Jones with me in your place."

"You can't do that!"

"When you scurried off to Viscount Wellington what did he tell you?"

"That you were in command!"

"Precisely! So?"

Through gritted teeth, he said, "Yes, sir, I will obey every order." I pointed to the tent. "And I will study the map."

I saw Sharp and Dunne in conference and I would speak with Alan later. I found that my hands were shaking for I did not enjoy such confrontations. It seemed I had had to face such situations since I had served with the Chasseurs.

The first two days were horrendous. It was clear that all Major Wilkinson had done was have the men parade in their uniforms on the backs of their horses. They had marched at the walk and the only time they had used their weapons was when they had unsheathed their swords to salute. Jack Jones had shaken his head at their display, "Sir, Colonel Fenton had the lads well trained back in England but the voyage here and the Colonel's wound means that they have forgotten how to be cavalrymen!"

"Don't worry, we have time."

Each day, while the troopers ate, I spoke with the officers. Some were not happy to have their mealtime interrupted by my harangues, but they endured it. I knew already, from Sharp, that Lieutenants Crosby and Jennings were still under the sway of Major Wilkinson. At the end of the first day, I rearranged the troop assignments and split them up so that one was with Percy Austen and the other with Brian Hargreaves and this simple act made a difference. The first time that the regiments fired from the backs of their horses it was a disaster. Despite what the Sergeant Major had said, Colonel Fenton had not practised this drill, at least, not enough. Some horses had not been schooled well enough and the carbines made them buck their riders. Three troopers needed medical attention.

At the start of the third day, I had the regiment around me in a square. "Yesterday was a disgrace. If we had to face a French regiment today, then I would need a week to write the letters to your families to inform them of their loss. I had expected, by now, that we would be able to practise firing by troop and at targets, that will, patently, not happen." I took out my Baker carbine. Quartermaster Grant had managed to get a pair for Sharp and I. "Your carbine could be the difference between life and death. Imagine the effect of ninety lead balls being fired at enemy cavalry. Even if less than half found a target it would mean fewer Frenchmen for you to fight!" I knew that there would be doubters, and, just at that moment, a crow flew above the regiment. In one motion I cocked and raised the primed carbine and fired at the unfortunate bird. It fell obligingly at my feet. "Now I am, I know, a good shot, but so can you be. It needs practice! From today we will spend a minimum of two hours a day in a shooting drill. Those of you with skittish horses have this time to eliminate those traits. If you do not then you may find yourselves left on a battlefield. Your comrades, who will be in the hospital, will be the lucky ones."

My demonstration had the desired effect. We had fewer incidents. When, on the fourth day, I was summoned to a meeting of senior officers I left Captain Lutyens in charge and took Major Wilkinson with me. I do not know if he understood the reason, he seemed pleased, but I would not leave him alone with the regiment to undo all my work. In the event, it was the perfect decision for he met Sir Thomas and if he thought that I was a peasant then his introduction to Sir Thomas was a rude one.

The irascible general strode into the farmhouse which he was using with a round hat perched on his head and a tattered frock coat. He had a cigar in his mouth, and he waved affably as he entered. "I don't like to waste my time filling the air with damned empty words. We will be close to the damned Froggies and if the bastards come close to us then we will give them a bloody nose and kick their arses!"

I recognised Colonel Donkin from the 88th and saw him smile. I had fought alongside the Colonel at Oporto and knew that this was his kind of language. Major Wilkinson, in contrast, appeared to be in shock. Major General Alten just looked bemused.

"We have a few squadrons of cavalry with us, but I will not have them charging off like a pack of wild Irishmen. They are there to find Johnny Frenchman and then let my lads finish them off. Is that clear, Major General Alten?"

He smiled, "Yes, Sir Thomas."

The entire room knew Sir Thomas, and none was offended by either his tone, language or manner; all except for Major Wilkinson who looked dumbfounded. I think, for the first time, he realised that I had spoken the truth. This was not the war he imagined.

When we left the main camp, my regiment was assigned the task of being the vanguard. As we had more squadrons than the Germans, we also had to guard the baggage. I assigned Major Wilkinson and Captain Platt to that task. They were the weakest of my officers. His face was as black as thunder when I gave him his orders but as Major General Alten was next to me he could say nothing.

As I rode to the head of the column with the Major General, he said, "I have spoken with some of those who know Major Wilkinson. They do not speak well of him. He has bought his way to this position and he is like a butterfly. He spends a short time with each regiment and then moves on."

"But, sir, how does he afford it? A majority in this regiment costs over three thousand eight hundred and eighty pounds."

"The captaincy he sold in the guards brought him more money, but he seems to make money when he is an officer." He raised an eyebrow and no more needed to be said. An officer was paid well but there were so many expenses that an honest officer was lucky if he broke even. It was clear that Major Wilkinson was being corrupt and there were many ways to accomplish that! As I joined A Troop half a mile ahead of the column, I ran through the various ways a dishonest officer could make money and realised which one Major Wilkinson had chosen. The young Lieutenants in the regiment all came from money. An unscrupulous senior officer could take money in return for easier duties and glowing reports after actions. If an officer was gazetted as a result of an action, then promotion could ensue. I put the thoughts from my head and concentrated on the matter in hand for they were an irrelevant distraction. We needed to find a camp and then look for the French. Major Wilkinson was a nuisance. It was Marmont and his army who were the problem.

Chapter 4

I could see why Viscount Wellington had put me with Sir Thomas' command. Brigadier Anson had the mobility of five regiments of horse. Sir Thomas needed someone who knew the country and was a cavalryman. And I remembered that the village of El Bodón was a perfect place for defence. The cluster of houses and farms lay on a low ridge between the two main roads which headed west. Even better was that it was just seven miles from Ciudad Rodrigo which meant we could be supported quickly if Marshal Marmont tried to catch us out. The six Portuguese guns which accompanied us would give us just enough firepower to slow down an enemy advance. We reached the ridge by ten o'clock in the morning and while it would take another couple of hours for the baggage and guns to arrive, we had plenty of daylight to begin to build a defensive position.

Sir Thomas looked happy when he surveyed the site, "Damned good spot, Matthews. I can see you have an eye for these things. It must be all the time you spend with Viscount Wellington. Never knew a man better when it came to spotting the best place to defend easily. Now take some of your blaggards and see if the French are close. Don't let the bastards in Ciudad spot you though, eh?"

"Yes, sir!" It did not do to argue with Picton and so I nodded and headed north with A Troop. I had made Percy Austen the troop commander and ensured that he had the best troopers in the regiment, by that, I meant the best shots. A Troop was supposed to be the best and was referred to as the Right Troop for that was its position in the line, on the right. When we fought in squadrons then A and B Troops were the Right Squadron.

Without turning I said, "Dunne, this is your first time in this country so get used to it quickly. If I have to take off, then I want you a heartbeat behind along with Sergeant Sharp! He will see that you are safe!"

"Sir."

Percy asked, "I thought you said that they had withdrawn men from the fortress, sir? If that is the case it is unlikely that the garrisons will probe."

"It is Marshal Marmont who will be doing the probing. He might use the fortress for accommodation, but he has over sixty thousand men and five thousand cavalry. He will be looking for weakness in our defences. The French, Percy, are not like us. Bonaparte makes generals into marshals and then they each become rivals trying to outdo the others. Masséna was the golden boy until Fuentes de Oñoro and now Marmont will be trying to impress the Emperor for this is his first major command. He has only recently been promoted. If he can defeat Viscount Wellington, then he will gain the favour of the Emperor and be given more armies to command. We are lucky to be serving under such a good general as Sir Arthur."

I reined in because I had seen something, it was animal spoor. I dismounted and examined the dung. It was French and I knew that because we fed our horses different food. There was enough to suggest that it had been at least a troop which had passed this way and was a day or more old. They had halted here and that explained why there was so much of it.

Remounting I said, "We can go back now for this tells me that the French have scouted here already. They may be back but," I took out my watch, "not today. We will send Captain Lutyens out here tomorrow. This looks a good spot to watch for the French as our camp is just a couple of miles down the road."

As we headed back Percy asked, "You must do an awful lot of this, sir, riding behind the lines. Does it ever get hard?"

I laughed, "Sergeant Sharp and I always find it hard. The French get better and we have to improve too. If it is any consolation to you, Captain, the French find it harder than we do as they have to contend with us and guerrillas!"

By the time we returned I saw that the 5th Foot had provided the piquets and the six guns were being manhandled into position so that they could cover the northernmost road. I rode to Major General Picton to report and as I did so I was able to ascertain our numbers. With a thousand infantry and five hundred cavalrymen, we could prevent any French patrols from closing with the main camp but if Marmont came in force then we would have a difficult time extricating ourselves. General Picton seemed pleased with my news, "I shall leave Major General Alten in command. I don't see the point in two senior officers having to sleep on the ground. Besides, I can report to Viscount Wellington."

Major General Alten was with us and he nodded, "If you think that wise, Sir Thomas."

He leaned in, "Between the three of us, I am having problems with guts! To put it delicately, gentlemen, I have the shits!"

We all knew the dangers of a minor complaint becoming dysentery! The Hanoverian said, "You should have said so, Sir Thomas. You need not have come."

He laughed, "After my speech the other day I had to come! Let me know if Johnny Frenchman comes eh?"

After he had gone, with his aides, we discussed the dispositions of our men. The Hanoverian was experienced and had thought this through, "We will use the 5th as our forward line and have the rest of the infantry hidden from view just to the west there. I shall have my Germans to the right of the guns if you would have your three squadrons to the north of the guns where you can cover the road."

"Yes, sir."

The plan made sense and I left to join the regiment. Someone, I suspect Captain Austen, had ordered the men to dismount. I pointed to the depression just a few yards from the left flank of the 5th. "We will make camp here! D Troop, you will be the piquets. After you have tended to your horses take the troop, Captain Hargreaves, and make a camp close by the road where you can be our piquets."

"Sir."

This is where the training in England, the esprit de corps of each troop, would come into play. D Troop would have to watch the road while cooking for themselves and arranging the watches so that someone was on duty all night. I would rotate the duty and include myself in the rota. I suspected Major Wilkinson would try to get out of the duty as it would be beneath his dignity!

Sharp and Dunne had already seen to the horses and were erecting our tent. These were simple affairs and I knew that unless the weather turned nasty, we would not need them. I think they were erecting mine first as I was the commanding officer. I took my glass and climbed to a high spot to view the road. One of the officers from the 5th, Major Henry Ridge, joined me. He waited until I had scanned the horizon and then said, "Do you mind if I have a look, Major?"

"Be my guest."

When he handed it back, he said, "You were at Bussaco." I nodded. "We showed them there, but they do like to charge in column, don't they? Very obliging of them to present the fewest muskets so that we can use our line and decimate them before they close with us."

"That they do and if we are attacked by infantry then we shall send them packing but it is their cavalry I fear."

He nodded. We were alone and he could speak freely, "Sometimes, sir, our cavalrymen are just a little reckless!"

I laughed, "Diplomatically phrased, Major, but don't spare my blushes, I know that some of our officers are as mad as fish! Don't worry though the Major General is a good sort and my lads might be new to the Peninsula, but they will do the business!"

"Aye, we should be alright. We are only a few miles from the main army!"

I got up twice in the night to visit the piquets, but Percy and his troop sergeant had impressed upon them the need for vigilance. We woke to a grey September morning. I went to Captain Platt who commanded E Troop. "You can relieve D Troop at noon."

"Right sir."

He did not seem enthusiastic about it. "Captain Platt, you have been given the easiest assignment in the regiment. You are the adjutant and I know you appreciate the extra pay but out here we need you as a soldier. Impress me or I shall inform Colonel Cummings that you are ill-qualified to be the adjutant!"

"Sir!" I knew I had made another enemy and I would be driving him into Wilkinson's camp, but it had to be said.

I found Captain Lutyens; he and his men were preparing to go on patrol. "You know what you have to do?"

"Ride three miles down the road, wait until noon and then, if no one appears, return."

"This could be a quiet duty, sir."

I shook my head, "It might be, but you never say such things out loud!"

He laughed, "Superstitious, sir?"

"Aye and not ashamed to admit it. Most soldiers have superstitions. They also believe in God! There may be atheists back in England, but I guarantee that there are none here!"

"Amen to that."

I went to the vantage point on the top of the hill and watched them leave. Alarmingly, I saw that the road east was hidden from view as it undulated through the rough ground. That was worrying and I walked over to Major General Alten. He was with his Hanoverians. "Sir, we have a limited view of the road from here."

I led him to my vantage point, and he nodded, "Then we must place the guns a little better. Has the patrol left?"

"Yes, sir."

"Good. I will have the 5th change their positions too."

Sharp had some food on the go by the time I reached the regiment. I saw that Major Wilkinson had, once more, surrounded himself with the younger, more impressionable officers. I would have to do something about that and rearrange the troops or the bad apple could infect the whole barrel. I had just returned to the high ground when I saw a movement on the road. I calculated that Lutyens could not have reached the end of his patrol yet and I took out my telescope. It was B Troop and they were galloping back.

I rushed back to our camp and shouted, "Dunne sound, 'stand to'! Troop Sergeant, send a rider back to Viscount Wellington and tell him there may be trouble on the road."

All but Major Wilkinson were busy preparing for action. He turned and said, "Are there Frenchmen coming for us or not, Major?"

"Major, you heard 'stand to'! Now obey the bugle!" I turned and mounted Donna. Sharp had saddled her first. I rode up to the guns and found Major General Alten and Major Ridge there.

"We heard your bugle, is there a problem, Matthews?"

"There may be, sir. My patrol is galloping back which means that whoever they met outnumbered them. This is not just a patrol heading this way. I have sent a rider to the General to inform him. It seemed wise."

"I see your point. Colonel, tell your men to get their horses!"

"Sir." The Hanoverian Colonel hurried off for the King's German Legion mounts were some four hundred yards from their camp. My men were already saddling their horses.

Major General Alten said, "Major Ridge, take command here and I will fetch General Colville and his men. Major Matthews, rejoin your men if you please."

"Sir."

By the time I reached my men Captain Lutyens and the patrol galloped in. He pointed behind him. "There are at least eight regiments of cavalry coming down the road, sir, with a horse artillery battery and infantry supporting them. I was unable to count the infantry but it looked to be a long column; more than we have here, sir!"

That meant over two and a half thousand cavalrymen. The horse artillery battery would be six guns. "Dunne, I want the regiment formed up in troops. Make the call!"

"Sir."

As the notes rang out, I galloped to the reserves. Major Ridge would be able to prepare the defences on the ridge. I reined in as the infantry were forming up into lines. "Major General, there are eight regiments of cavalry! They have what appears to be a large number of infantry and a horse artillery battery!"

To be fair to the Hanoverian he did not panic. "Brigadier General Colville get your men to the road and have them form up there. Colonel Bacellar, take your Portuguese and support the guns." He turned to me, "Have your chaps slow them down and I will bring the Hussars to support you. We may have to pull out!"

I nodded, in my view that was obvious. We had not prepared a defensive position, we had just built a camp. That Marmont had sent so many men would come as a surprise to Viscount Wellington. I could not waste time in idle speculation, and I rode back to the regiment.

"Draw carbines!" Standing orders were to keep them loaded. All that we needed to do was prime them. "Prime!"

I primed my new carbine quickly but then again Sharp and I had the most experience. Dunne would not load a carbine as he was the bugler.

"Dunne, sound the advance."

We moved forward with just six inches between the knees of each rider. It was an effective formation when charging but even better when we fired for when a whole troop fired its carbines then the effect of the musket balls would be so close together that it would be like a shotgun. We had not travelled more than two hundred yards when I heard the Portuguese cannons open fire. I could not see them for they were above and behind me. What I did see were five regiments of Dragoons approaching us and they were moving from a line of column to lines of troops. They were four hundred yards from us. They were not charging as changing formation was a tricky affair and so we approached each other relatively slowly. It allowed me to identify the regiments for I could see their standards. The one which we would be facing first was the 15th Dragoon Regiment. Thankfully they had not thought to use their muskets and for that I was grateful.

I waited until they were three hundred yards from us and shouted, "Halt!" The bugle's notes rang out, but I was annoyed that some troopers did not stop immediately. "A Troop, present!"

The Dragoons were still coming on. The 15th would be the closest as the other regiments were fanning out to try to outflank us. I waited until they were eighty yards from us and I shouted, "Fire!" The air before us became grey with smoke. "Open ranks!" Dunne's bugle sounded and I said, "A Troop retire. B Troop, advance." I was desperate to look back, but I dared not. From now on the work we had done over the last week would show if the message had sunk in. I heard the volley and Captain Lutyens words were lost. I could hear the battle at the Portuguese guns and hoped that the 5th and the Portuguese were managing. I saw the troopers struggling to reload while they rode. My Baker carbine took a long time anyway. B Troop had joined us and there had been two more volleys behind us before I managed it.

I heard a stentorian voice shout, "The infantry will form square!" That told me the French cavalry was threatening the 5th. A battalion in square, supported by artillery, would normally defeat cavalry; especially holding the high ground.

Captain Dunbar galloped up, "Viscount Wellington got your message and he came here in person. He is going back to the main camp to organise the defence. He has ordered Major General Alten to begin to withdraw. The infantry will retreat in square and the cavalry is ordered to keep their cavalry at bay."

"All eight regiments?"

He smiled, "He has great confidence in you, sir! I will see you back at camp." Turning his horse, he galloped back down the road.

"Dunne, sound 'fall back'. A Troop, hold your position and be prepared to fire when the last troop has passed us." I turned to Percy Austen." I will have to leave A Troop while I command the regiment. You have the best men and thus far they have acquitted themselves well. This will be tricky. The command I shall give will be to attack by troop, but I only want carbines to be used. Keep their swords sheathed!"

"Yes sir, but it is Major Wilkinson you will need to tell."

I knew then that I should have left him at the main camp! It was Major Wilkinson and his men who passed through our lines and were the last of the regiment. I saw that a couple of his troopers had wounds and I wondered how that had happened.

"Prime!" The Dragoons who came at us were not just one regiment, they were a number. This time I waited until they were less than sixty yards from us before I shouted, "Fire!"

"Dunne, sound about face and retreat!" They were two calls and the experienced bugler paused between them and then again before repeating them. Our last volley had halted the French and they gave us the breathing space we needed to retreat. As we came upon the flatter ground, I saw the infantry regiments and they were in square. Moving a square of infantry was the slowest pace for a quarter would be walking backwards and a half sideways! I watched the Portuguese artillery as it bounced along with the gunners running alongside it. The German Hussars were on the other side of the road and I gave another order to Dunne, "Form Squadrons."

This meant we would have three squadrons. Two would have two troops in each one and one, Major Wilkinson and his men would have just one troop and, even more worryingly, they would be on the exposed left flank. We had a long six miles or so to safety, I was reassured that Viscount Wellington was organising a defence and there was no one better at that, but we had an almost impossible task. The cavalry who opposed us would probe for weaknesses and they still had their horse battery. That could destroy any of our walking squares.

We had some moments of grace for, thanks to our carbines, the Dragoons were wary of approaching too close to us. I had no time to reload my Baker and now I would have to use my pistols. I was gratified to see A Troop all reloading.

I shouted, "Get the wounded to the rear!"

We made almost half a mile before the French reorganised and the Dragoons came for us. In a way, I was quite happy about this as the Chasseurs were the more dangerous foe and I had not seen the uniform of the 13th, my old regiment. I would not have liked to fight against them.

I shouted, "Walk the horses backwards to allow the infantry to gain some ground." I knew that we could not walk all the way backwards, but we could now and that would buy the infantry time. Behind us was the 1st Battalion of the 77th Foot, the East Middlesex. They were struggling to keep in formation. That wasn't unusual for few regiments had to practise marching backwards. I saw the French Horse Artillery gallop up and I knew what they intended. With so many Dragoon regiments they would easily stop just a hundred yards from the 77th, unlimber and then massacre a fine regiment.

"Captain Austen, when I give the command, we will charge those guns. You will have the men halt and fire at a range of eighty yards."

"Sir!"

"Captain Hargreaves and Captain Lutyens, you will support us and engage the Dragoons with carbines. Major Wilkinson you will continue to protect the infantry."

I heard the two captains shout, "Yes sir!" but the Major was ominously silent! There was no time for debate as I saw the horse artillery unlimber and I knew how fast they would be.

"Charge! Go for the gunners and the horses!"

It was a great deal to ask from such inexperienced men but there was no other choice. Sir Arthur had hung us out on a branch and circumstances had dictated the outcome! I drew a pistol and led the charge. We had no fire to face for the guns had yet to be turned and the Dragoons were still holding their swords. I heard Captain Austen shout, at eighty paces, "Halt! Fire!" As the carbines popped, I rode to within forty paces and aimed my pistol at the Captain who commanded one of the guns. Two of his men were already down and I fired my pistol at his chest. I then holstered my pistol and, drawing my sword rode directly into the guns where, ironically, I was the safest. I slashed at horses, men and traces. Behind me, I heard Dunne's bugle sound the retreat. I drew a second pistol and fired at the Dragoon who had charged from nowhere. At ten yards I could not miss, and his face disappeared as my ball struck his nose. I obeyed my own bugle and turned and galloped back towards our infantry squares. An artilleryman rose from beneath a gun and waved his short sword at me. Using my knees, I guided Donna to the other side and hacked down at his shoulder. He fell in a heap.

I was the last to reach the regiment and I was greeted by a huge cheer. I did not know so at the time but that was a mistake!

As I faced the French I saw that while few of the gunners had been killed, enough damage had been done to the horses and limbers to mean that they would not be able to use artillery against the vulnerable squares of infantry until repairs had been made. I saw that our infantry were now four hundred yards away. "The Regiment will fall back to protect the 77th. About face!"

The simple about face manoeuvre meant that A Troop, the best troopers, were at the back. I glanced over my shoulder and saw that the French had been disorganised and were busy sorting out their regiments so that they could attack us again. I did not expect all of the troopers to have reloaded for we had not practised that drill and only the most confident of troopers would attempt it. I still had two loaded pistols and so I kept an eye on the French as we neared the 77th who gave a cheer as we approached.

Brigadier General Colville rode up to me, "Good work, Matthews, but we have a long way to go. You know cavalry; what will they do, do you think?"

"They know they outnumber us. The odds are four to one in their favour. They will try to draw us into a skirmish with them and they will rely on the reputation we have earned and expect us to be reckless. If we hold our nerve, then your muskets can keep them at bay. I will keep the regiment to your flank, sir, and that way your muskets can have an uninterrupted field of fire."

Just then we heard a volley of muskets and saw, to the south of us, Brigadier Alten doing the same with the Germans and the 5th. The other British regiments were also marching in square with their flanks protected. The French could charge them, but they would be facing the grenadier companies of the 83rd and the 94th. That would be a daunting prospect. The order to form square had been vital.

We managed another three hundred yards before the French tried another attack. The infantry were the ones who alerted us for they had men who were marching backwards. I still do not know how they managed it without falling over! The Grenadier Major shouted, "The 77th will halt and present!"

"Dunne, sound about face!"

I turned Donna around and saw that three of the French Dragoon regiments were preparing to charge us. Their formation meant that they would charge us obliquely and minimise the effect of the muskets of the

77th. Once again, the reputation of the British cavalry meant that they saw us as weak.

"The regiment will not counter charge. Every trooper will discharge his weapon at the French but only on my command."

I reloaded the pistol in my holster, and I saw the troopers with discharged weapons loading them. The French bugle sounded, and the Dragoons began to charge. There were drills for charges as I knew well. When I had been in the Chasseurs, I had been trained to draw my sword only when the command was given and that was normally when we were just forty yards from an enemy. The sight and sound of blades being drawn were intimidating. The French began to increase their speed as they closed with us. Although they had experienced our carbines once they would not expect a second volley. It simply was not done, and I hoped the shock of our volley would tear the heart from them. Their oblique charge meant that the first troop they would engage was Major Wilkinson's. As the second most senior officer in the regiment, it was his place, but I wished that it had been Hargreaves or Lutyens!

Timing was everything and I shouted, "Fire by troop! C Troop!" As soon as I heard the carbines volley, I shouted, "B Troop, fire!" I saw that A Troop was anticipating the command and had their carbines raised. I could no longer see the French for clouds of carbine smoke masked them, but I heard whinnies, cries and shouts which told me that we had hurt them.

I was about to give the order for A Troop to fire when I heard Major Wilkinson shout, "C Troop, charge!" There was a roar from the troopers who followed their foolish and insubordinate leader to their doom.

Mentally cursing him I shouted, "A Troop, fire! E Troop, use your carbines to support C Troop." Captain Platt was no hero and he would do just what I commanded but we would lose troopers unnecessarily!

I had my pistol ready for I knew that I could not hit at the same range as the carbines and I awaited the first Frenchman to emerge through the smoke from A Troop's carbines. It was an officer and he loomed up just fifteen paces from me. I fired at his chest and I managed to hit him. I holstered the pistol as he wheeled away. To my right, I heard the command to present and then to fire by rank. The rolling volleys of the three ranks of the 77th had a dramatic effect and the French Dragoons withdrew. As the smoke cleared and the French bugles sounded the retreat, I saw that C Troop had been badly handled.

"Dunne, sound disengage! Sharp, come with me. Captain, take command!"

I spurred Donna who had to leap over the dead Dragoon laying before A Troop. I saw that we had hurt them. The clash of sabres told me that not all of the Dragoons had obeyed their trumpet. Major Wilkinson was duelling with a French officer, but I saw that the Major did not have the skill to do so on horseback. The fencing he had done had been with the earth beneath his feet and not the horse which twisted, turned and reared. Even as I drew and fired a pistol into the back of a Dragoon who was about to skewer a trooper, I saw the Dragoon's sword slash down the face of Major Wilkinson. It would be the prelude to a coup de grace. Next to me, Sergeant Sharp's pistol emptied another French saddle and the French Dragoons began to obey their bugle. Holstering my pistol, I drew my heavy cavalry sabre. Major Wilkinson's blade was already bent from the effects of the French blade. I watched the French Captain raise his sword to finish off the Major. With blood streaming down his face he could see little.

I shouted, in French, "Captain! I command you to stop!" The shock of hearing French and an order at that made him hesitate. It was enough for me to swing my sword in a slashing arc. The French Captain did two things. He wheeled his horse as he slashed down at the Major. My sword connected with the head of his horse and his sword hacked into Major Wilkinson's leg.

The Captain continued his wheel. His horse was wounded but could still gallop; horses were brave, and he rode away shouting, "I will remember you, traitor!"

"Get Major Wilkinson to safety." As his servant took the reins of his horse and galloped west, I looked and saw that the only unwounded officer was Lieutenant Gates. "Lieutenant, take command of C Troop and fall in behind A Troop."

"Sir!"

Thanks to Major Wilkinson's disobedience I would have to reorganise. Until that moment we had had few casualties but as I rode back to A Troop I saw that seven troopers lay dead and there were others who were wounded. Two officers had been wounded and we had been weakened! "Captain Hargreaves you will take your troop and guard our flank."

"Sir!"

To the south of us, I heard the sound of fighting and saw that the Germans were having to fend off the French Chasseurs. As I looked east, I saw the column of French growing ominously close. If the French could pin us with their cavalry then their infantry could break us! Brigadier Colville shouted, "The 77th will resume their march!" He raised his sword in salute.

"Dunne, sound reform!"

Once again, we would allow the infantry to move down the road a little before we followed them. The French Dragoons still had two regiments who had not joined in the last charge and they would be a threat, but they had lost men and, more importantly, horses. If I had been the commander of the Dragoons, I would have used their firepower against us for they outnumbered us five to one and their muskets had a longer range. As we reformed, I looked and saw that Major Wilkinson's servant, Private Short, had stopped to apply a tourniquet. We had no doctors with us and so I knew he would have to ride the few miles back to the main camp before he could receive medical attention.

"The 11th will about face and follow the 77th!"

I wondered if Brigadier Colville would rotate his regiments so that one of the others bore the brunt of the French attacks. They had lost one man during the attack as some of the French Dragoons had closed with the front ranks and used their long swords to cause some damage. When I saw that the other regiments were still in the same line of march, I knew that the Brigadier would continue to use the 77th.

We were just a mile and a half from the main camp when the next attack materialised. It was quite obvious to me that the French did not know where Viscount Wellington was keeping our men and that worked to our advantage. I knew that our clever commander would have made the camp like a fortress; he knew how to defend.

"The 77th will halt and present!"

Hearing the words, I shouted, "The 11th will about face." I had been aware of the French behind us and I had glanced around as they had followed us. As we turned, however, I saw that their infantry had caught up and there appeared to be at least eight regiments. That was almost six and a half thousand men. The French cavalry commander, we later learned from a prisoner that it was General Lamotte, intended to break us for he had his two largely intact regiments to the fore and he intended to charge us.

"Form line of squadrons!"

The formation meant that we could bring every carbine and pistol to bear. Lining up I saw troopers hastily reloading. If they did so badly then it would not matter overmuch as even a badly loaded carbine could send a ball, and sometimes a ramrod, in the direction of the enemy. As we had ridden back I had managed to reload all of my pistols and my Baker carbine. The regiment appeared more at ease than when the French had first appeared. In many ways, despite the losses, Major Wilkinson's abortive charge had helped for even the young lieutenants saw the wisdom of my commands. The Dragoons had a four-squadron frontage and intended to hit us and the 77th in one knee to knee charge. This was not an oblique charge; it was a frontal assault and would be a real test of all of us. I risked a glance to the south and saw that the three regiments of Chasseurs were employing the same tactic against the King's German Legion. This was a determined attempt to break us and win the battle.

"Present!" The muskets of the 77th outranged our carbines and they would be firing first. Sharp and I, however, had a carbine which had a greater range than the Brown Bess. "Sergeant, let us see if we can hit their officers, eh?"

"Good idea sir!"

We were both good shots and knew how to shoot from the saddle. We both held our carbines to the right of our horses' heads so that the sparks from the pan would not frighten them. I also rested my left elbow on Donna's neck. It gave me stability and it helped to have such a calm horse. "I will take the one to the right. You take the officer in the centre." The squadrons were led by either colonels or majors and if we could hit them then it might dismay those following. I fired at a range of one hundred yards. It was almost twice the range of the rest of the carbines and I knew the Dragoons would not be expecting us to fire. My ball was fired before Sharp's and not only did I hit my target, he was knocked from his horse and dragged along by his stirrup. His head cracking into a rock gave him a merciful death. Sharp hit his target and although he did not fall from the saddle, I saw that he was hurt. Then the muskets from the 77th and the 5th rolled out and grey acrid smoke filled the air to the right of me. I dropped the carbine; it would hang from its swivel and I drew two pistols.

"Prepare to fire!" The Dragoons were less than eighty yards from us when I shouted, "Fire!" The speed of the Dragoons brought them into the range of the two hundred and odd carbines. Smoke filled the air before me and I shouted, "Draw sabres and advance!" As I kicked Donna in the ribs, I fired my two pistols into the smoke, sheathed them and drew my own blade.

Screams, shouts and whinnies told me that we had hurt their front line and slowed it. To my right rolling volleys told me that the infantrymen were giving a good account of themselves. Entering the smoke was like waking up to find fog outside your front door. I had my sword raised and when the Dragoon who emerged through the gloom lunged at my middle, I swept aside his long sword with mine and Dunne urged his horse forward to hack into his arm with his own sword. The Dragoon's blade fell, and the rider turned his horse to flee.

Once more the French sounded the retreat and as the smoke cleared, I could see why. The ground before the 77th was filled with riderless and dead horses and some dead Dragoons. Others were clinging to the saddles of their comrades who were also falling back.

"Thank you, Corporal Dunne, now sound the reform!"

I saw that some of our troopers had wounds but the only dead we had suffered was because of Major Wilkinson's mistake. That was a problem I would have to deal with back in camp. If we made it that far.

As we began to make our way back, I saw that there were skirmishers ahead and artillery pieces. Viscount Wellington had prepared a warm welcome. We were so close that Brigadier Colville gave the order to change to column.

I shouted, "11th, about face!"

Until the infantry were safely behind the defences we would wait. I turned and looked to the other side of the road and saw that Major General Alten had done the same. This time the Dragoons did not charge but waited for their infantry and the horse artillery. The gunners looked to have repaired the damage. Our horses were exhausted, and I saw that the troopers were too but now was not the time for laxity. I rode along the line and spoke to the regiment. "You have all done well but this is not yet over. Until the infantry and the artillery reach the safety of Viscount Wellington's defences we wait here. You have all learned how to use a carbine and I am pleased but we can do better. Just a little while longer and we will have done our duty and you will be able to add El Bodón to our battle honours."

I returned to Sergeant Sharp who nodded, "The lads will appreciate that, sir."

We did not have long to wait, and we heard the notes of recall sound behind us.

"Columns of fours!" I wheeled Donna with Dunne and Sharp next to me and we led the regiment through the lines to the encampment.

As we passed Viscount Wellington he said, "Well done 11th! When you have the time, Matthews, I would appreciate a word with you."

"Certainly sir. I will see to the regiment first."

He nodded, "I think we shall be busy here until dark."

Chapter 5

I discovered that Major Wilkinson was being tended to by the doctor, but the wounds were not life-threatening. Private Short came to me to bring me the news, "Major Wilkinson is a decent chap, sir, but his family expects great things of him!"

I looked at him, "Short, he is not a cavalryman, and neither are you. If he stays in the regiment then one of you, perhaps both, will die. I do not say this with any kind of pleasure. You know that this is true."

He nodded, "I know, sir, and thank you for today. You saved the Major's life, but I do not think he will show you gratitude for it."

"Nor do I expect it. He is in my regiment and all the men of my regiment are precious to me."

"I know, sir. I know."

I did not ride Donna back to Viscount Wellington for she had done enough. Instead, I took Sergeant Major Jones' mount, Anna. She was not a warhorse, but she was a lovely horse to ride for she was gentle and obedient.

When I reached the front line, all was quiet, and darkness had fallen. I saw the French fires. They were beyond the range of our artillery. Viscount Wellington nodded and dismounted. He handed his reins to one of his aides, Lieutenant Hogg, "I was almost humbugged today, Matthews. What you may not know is that Marshal Marmont sent another eight squadrons of Chasseurs and Lancers further north. Brigadier Anson sent them packing but it has shown me that we need more cavalry. You and Alten handled yourselves well today. Colville has been singing your praises."

I nodded, "Considering that they were new to the Peninsula I think that the 11th did well."

"I am sorry, Matthews, for it is your regiment but we cannot afford second-best here. From what I have heard Major Wilkinson was almost responsible for a disaster."

I sighed and defended the indefensible, "To be fair, sir, Major Wilkinson is an infantryman and not a cavalryman. There are differences in the way we fight battles and skirmish. He needs to learn how to fight and lead from the back of a horse."

"Then I will make it quite clear what is expected of him." He showed me that he had put that minor irritation from his mind and lifted his telescope. "We hold here and when the French run out of food and fall back east then we reoccupy El Bodón. Major General Alten thinks that it is a good position which we can make better."

I bit the bullet, "And Sir Thomas?"

"I am promoting Brigadier Colville to Major General and until Sir Thomas is well again then he will command." He leaned closer, "When January arrives, we shall go on the offensive. The siege train is but a couple of weeks away. I intend to strike when Marmont least expects it. Now get back to your regiment. I can handle this!"

I confess that I was exhausted for it was not just the long day but the fact that I had had to use an inexperienced regiment against five of the best cavalry regiments in Spain and that took concentration which was as exhausting as fighting! However, before I could eat or even change, I needed to see Major Wilkinson. He had disobeyed a direct order and almost cost us the battle. I rode back to the hospital. I saw many of the men wounded in the battle. I was gratified by the cheers and the applause when I entered. These men did not resent their wounds. The two wounded officers were kept separate from the rank and file. Captain Jameson was already standing when I entered. He had his arm in a sling and he looked a little shamefaced, "I am sorry, sir, I disobeyed you and I should not have. If you wish to take disciplinary action against me then I shall understand."

I shook my head, "You obeyed Major Wilkinson, but it was a mistake. Learn from it."

"I shall, sir."

Major Wilkinson looked to be in a far worse state. His head was encased in a bandage and I could just see his mouth and eyes. His leg was wrapped in bandages. I waved the doctor over, "Can I speak with him, doctor?"

"It would do little good as I had to give him a large quantity of laudanum."

I nodded, respecting his professionalism, "And his wounds?"

"He will have a scar for the rest of his life, but it is not life-changing. His leg, on the other hand, is. I saved the leg and did not have to amputate but that was thanks to Private Short. His prompt action contributed greatly. However, there was tendon damage and he may never walk properly again." He tapped his head, "Much of this will be in his head. Some men can cope with such adversity whilst others…"

"Thank you, doctor, I shall visit again tomorrow."

The doctor smiled, "Those who were wounded spoke of your leadership and courage, Major, and I would take that as the greatest compliment. Those men would follow you to hell again if you asked."

"I know, doctor, and that is a heavy weight for a man to carry!"

Before I ate, I went to the Headquarter's tent. Jack Jones and his clerks and orderlies were there. They had much to do for there were reports to write and equipment and animals to replace. The Sergeant Major said, "Sit down, sir." He turned to one of his orderlies, "Jenkinson, fetch the Major a mug of rum, he needs it."

"There is no need, Sergeant Major."

"There is every need for you are out on your feet." Jenkinson gave me the mug and I downed it in one. The fiery liquid burned but Jack was right. I had needed it. "A close-run thing today, sir. Viscount Wellington had all of us armed and ready to join the line. The lads who came back first said it was a perfectly executed withdrawal under fire from superior numbers."

"But it wasn't just me. It was the whole Division."

"Nevertheless, we did our part."

"What is the butcher's bill?"

He sighed, "We had more casualties than any other regiment apart from the Germans. They lost forty-four men. We had eight men killed and fourteen wounded. Two officers were also wounded."

That depressed me more than anything. But for the Major's reckless and ridiculous charge we might have had a handful of wounded. No matter what happened he could not return to the regiment. I would see Viscount Wellington and have him court-martialled and to hell with the repercussions. I left Jack and went to the Officer's Mess where there was hot food. I was greeted by a cheer, but it sounded hollow to me for we had lost too many men.

I told them all the news they wanted to hear, "Captain Jameson is fine but Major Wilkinson is still in danger. Tomorrow we reorganise the troops as we have a winter of this type of thing. You all did well today but all of us know that we could have done better." They nodded for they were learning the difference between serving in England and on campaign.

There is more to running a cavalry regiment than simply mounting a horse and fighting the enemy. The next morning the farriers and the veterinary were all busy tending to the horses. Troopers had equipment to repair and to replace. That gave time for the officers and myself to reorganise the troops. Most of the losses had been in C Troop. Captain Platt had not impressed me during the action and so I disbanded his troop and added his men to C Troop as well as filling the ranks of the other troops. Platt could function as an adjutant, but I made certain that I had a word with him and suggested that resigning his commission might be a better option for him. I threatened him with putting him in the front line the next time we fought. I saw the fear on his face, and he said he would consider it. The result of all of this was that it was late morning by the time I was able to get to the hospital.

Almost all of the patients had been discharged. For one thing, there were not enough medical staff to care for them and the rank and file preferred to be with their tent-mates who would tend to them as well as any orderly. Captain Jameson had reported for duty and had been at the staff meeting. The action had been sobering for him and he had changed as a result. The doctor met me at the entrance to the tented hospital, "The Major will not lose his leg, but he is low in spirits, Major."

"But he is lucid?"

"What?"

"The medicine you have given him will not impair his judgement and thoughts."

"No, no, it is just for the pain. He can speak with you if that is what you mean."

I entered and saw Private Short tending to him. "I will see to that Major Wilkinson. Major Matthews is here to speak with you."

He saluted as he left and I sat on the camp-stool next to the bed. "Come to gloat have you, Matthews? Here to tell me 'I told you so'!"

"That is not my way. You are one of my officers and I came here to see how you fared. The doctor says that you will not lose the leg and that is good."

"If you expect me to thank you for intervening then you are also mistaken!"

"You truly do not understand soldiers do you, Major? Perhaps you should have stayed in the Guards where you could have paraded in polished boots and sparkling uniform. I came here to make pleasant enquiries, but I can see that is not what you wish. I will leave but you should know that I intend to speak with Viscount Wellington about your disobedience of my orders. At the very least there will be an enquiry, but I should warn you that I expect it to be a court-martial. Men died as a result of your lack of self-control. Good day, Major." He was stunned into silence. I do not think he had thought there would be such repercussions.

After I had lunched, I took Anna again for the farrier was tending to Donna and I rode alone to the front line. As I had expected, Viscount Wellington was there with Sir Thomas Picton. I saluted and asked, "Are you better, Sir Thomas?"

"Yes, Matthews, and I was damnably sorry to have missed the opportunity to hurt the French the other day, but I hear that you and Alten acquitted yourselves well. Thank you!" He turned his horse. "I shall go and organise the division then, Viscount Wellington."

Viscount Wellington shook his head as the idiosyncratically dressed Major General rode off, "Irascible, but none better in a fight. And your regiment, Matthews, how are the men? Could they ride soon?"

"Yes, sir. Today is make do and mend but I have reorganized the troops and we can field two strong squadrons."

He nodded, "And that Major of yours, what of him?"

"He will be on sick leave for some time, sir, but if I was to be honest, I believe he is a lost cause and I do not say that lightly. He is not a cavalry officer and I would not be confident with him as a second in command. Had I fallen at the battle then he would have charged the whole regiment and there would be none left to obey your orders."

"That is a stark assessment, but you are an honest fellow. Leave Major Wilkinson to me. His family is not without influence and we have little enough support in Parliament as it is. This requires diplomacy but, as you say, he is indisposed for a while and he will not be a problem. I want your regiment here tomorrow. The French are still there, and it is a waste of manpower just watching them. I intend to take Ciudad Rodrigo in January for the siege guns will be here by then and I want the men rested and prepared before we assault their walls. Let us see if we can make these chaps scurry back to Salamanca! And then Major General Picton can return to El Bodón."

We had not had a long break but sometimes that was what was needed. I had an officers' call and told them what we would be doing. Captain Jameson was keen to come along but I pointed out that he would be of little use with his arm in a sling.

I then addressed them all, "The action the other day showed me that the regiment has potential, gentlemen, but there is still work to do. When we are back in camp, we resume our training. When January comes, we will not be engaged as a regiment but as troops and we will be protecting our men from French attacks. That means each troop must act alone and the responsibility will be upon your shoulders." I allowed that to sink in. "We will be returning to El Bodón once the French have left. We now know what to expect so each of you must prepare your troop."

I went to speak with Sergeant Major Jones. "I am leaving Captain Platt here as adjutant when we return to El Bodón and I need you two and the Quartermaster to ensure that the regiment has all that it needs for the winter. When Colonel Cummings arrives, I want the regiment to be in the best condition. We owe him that."

"And you, Major Matthews, will you still be with the regiment or will Viscount Wellington whisk you away again?"

Bloody Badajoz

"You know, Jack, I have no idea and that is another reason why I want everything right for Colonel Cummings."

When the regiment reached the front line the next morning, I saw that he had ordered not only our brigade of cavalry but also that of Brigadier Anson. We now had four regiments of cavalry to face the Dragoons and Chasseurs. It took half the morning for Viscount Wellington to position us and I think that was deliberate to make the French think that this would be a major attack. The 3rd Division was placed in the centre in a huge line and at noon the order was given to advance. It was almost laughable for as soon as the line moved forward, we heard the French drums sound the retreat.

Viscount Wellington rode with us for the first few miles, "Have your swords in their backs and keep them moving until you reach El Bodón."

The carcasses of the dead horses still lay where they had fallen in the charges and the skirmishes. None were whole for the French infantry had hacked into them for meat. There was never enough food on the battlefield and here in Spain, the French soldiers would get nothing from the Spanish. We reached El Bodón by the middle of the afternoon and we halted. Having fought here already we knew the best positions to occupy and the guns were placed, and camps created before dark. This time we did erect tents for we did not expect to leave here before the weather changed. Once the rains came then we might be ordered back to the main camp but, equally, we could be left here until the siege.

In the end, although the regiment had to endure the winter there I did not. I was summoned back to Headquarters and I left Captain Austen in temporary command. He was dependable and if he had had enough money would have bought a majority in the regiment. It was still annoying that promotion was not through ability but coin!

When I reached headquarters, I found that Colonel Cummings had arrived and that explained my summons. He was with Sergeant Major Jones, Quartermaster Grant and Captain Platt when I arrived. I liked the Colonel as soon as I met him.

"Good to meet with you Major. Colonel Fenton has told me all about you and I know that the regiment has been in good hands. It will be some days until I can get to El Bodón; how is the regiment coping?"

I looked pointedly at Captain Platt whose eyes would not meet mine, "The fighting retreat seems to have made cavalrymen of them, sir. They can now patrol and perform piquet duty. They have learned from Elvas and El Bodón."

He nodded and said, "It is a shame that we lost irreplaceable troopers to do so. Officers we can get but troopers are another matter. Would you take the air with me Major? It is a little fresh, but I find that invigorating."

"Of course, sir."

Once we were outside with our cloaks wrapped around us, he said, "There are three problems that I can see and they are all officers: Major Wilkinson, Captain Jameson and Captain Platt."

I shook my head, "Jameson is not a problem, sir. He obeyed Major Wilkinson's orders. Major Wilkinson is a very forceful character."

He nodded and I was pleased that he seemed to accept my judgement. It boded well for the future. "I know, I have met him and a more obnoxious individual I have yet to meet." He chuckled, "He does not like you, Matthews!"

I laughed, "That does not surprise me, but I shan't lose any sleep over it."

"And Platt?"

"He has never been a good cavalryman. He has no interest in the war nor in the regiment. I suggested that he resigned his commission."

"And that might well work out for my sister's son seeks a commission and his father has money. I shall write to him. He cannot be any worse than Platt." He saw my look and continued, "Look, like you I know that the purchase of commissions is not always good for the army, but Ralph is a good chap and I can mould him."

"It is your regiment, sir, and, as you say, he cannot be any worse. Now Major Wilkinson is a problem and he has influence back home. We cannot be so cavalier with him."

"No, and there is another problem, Matthews, you."

I was so shocked that I stopped, "Me, sir?" I wondered what had been said.

He shook his head, "Sorry, those were the wrong words. Viscount Wellington has asked for you back again and my problem is that I need a good major and you are not going to be around all of the time."

"Then promote Austen and Hargreaves, sir, or Lutyens. They are all good men and the extra pay might help them to buy a majority. I would have done so already but I knew you were coming and did not want to interfere."

"That might well work but Major Wilkinson is another matter. Let us see Viscount Wellington and use the chain of command to our advantage."

We were not admitted straight away for Sir Richard Fletcher, Viscount Wellington's Engineer was with him and they were planning the assault on Ciudad Rodrigo. Regimental issues were secondary. When the three of us were alone he waved us to seats and sighed, "I know why you are here, and I fear that this is a distraction that I could do without. I have yet to find a solution to the problem."

There was silence. The Colonel was new to the Peninsula and Viscount Wellington had other things on his mind. "He disobeyed a direct order, sir, and he should be court-martialled."

"A messy affair, Matthews, and a difficult one to prove. He could argue that he had to charge to prevent the French from flanking you. He was the flank troop."

And that told me that Viscount Wellington had already broached the subject. I tried another tack. "Sir, the Major does not want to be in the cavalry. I think he would rather be back in the Guards or an infantry regiment. Surely, he could be persuaded to sell his majority and buy one in a line regiment."

Viscount Wellington looked interested, "That might work but he is an unpleasant fellow and he may choose to be awkward."

"Then how about this, sir. I will go to him, with the Colonel, and we will hint that a court-martial will take place and that win or lose his name would be dragged through the mud. If you were then to offer him the chance to change horses, as it were, then it might persuade him."

Viscount Wellington went to a pile of papers and began to scan them, "Ah, here is one which might do. The 28th is with Marshal Beresford, and they lost several officers recently including a major. That might just do." He looked happier. "Go along to see Major Wilkinson and when he erupts, as I know he shall tell him to come and see me. I will make the suggestion and couch it in such a way that refusal is not an option. Was there anything else?"

I looked at the Colonel who said, "Yes sir, as Major Wilkinson will be leaving us, and Major Matthews will have duties to perform for you then I would like to temporarily promote two of my captains."

He waved an airy hand, "Your regiment, Cummings, do as you wish!"

Major Wilkinson was not staying in the camp and he had rented a house in the village. The Colonel and I walked there to meet him. Private Short admitted us. The major's face was no longer bandaged, and the stitches were visible as was the red and angry scar. It would make him look permanently angry. The colonel began, "Major, I have had the opportunity to speak with Major Matthews and the other officers in the regiment. I am of the opinion that you deliberately disobeyed Major Matthews' order."

He gave a smile which might have been intended to be sly but the scar just made it look lopsided and the effort caused him pain, "I had to react and defend the flank of the regiment. I should be honoured for my efforts and not hounded."

"Nevertheless, Major, a court-martial is a messy affair and you would not like your name dragged through the reports, would you?"

The Major jabbed an angry finger in my direction, "This is your doing! You are trying to get me to resign my commission and I will not do so!"

"Then you leave us no choice, Major, we will go back and prepare the paperwork. Would you like Captain Platt as your defence?"

He knew the worth of Platt and he shook his head, "I will see the General myself! I still have influence. Damn you all to hell!"

Captain Dunbar rode into our camp that evening. With most of the regiment away, it was quiet, and the Colonel had arranged for all of those left in camp to dine together. Captain Dunbar said, "Colonel, Major if I might have a word?"

"Of course." We rose and went outside.

"Major Wilkinson has resigned his commission and will be joining the 28th the North Gloucestershire Foot. The appointment is immediate. When the majority in the 11th is sold then the proceeds will go to the 28th."

The Major had managed to avoid losing a single penny. The 28th must have been desperate!

"Thank you, Captain, would you care to join us?"

"As much as I would like to, I am afraid I have work to do for Viscount Wellington and he said, Major Matthews, that as soon as you have shown Colonel Cummings El Bodón then you are to rejoin his staff and help with the preparations for the siege."

He turned and left. "And that, Major Matthews, just leaves us with Captain Platt."

"Let us try honesty, eh sir? He will not wish to leave what he sees as a comfortable life so tell him that he has to be a troop commander once more. He did not enjoy the proximity of the French Dragoons and if you suggest that he might wish to sell his commission. Two thousand seven hundred and eighty-two pounds is the fixed price, as you know but cavalry regiments nearly always cost more. Suggest that he might have three thousand pounds coming his way. As the alternative is danger then I think he might jump at it."

And it worked. In one week, the regiment lost its two worst officers and two good ones were promoted. I felt sad as I headed west from El Bodón for the regiment was now becoming a good one once more.

However, Viscount Wellington commanded, and I obeyed. I had enjoyed my brief spell with the regiment, but it was now over, at least for a while and I would learn about sieges!

Chapter 6

I soon discovered my mission; Sharp and I were to become Sir Richard Fletcher's bodyguards along with Captain Dunbar and a young lieutenant. Lieutenant Broome was unusual in that he was a young officer who wished to be like Sir Richard, an engineer. As such he would learn a great deal about sieges but would be of little use if there was to be any action and the bulk of the protection duties were down to Sergeant Sharp and me. We left the camp on a cold December day with an icy wind whipping across the dead land of Spain. Any sensible person was indoors and even the forward encampments had been withdrawn to the main camp. Wrapped in our cloaks we left under brooding skies filled with what might be rain but, equally, could be sleet or snow! As well as the young officer Sir Richard had with him he also had four of his Royal Engineers and their horses. We were equipped to camp if Sir Richard deemed it impractical to return to the main camp. Until we reached Ciudad Rodrigo then I was in command for I knew the land and I took us on a circuitous route to avoid any cavalry patrols. My instincts told me that the French would save their horses for more important tasks. Having bloodied Marmont's nose he would look further north and he would try to turn our flank. We had an unpleasant and wet crossing of the river which did not improve our spirits. Sharp and I rode with loaded Bakers although we did not prime them. We led the others who followed us thirty paces behind our horses' tails. Any fighting would be done by Sharp and me and Captain Dunbar would get Sir Richard to safety.

I stopped just three hundred paces from the fortified convent of San Francisco which lay close to the walls of Ciudad Rodrigo and would be the first obstacle Viscount Wellington had to negotiate if he was to take the fortress. We were, of course, seen and I heard the drum which caused men to man the walls. They would waste neither shot nor shell on us. We were too few and I knew from my previous visit that they had no horsemen. Sir Richard and his engineers used their equipment to take measurements and to make a map. I had already sketched one out, but they needed accurate ranges and elevation. It was after the sun, had we been able to see it, had reached its zenith when we moved on. We climbed the Great Teson and I saw Fort Renaud for the first time. It was, in effect, a redoubt and I saw cannons poking over the defences. The purpose of the fort was clear; it would deny an attacker the ability to fire directly at the town's walls. I estimated no more than sixty or so men were within and while Sir Richard and his Royal Engineers measured and calculated I took out my telescope to confirm the numbers. I recognised the Light Infantry uniforms.

Sir Richard and his men seemed to take longer over this calculation, and I rode over to them and said, diplomatically, "Trouble sir?"

I had got to know Sir Richard when he had worked on the defences of Torres Vedras and we had a good relationship; we respected each other. He smiled at me, "You are keen to move, eh Robbie? I fear that we will need longer as it is obvious to us that this is where we will attack. Do you see there at the corner of the fortress there is a two-hundred-yard stretch of wall? We are above the glacis here and can hit the wall at will. That means we need to take this fort first and then place our guns to pound that section of wall."

I sighed, "Yes sir."

He and Lieutenant Broome went back to their calculations and the Royal Engineers used all manner of equipment to help them. I took out my Baker and primed it and Sergeant Sharp emulated me. Captain Dunbar asked, "Do you see something, sir?"

"No, Captain, but we are less than two hundred and fifty paces from the fort. They have no horses and they will not waste powder on us, but they are French Light Infantry and think themselves the equal of Black Bob's men. Life inside that fort will be dull and boring. I am not a gambling man, but I wager a guinea that they will try to shift us from here before Sir Richard is finished with his plans to take the fortress!"

John Dunbar was a gambler and he grinned and said, "You are on, sir."

I, of course, had no intention of taking his money but I nodded. With my gun loaded and primed I mounted Donna and rode a little closer to the walls. I wanted to see the defences close up. I could not hold my Baker and the telescope and so I just used my eyes. The wooden fort had a ditch and I saw that they had used chevaux-de-frise to make its capture difficult. Chevaux-de-frise were long pieces of wood and embedded in them was anything sharp: nails, broken knives, bayonets, broken glass. They were nailed to the walls and that meant that any attack would be channelled through the doors. The wooden walls of the fort were also angled so that cannonballs might just bounce off them. At the foot of the fort was a soil mound. That would be effective in reducing the effect of cannon fire. I did not make notes but when I returned to the camp, I would write a report. While Sir Richard would be planning on reducing the fort, I would be able to speak with the commander of the attackers and give him fair warning.

"Sir!" Sharp's shout drew my gaze to the door of the fort. Fifteen light infantrymen led by a Lieutenant and a sergeant were racing towards us. The rough ground meant that they could probably move almost as fast as the Royal Engineers on their pack horses.

"Sir Richard, time to move! We have outstayed our welcome."

Sir Richard trusted my judgement, "Right boys, pack it away!" The Engineers were as precious about their equipment as we were about our horses and weapons and they packed everything very carefully.

I wished then that I had brought my Baker rifle which had a range of almost five hundred yards. I raised the carbine and aimed at the Lieutenant. It was not an easy shot as he was dodging and dancing, added to which the wind made the end of the barrel move too much. I fired and hit him in the shoulder. The Sergeant and the others dropped to the ground. I turned and saw that the Royal Engineers were still packing away their gear. As I reloaded, I said, "I hope that you have a brace of loaded pistols, Captain!" When I heard the sound of the ramrod in his barrel, I knew that he had not. The French sergeant sent one man to deal with his wounded officer and then ordered the rest to their feet. This time they used our light infantry tactics and one fired while the other ran. Sharp fired at the sergeant, but he only winged him, and the Frenchman continued to exhort his men to close with us. In another thirty yards, they would be in range and light infantry knew how to fire muskets. Having reloaded I fired at a Corporal who was also trying to rally them. This time it was a killing blow and I hit him in the chest. There was no leather to slow down the ball and it flattened as it hit his chest. Now expanded to the size of a Spanish gold piece, it would make a hole which would exit the size of a fist. I would not have the opportunity to reload and so I drew my best pistol, the French one with the longer barrel. I rested it on my forearm which, in turn, rested on Donna's neck. Sharp's Baker rang out and another Frenchman fell. A musket ball from the Charleville whipped over my head but I ignored it and squeezed the trigger. Although I hit one of the Frenchmen, I merely nicked him, and he carried on.

From behind me, I heard, "Ready Major Matthews!"

"Then ride!" As I heard the horses' hooves I shouted, "Captain, Sergeant, on my command fire every weapon and then turn and ride."

"Sir!"

"Sir!"

I holstered my pistol and took out a brace, "Fire!" Six pistols sent six balls in the direction of the French, more importantly, the smoke obscured us a little especially as the French fired at us at the same time. I felt a tug at my hat as I whipped Donna to follow the engineers. It

73

sounded like angry wasps behind us as the French made one last attempt to stop us. They failed. I caught up with Sir Richard north of Ciudad Rodrigo.

"Damned close, Matthews."

"Yes, sir,"

He took my hat off and handed it to me, "No, Matthews, I meant this."

A musket ball had passed through it, "Damn it! I shall have to buy a new one and I liked this one!"

John Dunbar took out a guinea, "You can buy one out of your winnings, sir."

Shaking my head, I said, "You are not a line officer, John, and it was unfair of me to take advantage of you. Keep your money and regard it as a lesson learned. Sir Richard, do you wish to camp, or shall we head back home?"

"Back home, I think."

"Then we either risk a long route back the way we came, or we try to ford the river. I hope your chaps know how to swim a horse!"

Sir Richard said, "We will try the ford and you, gentlemen, will learn a new skill." He was, of course, talking to the Lieutenant and his Engineers.

Crossing the river we almost lost an engineer who fell from his horse. He was saved by the mighty arm of Sergeant Sharp who reached under the water to drag the spluttering and coughing Royal Engineer from the river and deposit him across his horse's neck. I grabbed the reins of his horse and the packhorse he was leading. Once on the bank, he coughed his thanks. When we reached Fuenteguinaldo we were cold, wet and thoroughly miserable.

"Will you need us on the morrow, sir?" I looked up at the dank and miserably sky. I did not relish another patrol.

Shaking his head Sir Richard said, "I think not. I have enough information to make a preliminary plan and if we need to go again it won't be for a day or two."

That suited me and we rejoined our regiment to enjoy Christmas, albeit a fairly cheerless one! I was flattered by the fuss the regiment made when they discovered that we were able to spend Christmas with them. The wet ride of five days earlier seemed a lifetime ago as the cooks excelled themselves cooking a Spanish version of Christmas dinner! The newly-promoted majors put their elevation down to me, but I had only spoken the truth. Now that Captain Platt had accepted Colonel Cumming's offer and was on his way home then there was harmony in the regiment. I also received letters from home. One was from Mr Hudson, the d'Alpini agent from London. I had written to him to tell him of my new state and asking him to send half of my income to my wife. The other four letters were all from Emily and I opened them all and looked at the dates. I would read them in order. I sniffed them and could detect the faint smell of the eau de cologne she used. The days were not only short, but they also were dark, and I lit an oil lamp and opened some port. I knew many of the men who produced that wonderful drink from my time with Donna Maria and I always had a good supply. With a large glass next to me I read. It was both joyous and sad for I could hear her voice in every line and yet I could neither see nor touch her. I was able to deduce when she had read my letters, but it was infuriating that I had received her letters all together. I suppose I was lucky that I had any letters at all for many others, even married men like Quartermaster Grant, had yet to receive one. I read them all over and over. It was a touch of home. She and Annie had begun to refurnish my home, Matthews Farm, and I could tell that it was a joyous experience for her. In her last letter she spoke of planning a good Christmas in honour or me and I felt real regret that I was here in a chilly and soulless Spain.

In England we call the day after Christmas, Boxing Day, and it was on that day when Sharp and I, along with Captain Dunbar, rode forth once more. Now that the batteries and their gunners had finally arrived, Sir Richard could begin to plan properly. We had to go back and find the best site for his engineers. As well as the guns, howitzers and mortars we had great quantities of spades, sandbags, nails, pickaxes, shovels not to mention axes and spades. We needed a site which was safe from attack and yet close enough for the men to be able to get to work as quickly as possible. We knew where we were going. It was to the northeast of the Great Teson and so we could avoid the two forts. In theory, it would be simpler, especially as there were just five of us this time and we had no pack horses. The Royal Engineers were left in the camp. As we rode, I asked Sir Richard about the art of siegecraft.

"I fear it is easier to defend against a siege than it is to storm walls and to be truthful, Robbie, we English are not very good at it. We can use regular artillery to reduce the two forts but then we must dig trenches to enable our men to get to the guns. For the first few days, I anticipate that the men will just be digging and that rarely suits soldiers! They want to fight. When Fort Renaud is taken then we will dig a trench which is parallel to the lines of guns we shall use and then we will dig individual trenches to the batteries. We will place four of them on the high ground where the fort now stands. They will be almost eight hundred yards from the walls. We shall keep one battery in reserve for we need a second parallel and another battery which will be less than two hundred and fifty yards from the walls. At that range the walls will crumble; at least I hope that they do."

I had a better idea now of what to expect. We reached the site without a problem. We were more than half a mile from the fort and the battery. We spent just long enough for him to confirm that we had the best place for the artillery and engineers park. It was as we were heading back that we were seen. We had to cross the main road from Salamanca and there was no way to avoid crossing it. I tried to minimise the risk by watching until I was certain that there was no one riding from Ciudad Rodrigo. That was my mistake for the horsemen were riding to Ciudad and we had just crossed the road when I spotted them. They were half a mile away and, had it just been Sharp and I then we would have outrun them for we had good horses and were good riders. Even Captain Dunbar was not a good rider.

"Let your horses open their legs and make for home. Sharp and I will be the rearguard and try to slow them down."

We only had six miles to ride but that would be a long six miles. As was our usual practice I had my loaded Baker carbine but this time I also had my loaded Baker rifle across the back of my saddle. Sharp and I slowed down both to conserve our horses and to give the other three the chance to escape. I looked over my shoulder and saw that there were eight Lanciers de Berg. These were lancers from the German Confederation, and they were allies of the French. They had been defeated by General Anson on the same day that we fought our retreat. With their Polish hats and lances, they were distinctive and used in the right way, then their lances could be effective, but they had no guns!

"With luck, sir, they will give up!"

"I wouldn't count on it. This regiment was raised by Murat and you can bet that he handpicked them all. They will be fanatics and I can see them doing all that they can to capture us. It was our cavalry that defeated them!"

Sir Richard and Lieutenant Broome were struggling and even though we had slowed we were gaining upon them. Riding across country was a skill and they were not choosing the right path. If I had been leading them then we would have been. Behind us, the lancers had cut the gap by half.

"We need to slow them down. Perhaps if we can hit a couple the others might be discouraged. Look for somewhere we can ambush them."

Alan Sharp had good eyes and a poacher's instincts. He saw the shepherd's hut ahead. The other three were just passing it. "Sir, we will be briefly out of sight when we reach there; if we stop, we can get one shot off with rifles and another with our carbines. We have four pistols each. What do you say?"

"It is worth a try!"

I saw that Sharp had used his head for the other three did disappear briefly and as we rode towards the shepherd's hut, I counted to six before they reappeared. That gave me about ten to twenty seconds to dismount, prime the rifle and fire. To give me more time I reached back and unfastened the straps as I rode. We could now hear the hooves behind us as the eager lancers anticipated skewering us. Donna was the stronger horse and as I turned around the hut, I reined her in. Leaping down and priming the rifle I used the side of the hut for support and aimed at the nearest riders who were more than a hundred yards from us. I fired and knocked one rider from his horse. I dropped the rifle, as Sharp brought down a second lancer, and picked up the carbine. I primed it and aimed. The next lancer was less than eighty yards from me, and the shot was a little hurried. I hit his shoulder and he dropped his lance. As Sharp's carbine bucked, I dropped mine and drew two pistols firing both as the last four riders and the wounded lancer rode at us. The smoke obscured the result and my original plan to remount and ride away was now in tatters. I drew my sword as a lance came through the smoke. I managed to grab it behind the head and, dragging it to one side, slashed at the shaft. The wooden shaft broke. I heard Sharp's pistols fire and I waited for the next lance to come from the smoke. As a breeze shifted it, I saw that four lancers were riding away. Between us, we had killed or unhorsed four of the lancers. The last one had been hit by both of Sharp's pistols and the poor man had no head. One of the horses had stayed by the hut and was grazing. We grabbed our weapons and I peered at the fleeing lancers. One at least was wounded.

"Well done Sergeant, now, let's get back. Fetch the horse." I picked up the lancer's helmet and lance as a souvenir. I hoped that Sir Richard had all he needed for after our two expeditions the garrisons would be alerted!

Sir Richard and the other two had obeyed my orders but were waiting for us at the piquet on the road. Sir Richard appeared concerned, "I thought they must have caught you, Robbie, I am sorry that I took so long but everything has to be just right, don't you know?"

"Don't worry Sir Richard, it was just bad luck and no harm was done. We have a spare horse and we completed the mission."

When we reported back to Viscount Wellington, he was concerned that there were the allies of the French, German cavalry close to Ciudad

Rodrigo. "We need to strike sooner rather than later. Sir Richard, how long will it take to get your equipment into position?"

"It could take almost a week if the roads are bad."

The General shook his head. "You will have two days! I intend to begin the attack on the eighth of January. I know which men I shall take. Matthews, find General Alten and tell him that I want the cavalry to cut off Ciudad Rodrigo by the seventh! I want you and Dunbar with them to report back to me."

"Yes, sir."

As I was about to leave, he said, "And try to stay out of trouble, Matthews. There are junior officers who can take the risks. You are a passable aide and I would hate to have to train another to take your place!"

"Sir."

General Alten and General Anson both had quarters in the village. They did not have to endure tents. We reported to them both. I told them of the lancers and of the terrain. There were only a few of us who had been east of Ciudad Rodrigo.

"That will be hard for the horses as it is winter and there is little grazing."

"Yes sir, and that means wagons with oats."

General Anson was a cavalryman and he nodded, "However, we will have enough grazing for a day or two. If the attack begins on the eighth, then we will not be riding in numbers. Matthews, have you seen any other sign of cavalry apart from these eight lancers?"

"No, sir. The infantrymen have sallied forth aggressively, but I have seen little sign of horses. It is winter."

"And that is the genius of Viscount Wellington for who else would attack in winter? If Marmont had been as vigilant then we would not be able to assault the walls."

General Alten nodded his agreement, "And perhaps what some people said was a defeat, when we had to retreat before that probe, may actually be a victory for it made Marshal Marmont put his head back in his shell. Are you to be with us, Matthews?"

"Yes, sir. Captain Dunbar and I will be liaising with Sir Richard and Viscount Wellington."

"Good. You are a clever fellow and I think your Colonel Cummings will appreciate your support."

I returned to the regiment to tell them that they ought to be ready to move quickly. Colonel Cummings had brought replacements from England and had been able to fully reinstate E Troop as well as F Troop which had been a troop in name only. The regiment was still not at full strength, it rarely was, but each troop had sufficient men to make its presence felt. There were also many men in the hospital. It was rarely wounds and deaths which hurt our regiments but disease. The beer which they were used to in England was replaced by watered wine and the change had a major effect on some men.

We left just after midnight and rode through a frosty landscape where breath from horses and men looked like a moving fog. I led and I followed a now-familiar route until, as the sun rose on the seventh of January, we sat astride the Salamanca Road just three hundred yards from Fort Renaud and the four regiments of cavalry were placed in a long line anchored at each end at the Agueda. While the river could be forded, as we had discovered, it could not be crossed in large numbers. Each regiment had a squadron kept in reserve and General Alten had made it clear that the watchword was caution. We had too few cavalrymen for us to be picked off by the superior French horsemen. The experience of the 11th and the 2nd King's German Legion had chastened those enemy regiments of Dragoons and Chasseurs.

We were rewarded within a few hours as two French despatch riders left Ciudad Rodrigo and galloped up the road. They had a real shock when they found themselves being fired upon by some eager German piquets. Unhurt, they turned tail and galloped back to the fortress.

Major General Alten said, "Captain Dunbar, ride to Viscount Wellington and tell him that we think the army has been spotted heading this way but that Ciudad Rodrigo is now cut off."

I nodded as John galloped off, "And that tells us that Marshal Marmont knows nothing about our impending attack. If he did then General Barrié would not risk riders going to warn him."

The Portuguese to the north of us had told Viscount Wellington that Marshal Marmont was still trying to probe our left flank, held by our allies. The Emperor was relying on generals who were simply not good enough. Marshal Masséna had failed and, from what I had seen, Marshal Marmont was little better.

We had a chilly camp and men wrapped themselves in their blankets and cloaks. Until Sergeant Major Jones and the other support troops reached us with tents and camp kitchens, we would all have to endure crude conditions. I made sure that the sentries who were close to the headquarters were all alert. That was as much for their own safety as anything else. While I did not think that the French were abroad, the fifteen men who had sortied from Fort Renaud told me the men we fought would not simply give up.

Chapter 7

Viscount Wellington and the army began to arrive by mid-morning on the eighth. He rode up to me with Major General Craufurd and Colonel John Colborne. They dismounted and waved me over for a discussion. "We intend to attack Fort Renaud as soon as the Colonel's men arrive. We are here for your opinion."

I nodded and Black Bob said, "Viscount Wellington tells me that you think there are just fifty or sixty men in the fort, Matthews."

"Yes, sir. It is not that big and has been quickly thrown up. The biggest problem will be the chevaux-de-frise."

Colonel Colborne nodded, "Yes, Matthews, I read your report. We have some hides. We will throw those over the blades and that should minimise the risk. Are you coming with us?"

"If you wish me to, sir."

He nodded, "You know this fort better than any." He smiled, "Sir Richard told me how you studied it. You don't need to put yourself at risk, I know how much Viscount Wellington values you, but your presence would be welcome for you have been closer to it than any other."

"Then I shall be honoured."

"Matthews, remember what I said!" Sir Arthur's words reaffirmed his instructions.

"Sir." Turning to the Colonel I said, "I will go and get my gear."

I found Sharp and told him what I intended. "I will fetch my guns too, sir."

"No, Alan. I don't need you."

"But sir!"

"I am just taking my pistols and sword." I handed him my cocked hat. "Keep this for me. I don't intend to make a big target."

Sighing he took it, "Sir!"

I saw the ten companies forming up. Four of them were from the 52nd, Sir John's own regiment. I saw that they were all light infantry and that there were rifles with them. That was reassuring. I joined Sir John. He saw that I had taken off my hat and he smiled, "I can see why you have survived so long." Turning to the green jacketed rifleman next to him he said, "Captain Richards, if you and your chaps would begin the attack. Clear the fighting platform if you please."

"Sir."

I saw that each of the other companies had scaling ladders. The Colonel had obviously briefed his officers for as he nodded, I heard orders rattled out and the light infantry quickly ran to surround the fort. I heard the crack of the Baker rifles as Colonel Colborne raised his sword and shouted, "The 52nd will advance."

Light infantry rarely attacked in the same manner as line infantry and we ran ducking and dodging, jinking from side to side. The cannon I had seen managed to get one ball off before lead balls from the rifles cleared the gun of its crew.

I pointed to the main gate, "That is the best place to get in, I believe."

He said, as we both ran with the 52nd, "We have some of the 43rd with axes. They will make short work of it."

The first of the light infantry had reached the ditch and had thrown down their ladders. I saw a couple of them fall and then, as they began to cross, and the axemen began to pound on the gate with their weapons I saw French arms raising grenades. Unlike the other officers I was not holding my sword but my pistols. As one grenade exploded, I reached the edge of the ditch and I fired both pistols at the sergeant who raised his arm to throw another. He fell backwards and I heard a dull thump as the grenade went off inside the fort. With the hide over the chevaux-de-frise the agile light infantrymen clambered up the sides and the door crashed open. I holstered my pistols and followed the Colonel into the fort. As we did so hands came up and the French surrendered. I could not remember such a swift action nor such an easy victory. The signs were looking good.

"Captain Poulson, if you wouldn't mind, have the prisoners disarmed. Sergeant Major let me know how many casualties we suffered!" He turned to me, "You are a handy man to know, Major. We don't bother with pistols!"

I shrugged, "I am a cavalryman and they are quite handy. These are particularly good as they are French and have a longer barrel."

The Sergeant Major saluted, "Six of our lads are dead, sir, and twenty have wounds, mainly cuts, sir."

"And the French?"

"Three dead and three escaped. The rest have been taken prisoner."

Viscount Wellington was delighted and even Black Bob Craufurd allowed himself a rare smile. Rubbing his hands Viscount Wellington said, "And tomorrow, while the batteries are being sited, we will do the same to the convent. A promising start which bodes well, I believe."

As I had expected confusion reigned as the Engineers' Park was built and the regiments who would not be assaulting the convent began

81

to dig the trenches. The 1st Division had the first shift and each of the others would take their turns. Sir Richard's scouting expedition had yielded some useful piece of information. He had discovered the parallel, the trench which the French had dug when they had attacked and captured the Spanish fortress. It made the excavation slightly easier although the bitterly cold weather made the work hard and unpleasant. However, the men digging were at least moving and were warmer than the cavalry who were, generally, sitting on their horses watching for an enemy they hoped would not appear. I was actually glad to be where the real work was taking place. Braziers gave warmth to the engineers who directed the soldiers doing the digging. Each Division had twenty-four hours of work and a thousand men at a time toiled. The work went on even in the freezing night-time. When a shift came off duty, they ate some hot soup and then slept until they were woken to begin again. The other divisions huddled around their fires knowing that soon it would be their turn to begin digging. The French gunners knew the range and they sent cannonballs at the trenches. As the spoil was thrown up on the French side and afforded protection to the diggers the casualties were not great, but it slowed the work down as, each time a cannon roared, men quite naturally took cover.

Five nights after the first assault The King's German Legion was given their chance to attack and they were given the task of attacking the Convent of Vera Cruz. They were keen to emulate the success their cavalry had already achieved. As soon as the defenders were driven off then the batteries began to open fire. It was an anti-climax and Viscount Wellington was furious. The guns had been placed too far forwards and were smashing into the top of the wall and not the bottom. While they were re-positioned the 40th were given the task of taking the Convent of San Francisco and the siege batteries were able to add their weight of shot to the foot artillery and within an hour the fortified convent was in our hands and Viscount Wellington smiled once more. The Convent of Vera Cruz was more important as taking it would mean we could start another trench which would be much closer to the walls.

This was a strange kind of warfare to me for it was a mixture of men charging defensive positions and then digging trenches! I knew, from my scouting expedition that the defenders were few in number and each time we captured a fort we reduced that number. Sir Arthur became quite cheerful for a day or two as the guns battered the walls and the trenches drew closer to the French. Viscount Wellington's joy was short-lived for the divisions had been too predictable and the French were able to anticipate when the shifts would change. The departing division would leave the siege works and when they reached the main camp the next division would leave. On one such day, with just a handful of Engineers at the works five hundred Frenchmen poured from the walls of Ciudad Rodrigo to try to destroy the newly dug defences. They smashed and stole tools for only the shirt-sleeved engineers were there to defend them. As luck would have it Sharp and I had been assigned to protect Sir Richard and Lieutenant Broome as they inspected the almost finished trench. Sir Richard had chosen that moment to inspect the works as he knew that there would be the fewest number of men to obscure his view.

As soon as we saw the blue-coated French pour from the walls Sir Richard shouted, "Lieutenant Broome, fetch General Graham if you please!"

I drew a pistol as did Sharp. The Engineer just had a sword, but he drew it. He shouted, "You fellows! Pick up any sort of weapon and defend the works! Do not let them undo our hard labour!"

I ran forward for this was not a time to stand off and leave the Engineers to be butchered. The French did not bring muskets but short swords and axes. They were intending to destroy the work of the last six days! "Stay behind us, Sir Richard and Lieutenant Broome!"

This was not the fight for a gentleman. Fencing would be of little use. I watched one of the engineers swing his spade like a long axe and when it connected with the knee of the Frenchman above him it had a similar effect to that of an axe. I first heard the crack as the kneecap was broken and then the scream as the Frenchman fell into the ditch. I ran forward and fired up under the chin of the Frenchman who was about to leap down into the ditch with an axe. I blew the whole of the top of his head off and then, holstering my pistol I drew a second with my left hand and my sword with my right. The weapons which the French had brought were not sophisticated, but they could do great harm however, my sword outranged theirs. I did not worry overmuch about the damage they did to the defences for they could be repaired. Men could not and so I shouted, "Engineers, to me!"

A grizzled and moustached French sergeant wielding an axe as though it was a kitchen knife came racing towards me. I did not hesitate and as he swung back his axe, I fired my pistol into his face. I would now have to rely on my sword, but more than half of the engineers were now close to the three of us and our swords could, hopefully, keep the French, armed with short swords and axes, at bay. Sharp slashed his sword sideways across the faces of two over-eager Frenchmen. One had his face laid open while the second suffered a nasty looking wound to his arm. Sir Richard was just keeping them at bay while the engineers were using spades and shovels to keep the French away. The majority of the French began to uproot the fascines and palings while others used our shovels to fill in the trench. What they did not do was to attempt to spike the guns and that was a mistake. Sharp and I moved forward, parrying the clumsy strikes from the short swords used by the French. We then slashed our razor-sharp weapons across flesh and hands. Our blades were bloody, and the wounded fled back.

I heard a bugle from behind us and General Graham led the next shift to fall amongst the French raiders. This was more to the taste of British soldiers and the sight of the bayonets backed by the red tunics was enough to drive the French quickly back into the fortress.

Viscount Wellington rode up as those who were either wounded or too slow to move surrendered. "Take those prisoners away! This is a damned mess, Sir Richard!"

"It could have been worse, Viscount Wellington, and we have learned a lesson. From now on the division who is working waits to be relieved by the next division!"

Viscount Wellington nodded and seemed to notice the men we had shot and slashed, "Well done, gentlemen. I think, Major, that we keep you and your sergeant close by until this attack is over. Watch Sir Richard for if he falls then our chances of success diminish!"

And so, we became his shadows. It was not an easy duty for, as we later discovered, Sir Richard liked to get as close to the walls as the Forlorn Hope of volunteers! He supervised the entire network of trenches and the emplacements. Once the second parallel was begun then the diggers started work on a third one which was almost under the guns of the fortress. That work was done at night and, on the night that the Foot Guards were digging, the French threw fiery brands to illuminate the night and the work was, perforce slow as men took cover to avoid the sharpshooters. I was with Sir Richard when the Great Breach, as it became known, started to appear. The pounding on the base of the walls, despite the shoring up from within, soon showed cracks. As the damage increased Sir Richard, directed by Viscount Wellington ordered the fifth battery to begin to fire at a small tower on the wall just in front of the cathedral and some two hundred yards from the Great Breach. Nature, however, intervened in the form of a thick fog which prevented the guns from firing. Powder and shot were too valuable to be wasted but while the fog persisted Viscount Wellington sent some the 95th closer to the walls where they dug rifle pits under the cover of the fog and mist. They had plenty of time to make stone defences and they made their pits relatively invulnerable to attacks from the defenders, and they would still be able to pick off any who appeared along the walls. When part of the corner of the wall fell it became clear to all that soon we would have a breach and so I went with Sir Richard to meet with Viscount Wellington who sat as close to the walls as he could without being fired upon. We were all grateful that the French did not use rifles! He took Sir Richard's advice and scribbled notes down. The plan he created ran to sixteen paragraphs and was as detailed a piece of work as I have ever seen.

We had spent a lot of time with Lieutenant Broome and I liked him for he had a curious mind. "Sir, what is the Forlorn Hope?"

"They are the volunteers in each division who will be the first through the breach."

"They volunteer, sir?"

"Yes, every man is given the chance to volunteer to be the first up the wall and through the breach."

"But, sir, it is suicide!"

I smiled but it was a sad smile, "If you wished to be a captain, Lieutenant Broome, then it would cost you more than two thousand pounds. If you led a Forlorn Hope then you would be guaranteed a captaincy and all the men who followed you could expect promotion."

Sharp said, quietly, "Aye, Lieutenant, if they survived. Few do but men will do a great deal for pay and promotion!"

I could see that he did not understand the concept but then he wished to be an engineer and not a soldier. When we had been attacked, he had stood behind Sir Richard and waved his sword about, somewhat ineffectually.

By the next day, the fog had lifted, and the bombardment resumed. The Great Breach and the Lesser Breach both appeared within a short time of each other. I do not know how many men died when the two sections of walls collapsed but I am guessing it was a considerable number. Viscount Wellington sent for me. "Matthews, go under a flag of truce and ask the garrison to surrender, will you? I would if I could avoid a great loss of life on both sides." By the time I reached the breach night had fallen but there was enough light for my flag to be seen.

I went with Sharp and stood before the Great Breach. I knew that all around the fortress the various attacks were being prepared. The 3rd Division led by Major General Mackinnon would attack the Great Breach from the Lesser Teson. They would be supported by the 5th Regiment, led by Major Ridge, who would attack from behind the Convent of Vera Cruz. The Light Division would attack the Lesser Breach. On the other side of the Agueda, the Portuguese would attack the guns which were close to the Roman Bridge. Finally, General Pack's Brigade would make a feint attack at the St Jago Gate. All this was in my mind as I approached the walls, but the French would just expect an attack on the two breaches. Viscount Wellington had been very clever and having met General Barrié, I did not think that he had enough ability to thwart Viscount Wellington.

Sharp waved the flag and a French face appeared. Although I recognised Lieutenant Debussy, who now sported a bandage upon his head, he did not seem to recognise me for I wore the uniform of the 11th and I had upon my head a Tarleton helmet. Sir Arthur Wellesley, Viscount Wellington, commander of the Allied army calls upon General Barrié to surrender. You are surrounded and your walls are breached. There is no likelihood of relief and the fortress will inevitably fall. My general asks that General Barrié surrenders to save a great loss of life. The men who do surrender will be allowed to march back to Salamanca."

The Lieutenant shouted, "I will speak with him. Wait there."

The delay could only help Viscount Wellington for our men were getting into position for the attack and it allowed me to examine the walls. The tumbling masonry had cleared all of the defences and could be scaled. The rifles of the 95th would be able to give covering fire to the men who were attacking. I knew then that the attack would succeed but what I could not know was the cost!

The Lieutenant returned and said, apologetically, "I am sorry sir, but the General cannot surrender, and you must do what you see fit."

I nodded and headed back to Viscount Wellington. His headquarters was between the Light Division and the 3rd Division. As I passed the Light Division, who were all standing to, General Craufurd asked, "Well, Matthews, do we fight or not?"

"You fight, General Craufurd."

He nodded and began to speak to his men as I made my way to Viscount Wellington who was waiting patiently with Sir Richard Fletcher and Major General MacKinnon. I heard Black Bob's speech which seemed to sum up the man and the division he led.

"Soldiers, the eyes of your country are upon you. Be steady, be cool, be firm in the assault. The town must be yours this night. Once masters of the wall, let your first duty be to clear the ramparts and in doing this keep together." He saluted Viscount Wellington with his sword, "Now lads for the breach!"

That he should have waited for the order never occurred to Black Bob whose men had five hundred yards to cover to reach the breach. I stood before Viscount Wellington as Major General MacKinnon saluted and began to run to his division to begin their attack. "Sir, they say no!"

"A man should know when he is beaten. This will not end well for the French. Make the signal Dunbar!"

Every gun we had opened fire at once. Everything from six pounders to the monstrous twenty-four pounder siege guns. The air was filled with smoke and the walls disappeared. The guns would only fire a few shells and balls for their purpose was to keep down the heads of the defenders.

Sir Richard said, "Well then, Matthews, I suppose we ought to go and see how they do, eh?"

With my brace of pistols, we followed Colonel Colborne's 52nd. I nodded affably at some of those I had previously met.

"We'll show these Froggies, eh sir?"

"It'll be like Fort Renaud!"

"Silence in the ranks, Murphy!"

"Sorry, Sarn't!"

At the head of the column, the men with the ladders were throwing them across the ditch for the spoil from the breach had not completely filled it. Now darkness had descended and with the silencing of the guns, it was just the huff and puff of men moving towards the walls and the sound of boots scraping over fallen masonry which could be heard. And then both silence and darkness ended as the French opened fire and hurled grenades into the ditch. I was just grateful that neither Sir Richard nor myself would have to follow the Light Division. The breach was smaller than the Great Breach and the walls on both sides were still standing. We were making our way to the Great Breach and the 3rd Division who were attacking there led by Sir Thomas Picton. Sir Richard would have to assault Badajoz one day and he knew he would learn lessons from watching the men attack. It took us some time to work our way along the wall for it was dark and although the Lesser Breach was lit by muskets and grenades, not to mention cannon fire from the French, the three of us were walking in darkness. It was, therefore, shocking to see Black Bob silhouetted at the top of the breach, exhorting his men on as a musket ball hit him and knocked him down to the ditch; he fell a long way. As much as I wanted to run back, my duty was to protect Sir Richard.

I saw the 3rd Division as they formed up. As with the Light Division's attack, the French were waiting until the red-coated soldiers of the 45th were packed together and then they would unleash hell. General Campbell's attack to support the 3rd Division had already begun but was hidden from view. I could hear the firing. "Come, Matthews let us hurry!" Sir Richard was keen to see how men used an escalade to attack walls.

I hid the smile for Sharp and I would already have been at the wall if we had not waited for Sir Richard and his Lieutenant. The picture we saw was the same. The French waited until the British were ascending the rubble before they opened fire. The red-coated soldiers who climbed over the rubble were brave men and I wondered what drove them on but, even though the French were making the breach a maelstrom of lead and fire they were making progress. I saw General Mackinnon himself make the top and then, all of a sudden, a mine was exploded at the top of the breach. I wondered then if the French General had deliberately delayed his response so that his men could conceal the mighty mine. All those who had made the top were thrown into the air, their bodies like so many rag dolls and then they crashed to earth, some of them to be buried by the falling rocks. All of this proved too much for Sir Richard. He had seen two of his friends killed within a few moments of each other.

"Right, Matthews, those men need leadership!"

It would have done no good to tell him that they needed the leadership of a soldier and not an engineer. I said, "Then stay behind Sharp and me!"

We ran towards the breach and I saw the 88th and Colonel Wallace arriving from the direction of the convent of Santa Cruz. Sir Richard shouted, "Wallace, the General is dead, follow us!"

"Connaught Rangers, you heard the officer!"

Pausing only to pick up an unfired musket I ran towards the breach. "Sharp, stay close. If Sir Richard falls here, then Viscount Wellington will have our guts for garters!"

He laughed, "Major Matthews, if Sir Richard falls then we will be already dead and past caring!"

We ran and I found myself surrounded by the wild men of the 88th and the 74th, the Highlanders. They were fearsome fighters. A platoon had just made the top when two guns flanking the breach opened fire with grapeshot. The men who had made the top fell. That was too much for the Irishmen and the Highlanders. To a man, those around us took their bayonets from their muskets and just charged the two guns like some medieval warriors! I fired at the gunner who was about to touch the linstock to the cannon and he fell dead. I dropped the musket and, drawing my sword, ran at the nearest gun. I knew that it was loaded and ready to fire. This would be a race between the Irishmen who were around me and the sergeant who was blowing on the linstock and trying to fire it. One of the 88th was faster and perhaps wilder than those with him and he leapt on to the barrel and then hurled himself at the sergeant. His bayonet plunged into the soldier's neck, but the wild man repeatedly slashed and stabbed at him. The rest of the guns' crews were similarly despatched by the men who had seen their comrades killed. It was not pretty.

I turned and saw a shocked Sir Richard Fletcher. I said, "Sir Richard, we have the breach!"

He shook his head, "These are wild men and not civilised."

Colonel Wallace appeared next to us hatless and bloody. He had a sword in his hand. "Sir Richard, these are men, but the blood is in their heads. Get you back to Viscount Wellington and Major Matthews and I will try to stop their worst excesses. They are good men but when their blood is hot then God help their enemy!"

I saw that this mild-mannered engineer was shocked, and I said, "Sergeant Sharp, take him back and I will join the Colonel."

In the short time it had taken to have the conversation, the survivors of the two regiments had poured into the town and I could hear the screams, not of soldiers but of the townspeople who would suffer at the hands of men drunk on blood. The two of us, along with the Regimental Sergeant Major and a young ensign, ran after them. The garrison had still to surrender but I knew how many men they had in the castle and the men of the two regiments we accompanied would outnumber the survivors. It made no difference to the Irish and Scotsmen that some of the French soldiers were surrendering. They were butchered. I saw one of Colonel Colborne's men remonstrating with a pair of Highlanders who were hacking at a dying Frenchman. They turned with fire in their eyes and were about to assault him. In two strides I was next to him and I smashed the basket hilt of my sword into their faces in rapid succession. They collapsed with glazed eyes.

I turned to the Captain, "Keep a couple of your own men around you, Captain. These men have lost all reason. Losing your comrades like that is not an excuse but it gives a reason for their behaviour."

"Thank you, Major."

Colonel Wallace and his Sergeant Major had raced off after the Connaughts and I found myself alone. I ran towards the castle. If I could find the French General and make him surrender, then all might be recovered but so long as the flag still flew from the castle then the battle would continue, and the excesses would merely grow! Some Scots had already found a tavern and were drinking. So long as they stayed there then they would just drink themselves into a stupor and innocent townsfolk would not be harmed. I could live with that! I found myself running down a narrow alley with the bodies of English and French soldiers. There had been a fierce battle. I was about to move on when I heard a scream; a woman's scream and it was coming from the upstairs of a deserted shop. I ran in and saw an elderly man; his throat had been cut. The screams were growing louder. I took the stairs three at a time and ran towards the dimly lit room. A red coat had his back to me and was forcing himself on a Spanish woman.

I poked him in the back with my sword and said, "Get off her now! That is an order!"

The red coat jumped up and I saw that it was Private Woods, the Foot Guard! The woman was sobbing, and I said, in Spanish, "Get out of here, now!"

The soldier had pulled up his breeches and now held his musket. It was pointed at me. "You bastard! You ruined my life! I had to join the Forlorn Hope just to stay in the regiment! Well, you are going to die here!" He lunged at me with the bayonet. It was a room filled with things to trip me up and, as I danced back out of the way I hoped I would not fall. The guardsman would not give me a second chance.

"Woods! Think! This is a flogging offence but if you kill me then that woman will remember you and that will be a hanging matter!"

"I'll take my chance."

He lunged again. This time I did not dance out of the way, but I swayed to the side and as the end of the musket moved, I tried to grab the end of the barrel. I almost succeeded and I moved the bayonet so that it would not impale me, but the bayonet scored a long wound down my palm.

He laughed, "Not so easy when you aren't on the back of a horse is it, Major?"

He was a street fighter and I had to fight like one. Before he could lunge again, I reached down and, despite my bloody palm, managed to grab my stiletto from my boot. When he saw it, his eyes widened. It was not an officer's weapon. "Now put down the gun. Take the stripes and start again!"

"I can take you. The fancy sword, your boots and your purse will help me to disappear! I will get a new name and find another regiment, but you will be dead."

This time he did not lunge but swept the bayonet across my face as he stepped forward. I think he thought I would step back but I was at the doorway and if I had done that there was a chance I might have tripped and fallen down the stairs. I stood my ground and whipped up my sword to smack into the barrel of the Brown Bess. Unfortunately for the soldier, he had not been watching his feet and he stumbled on his shako which had fallen from his head. As he came forward, he impaled himself on my stiletto. Screaming, he pushed the barrel of the musket across my head and I cracked my head on the door jamb. As he stepped out, he lost his footing and as I groggily rose to my feet, his body tumbled down the stairs. When I reached him, I saw that his neck was at an awkward angle and he had died. His neck was broken. After putting my stiletto back in my boot, I took the stock from around his neck and used it to bind my hand. The fact that he had tried to kill me did nothing to assuage the guilt I felt at having killed a fellow countryman. If this was what sieges were like, then I hoped I had witnessed my last.

By the time I reached the castle, the tricolour was down, and Viscount Wellington had sent in German Hussars to control the mob which threatened to rampage through the streets. I found Colonels Wallace and Colborne. Both of them were shocked and disgusted by the behaviour of the men.

I said, "I was on the retreat with Sir John Moore. When the French attacked us then the men were magnificent but once they reached a town or found drink, they became like wild animals. It is something in their nature. I don't envy you two officers for we will have the same when we reduce Badajoz and that is a harder place to take."

Colonel Colborne said, "And Sir Robert is unlikely to recover. What will the Light Division do without him?"

"He trained them well and they are his legacy."

I was proved right, and the death of their leader merely served to spur on the men of his division. It was as though his spirit watched over them in every battle.

Viscount Wellington and Sir Richard found me as dawn broke. Sharp was with them and when he saw my bloody hand, he shook his head, "I can't leave you for five minutes can I, sir?"

Sir Richard laughed, "Are you his mother, Sergeant Sharp?"

Sharp shook his head, "I think I need to be! Here let me clean it!"

As he took out some vinegar and began to clean the wound Viscount Wellington said, "We managed to take it easily enough Sharp, but I have to ask was it worth the price of two damn fine generals?"

"It is not my place sir, but both were brave men. They could have let others lead but that was not their way."

Sir Richard nodded, "And this siege has taught this old dog a few tricks and next time I shall do it better."

"Aye, and we have the French siege train but that will not be until spring. We shall consolidate and you, Major Matthews, when you are healed, shall go scouting for me once more!"

Part 2

Badajoz

Chapter 8

Before I could be given the details of my next mission we had to bury our dead and the last to be buried was Black Bob who took four days to die. It was a hard death for a hard man, and I saw that Viscount Wellington was moved to call it the *'bitterest blow in the war'*. In Sir Arthur's mind, both the generals who had died had fallen unnecessarily as they had placed themselves in the greatest danger. I did not agree for in my experience leaders had to lead and it was not right for the ordinary rank and file to bear all the risks.

As soon as the last sod had been replaced, Viscount Wellington became all business once more. He sent the artillery to Oporto to be transported by sea to Lisbon. A lesson had been learned as he had waited for the guns to arrive; this way they would travel faster. He also began to send, one by one, the infantry regiments south to Elvas where they would wait for the next assault, on Badajoz. He suspected that there might be French spies and he did not want them to see a mass exodus to Badajoz. My task became clear when he invited me to dine with him. That in itself was an unusual event. In fact, in all the time I had known him this was the first time and, I think, marked a change. It had been the death of Black Bob which had affected him. I think he now understood the value of such men as Black Bob and perhaps myself. Certainly, he was more affable as, at the end of January, we sat and ate in the dining room of the house he had commandeered.

"You did well in this campaign, Matthews. Would that all of my aides were as competent as you."

I smiled, "They are young, Viscount Wellington, and as you know I have been fighting since I was a stripling and I have some unique gifts."

"Quite, your languages. And that brings me, neatly, to your next task. I need you inside Salamanca." He must have seen my face fall for he smiled, "I know you have done this many times and each time you do so you think that you will be caught. However, Salamanca is not a fortress. This time I need you to find out what the French are planning and the mood of their soldiers. You know the sort of thing, listen to conversations in bars, identify senior officers. Before Fuentes de Oñoro and Talavera that proved invaluable and saved lives."

"And how long do I have to complete this task, Viscount Wellington?"

"I intend to stay here to give the French and any spies they have the impression that I intend to remain here for some time. I will head south with the light cavalry at the beginning of March by which time the army should be ready to take Badajoz. You have less than one month."

I shook my head, "If I stayed in Salamanca for a month then I would be identified and caught. I have done this so many times, Viscount Wellington, that there are men who will recognise me. I was remembered in Ciudad Rodrigo and Badajoz although I was lucky, and no harm was done. The next time might prove fatal." I did not mention that there were also men who remembered me from the time I had served in the French Army."

"So long as you get me the information which I need then I am content. Come back in days if you discover all that I need to know."

Before I left, he handed me a purse of French coins captured at Ciudad Rodrigo and I knew they would help. I was also able to read the letters which Marshal Marmont had sent to General Barrié as well as General Barrié's journal which bemoaned the lack of communication. It was clear that the guerrillas had intercepted most of Marmont's missives. I still had the captured lancer horse and I decided that I would use that horse as Donna was a distinctive animal. The French brands would also help me to blend in. We found a horse in the stables of Ciudad Rodrigo for Sharp, a good officer's mount so that he, too, would not attract attention. Wearing our civilian clothes, we slipped out of camp before dawn on a desperately cold February morning.

The Spanish army now occupied Ciudad Rodrigo. As we had captured, intact, the French siege train then there was little chance that Marmont could recapture the fortress. Already the Spanish were repairing the damage we had done and this time they would hold it. We would not have far to ride but we would need a good story. I decided to use one we had used before but not since before Bussaco and that was a lifetime ago! We would pretend to be Portuguese wine merchants seeking to buy grapes and to sell our wine. That there would be little to be had was immaterial. It would explain our extended stay and why we visited so many inns. I knew enough about grapes and winemaking to get by and Sharp's poor accent would go, largely, unnoticed as he would be speaking Portuguese. We did not bother with a packhorse and carried our spare clothes on our horses.

It was our horses which almost ended our mission just four miles from Salamanca. Had we had Donna and Mary, then they would have alerted us to danger. Guerrillas found us. I did not doubt that the spot they used for an ambush was more than familiar to them. Indeed, as we had approached the narrow part of the road where the hills rose on both sides and there was plenty of cover, I identified it as somewhere which might help the French to slow down Viscount Wellington should he ever advance against Salamanca. They appeared, almost from beneath our feet. Had I been riding Donna then she would have warned me. As it was a dozen muskets were aimed at us and flight would have been futile. We both raised our hands and then I said, before they could speak, "I am a British officer, Major Matthews and a friend of Juan of La Calzada de Béjar!"

I used the guerrilla's name even though he operated much further south. I just hoped that someone had heard of him. The silence was deafening as I waited for hammers to fall and balls to fly. Then one of them smiled, "I know this man and I think I have heard of you. Were you not the officer who gave the fine rifles to our friends in the south?"

It was my turn to smile but I did not lower my arms, "I am that man."

"You may lower your arms. Where are you bound?"

"To Salamanca."

"It is full of French soldiers."

"And I must go there to count them for my general."

He laughed, "Then save yourselves a journey for we can tell you their numbers. General Francisco Espoz y Mina, our leader, has Salamanca ringed with men who watch."

"And I will heed your words but if we are to retake your land for you then a soldier must look at the town and see how we can take it!"

"And that is a good answer. I am Miguel the Dagger. Come to our camp and I will give you the numbers of men that you will find."

It was not just a camp it was a fine house in the hills. It showed the power of the guerrillas for the French must have known of its existence and yet they had made no attempt to take it or eliminate the band. We dined well and Miguel asked us to stay the night. He wished to know of the battles further south and how Viscount Wellington had defeated the French. They had known of the victories and seen the results, but these were all ex-soldiers and were interested in the battles. I made copious notes, but I did not take them with us when we left the next day. I left them in the fine house for if they were discovered in my possession then I would be shot out of hand. They were as safe with Miguel as though they were in the Bank of England!

The next day we crossed the River Tormes using an ancient bridge and the first thing I noticed was the pair of forts which guarded it. An assault on this side would be difficult. I stored their position in my memory for I dared not commit anything to paper. At the end of the bridge were a handful of soldiers. They spoke to us in French and I answered in Portuguese. One of them spoke a little Portuguese and he questioned me. They seemed satisfied with our answers and we entered the town. Once inside I saw that the French had cleared the ground of houses close to the forts so that they had a good field of fire and they would be hard to take. I followed the line of the remains of the destroyed houses and saw another two forts. They had no walls around this part of the town but the four forts we had seen could hold up Viscount Wellington. However, the walls of the town were not the equal of either Ciudad Rodrigo or Badajoz. We ended up staying at a small hotel in the town.

The war had ended much of the commerce of this part of Spain and we were able to acquire a room easily. When I offered to pay in French coins, I saw the relief on the face of the owner for Spanish money was largely valueless. He seemed more than happy to help us source out customers. Miguel had given us the names of men in the town whom we could trust but I would only use those if we had to. For one thing, I did not know if these men were being watched and for another, I did not wish to jeopardise them. The French were ruthless.

As we had not travelled far that first day, we had time to explore the town and its defences. I could see that Marmont's headquarters was closely guarded by Dragoons. Because it was close to the centre of the town we were able to pass by and, as we did not appear to show much interest in it, we were ignored once we passed. I saw the French camp outside the town. The forts had been garrisoned and the gates were all manned. Marmont was keeping his army away from the Spanish populace. That was good for us as it meant the officers would be more likely to visit the town in the evening. For an egalitarian army, the French one could be as elitist as the British Army!

As was our usual practice we spoke only Portuguese even when alone. Thanks to our time in Lisbon and with Donna Maria our Portuguese was much better than our Spanish and to the untrained ear, we did not sound like foreigners. That first evening we dined in what looked like an expensive dining establishment and, as we had discovered in Talavera, it attracted more senior officers and that was what we wanted. The table we had was between two larger ones. A handful of officers from the same regiment appeared. They were from the 62nd Line regiment. There was a colonel, a major and a captain.

When they saw us, they frowned and so I proceeded to tell a bad joke in Portuguese. Sharp laughed and I saw the relief on the faces of the four officers.

The colonel said, "Do you two gentlemen speak French?"

I had been caught out like this before and so I just shrugged and spread my arms.

The Captain said, deliberately, in French, "They are just ignorant Portuguese peasants."

When I just smiled and continued to talk with Sharp the Colonel said, "We can talk, gentlemen, but keep it low. The Spanish guerrillas are more dangerous than a pair of Portuguese."

I nodded to Sharp who then began to ramble on about nothing, but it was nothing in Portuguese. I just nodded, laughed and scowled as I eavesdropped their conversation.

"The Marshal has been outwitted, gentlemen, the British have captured Ciudad Rodrigo and now it is too late to do anything about it."

"How do you know that it is too late, Colonel?"

"Brigadier General Thomières told me when he briefed the brigade's officers this morning. We are to be prepared to march north. The guerrillas are threatening there.".

One of the two majors snorted, "And that means we will chase our own tails and haemorrhage men at night."

"As soon as it is summer, we will head south but we have no siege weapons. They were lost in the siege."

The waiter came and took their order. While he did so I took the opportunity of speaking to Sharp about the prospect of buying grapes and selling wine. I did not think that anyone would understand us but, in my experience, the more you spoke of real things the more plausible was your cover. When the waiter had gone, they spoke once more.

"And I hear that more regiments are being withdrawn to join the Emperor in Russia."

The Captain gave a wry laugh, "So the choice is to risk freezing in Russia and having Cossacks take your private parts or bake here in Spain and have the guerrillas do the same. Why cannot the Emperor find some more civilised enemies?"

The Colonel said, flatly, "Because he has defeated them all."

"All except the roast beefs!"

"Quite, Marchand, but as we now have over three hundred thousand men against the ninety thousand spread across Spain then I think the tide may turn. Now enough of war, let us drink and enjoy these few hours with a roof over our head and pleasant company!"

We heard no more and the other officers who came to dine seemed of the same opinion. What I managed to confirm was that the guerrillas had been correct. Over the next few days, we made more enquiries about the purchase of grapes and the selling of wine and we learned more about the various regiments and their commanders. We learned that the heaviest cavalry they had were the Dragoons and that the Cuirassiers were all in Spain and that the Lanciers des Bergs had also been sent thither. It left just Chasseurs and one regiment of Hussars. I learned that my old regiment, the 13th was here and I hoped I would not run into any of them!

It was inevitable that we would be noticed and after five days I spotted the men who were following us. I think we had stayed too long and the local French police had become interested in us. We did not change our routine for that would have been a disaster and invited arrest. We assiduously avoided eye contact and pretended that we had no idea they were there. That night, when we returned to the hotel the owner was most upset and apologetic. Five of the Gendarmerie had come into the hotel and searched our room. That they would find nothing was immaterial, it meant that they suspected us and the fact that they would have found nothing incriminating might make them even more suspicious. When we reached our room, we found that they had not hidden the fact that our room had been searched. Our bags had had their linings slashed and our clothes and belongings were scattered all over the room.

I feigned outrage and said, loudly, that we would be making a formal complaint. The owner waved me over and said, quietly, "That is what they want you to do, and they will arrest you, sir. I would leave in the morning. I will reduce your bill by half for the inconvenience and I will ensure that your horses are ready."

It made sense but I was not happy about it. We had most of the information which Viscount Wellington would need but we had been identified as a potential danger and I felt angry with myself.

The next morning, we rose before dawn. It would make us look guilty if we left while it was dark and so we breakfasted and then, after paying our bill, we left but instead of heading south, which was the way the Gendarmeries would suspect, we headed east, towards Madrid. Surprisingly we were not stopped, and it was only later that I realised they were expecting us to leave by the bridge over the Tormes. We did not and I followed the River Tormes to the east. If all else failed then we would swim the river, but fortune favoured us and, at Cabrerizos, a tiny village, we found a ford and reached the southern bank relatively dry.

I realised that I could still do work for the Viscount for if he came north to take Salamanca then he might have to fight a battle and I knew what kind of ground he liked. The road south and west was relatively empty, and we were able to talk. As we rode, we reloaded our pistols for I was certain that we would need them. I was not complacent. The Gendarmerie suspected us, and I wondered why we had not been arrested. They had been so obvious in their search of our room that I now knew they wished to frighten us. Our disguise had been too good. They did not suspect that we were English, and I deduced they were hoping we would lead them to the guerrillas in Salamanca. Having been thwarted they would come after us and could be ahead of us. Our two horses had rested well and so we pushed them until we rejoined the road to Ciudad Rodrigo. I thought we had outwitted them but they were waiting for us. I saw the blue uniforms as we neared the road. They were in four groups of two and spread out. As soon as they saw us, I heard a command and all four groups converged. There was little point in retracing our steps and so we took off and headed due south. The land rose and fell towards ridges and hollows. It was the sort of country which Viscount Wellington loved to defend and even though we were fleeing for our lives I could not help noting that the land around Garcia Hernandez could be used by him for the river was relatively shallow and easily forded.

In a race like this, we had to use our own skills as horsemen as well as our ability as soldiers. The Gendarmerie were not soldiers. They could fight but not as well as we but with odds of four to one they were in their favour. We just had our swords and a brace of pistols each. We needed to either lose them or spread them out and fight them.

"Right, Sharp, let us make this a horse race!"

"I wish these were our own horses, sir."

"So do I but beggars can't be choosers."

As we dug our heels in Sharp said, "Any idea where we are heading for, sir?"

"We use the hills to tire them and then look for a road south or somewhere that we can surprise them."

I looked over my shoulder and saw that they were thrashing their horses and gaining with us. That meant that in the long run, we should win but I could not count on that! Inevitably things did not go the way we had planned. The French horse which Sharp was riding was not as sure-footed as Sharp's own horse, Mary, and the horse stumbled, almost throwing Sergeant Sharp from the saddle. Although he recovered, the horse stopped and I reined in and turned while my sergeant regained control of the animal. I drew a pistol, but they were too far away for me to hit. However, Sharp's stop had encouraged them, and they urged their horses on so that two of them were less than forty paces from us. Sharp's French horse was not happy about moving on and so I raised the pistol. The range for such weapons was close but, as the two horses galloping towards us were close and such a big target, I took a chance and aimed to the left of the chest of the nearest animal.

"Right sir!"

Sharp had got his horse under control and as I whipped around the Lancer's mount's head, I saw that I had hit one of the horses and he was veering off. I suppose I could have fired at the other man and horse, but I did not and rejoined Sharp. I saw the crest of the ridge ahead and risked looking around. The nearest Frenchman was just twenty paces behind us and the other six were forty yards further back and the one whose horse I had hurt had stopped. All of them held their swords in their hands. Sharp's horse had hurt something, and she was labouring. The rider behind was closing with us and whilst one man was not a problem the others were. As I heard the hooves closing behind me, I knew we had to do something. There was no cover but there was a single large rock ahead. Although it would only cover half of our horses it was something and I was clutching at straws.

"Sharp, head for the rock, stop and dismount behind it. You use your pistols and keep reloading. I will try to deal with them!" We would never simply give up.

"Sir!"

As soon as he turned, I whipped around my horse and the French Gendarme who was chasing me was uncertain which of us to follow. He chose me and I simply fired at his head when he was almost next to me. He was thrown from the saddle and I holstered my pistol and grabbed the trailing reins of his horse. We now had a second horse but as the Gendarmerie were just forty yards from us, Sharp could not mount and we would not be able to escape. We would have to fight. I led the horse to Sharp and tied the reins to the lamed horse. I turned just as the next six rode up. They made it hard for us as they came together. As soon as Sharp fired I spurred the horse. She was not as good as Donna, but she obeyed me. I saw one Gendarme hit by Sharp's pistol and a horse was grazed by his second ball, it galloped off with the rider trying to control it. That left me four men to deal with and I had to buy Sharp time to reload his pistols. They did not think that one man would charge four, but I did. I rode through the two on the extreme left for that meant Sharp could shoot at the others. I was sword to sword with one of them and the other had to strike over his horse's head to reach me. Before he could I had smacked his horse on the side of the head with my fist as my sword rang together with the other. The horse did not like the blow and it veered away making the Frenchman strike fresh air. I heard another pistol shot and I riposted the French gendarme's sword. It flew from his hand and I lunged at his face. I raked his cheek and he wheeled away. I rounded on the man whose horse I had punched as he tried to turn. Sharp was outnumbered and when I heard his second pistol fire, I knew that he would have to resort to his sabre. He was not as skilled as I was! I stood in the saddle and brought my sword down hard. As I did so I heard muskets and my heart sank. French infantry would not be defeated as easily as policemen. The Gendarme raised his sword but the power behind my blow bent and buckled his cheap sword and struck him in the head. Gashed and bleeding he fled. I turned to face the French infantry and saw, to my delight, it was not the French but Miguel and his guerrillas. The only one to escape was the one whose horse I had first hit. The guerrillas fell upon the dead Frenchmen and stripped them of all that they had.

Leading the injured horse, we followed the guerrillas to their hideout. As we went, I told them of Marmont's plan to trap and capture their leader. Miguel nodded, "They will fail but I thank you for the information. You have brought us horses and weapons and so we are in your debt."

"No, my friend, there are no debts until the French are driven from this land and you and I can live at home with our wives and make little soldiers!"

Chapter 9

We reached the General's headquarters two days later and it was almost deserted. Only two squadrons of German Hussars and some Portuguese Cavalry remained but their patrols and the aggressive stance adopted by General Castanos in Ciudad Rodrigo kept any spies well away. I spent half a day adding to the information given to me by the guerrillas and drawing a map for the General. Then we sat and went through it all.

"The land south of Salamanca, what is it like?"

"There are ridges and dead ground, sir, just the kind which suits our infantry but there is scope for cavalry."

He nodded. "I have sent for heavy cavalry and they should be on their way. I also have two excellent cavalry officers, Le Marchant and Ponsonby, along with Anson and Alten we might just surprise the French. You have done well. You can stay with me for we leave in four days." We spent some hours discussing the ground. I knew the General and his mind and I had a good recall of the land. By the end of it, with the aid of some maps, he was a happy man.

And so, we had a roof over our heads as spring rains swept across Spain. When we left, we managed to make Elvas in six days. The infantry battalions were there as well as most of the cavalry, and the artillery was in place. There were even twenty eighteen pounder Russian guns. Alexander Dickson, Viscount Wellington's chief of artillery, was a resourceful man and even though British and Portuguese shot would not fit he scoured every arsenal in Lisbon until he had enough. Viscount Wellington had listened to my reports and there were two bridges made for us to take. Fascines, gabions and ladders were all ready, having been constructed by the infantry while they awaited the arrival of the General. On paper, all looked well and there was a general air of optimism in the camp. The deaths of the two generals, whilst not forgotten were no longer as raw.

More importantly for me, the 11th had risen so highly in the estimation of the general that when the 3rd, 4th and Light Division crossed the River Guadiana north of Badajoz, I was sent with my old regiment to scout out the land to the south for General Graham would follow with the 1st, 6th, and 7th Divisions. Our job was to ensure that he and his men remained unmolested whilst they did so. I was the one given the task of passing on the orders. The 11th was a very different regiment to the one which had first come to Spain. Trounced on their first outing, they had been demoralised and thanks to Major Wilkinson, leaderless. I like to think that I helped change them, but I knew that most of the credit was due to the new colonel aided by the backbone of any regiment, the non-commissioned officers. The Colonel and I led A Troop on the first patrol while the rest of the regiment acted as mounted skirmishers before the huge column which would, effectively, cut off Badajoz. We crossed the twenty-two pontoon bridge while the General and his ponderous column were still three miles behind us.

The Colonel was keen to pick my brains for he knew I had more information than anyone else below the rank of General. "So, Major, what exactly are we looking for? I mean will General Phillipon try to interfere with General Graham's dispositions?"

"No, sir. I believe that the three divisions are intended as support and to stop Marshal Soult advancing from the south. I don't think the French will be worried about our attacks. We have failed twice, and we didn't even try to scale the forty-six feet high walls then. They also have three times the men who were in Ciudad Rodrigo. You can be glad that this regiment doesn't have to assault the walls."

He looked at me with genuine interest in his eyes, "You were at the breach were you not?" I nodded. "And what was it like?"

"In one word, sir, hell. Imagine trying to climb up a steep slope made up of shifting masonry. All the while the defenders are shooting at you and dropping grenades and stones on you. If they are clever, as at Ciudad, then they will have cannons enfilading the breaches. If you do make the top then you risk having your hands slashed as you try to shift the chevaux-de-frise and if you get beyond those there will be a huge drop to the ground below. All of this will be done at night where you can mistake a foe's uniform for a friend's. Such mistakes are fatal. No sir, I take my hat off to the men who will assault the walls but achieving the walls is not the end. Our men are brave lads, but they lose their heads. Ciudad Rodrigo saw the best and the worst of the British soldier. I pray that we don't see it's like again."

We had reached the River Rivellas and could see the mighty walls of Badajoz. As we reined in on the bank above the river there was a collective intake of breath. The walls bristled with artillery and although there was just one fort on this side of the walls, the lake the French had built, although shallow, looked impassable. I looked north and saw that they had two more forts on the other side of the inundation.

Percy turned to me, "And we have to take that beast, sir? Why?"

"Because, along with Ciudad Rodrigo, the two fortresses guard the main routes into Portugal. If we hold these then we can move forward into Spain knowing that we can escape. We did not have that luxury in '08 with Sir John Moore and that is not a nightmare I wish to relive."

Trooper Foster shouted, "Eh up sir, Froggies are on the move!"

I smiled as Troop Sergeant Seymour roared out, "Foster, you horrible little man! Make report properly as you have been taught and don't embarrass Major Austen!"

"Sorry sarge! French cavalry leaving the fortress!"

"Recognize them, Matthews?"

I took out my telescope and looked at the horsemen. "When I was in Badajoz there was no cavalry regiment, but they were expecting reinforcements. However, they are a mixture of Chasseurs and Dragoons. It looks like they have cobbled together a small squadron from the remnants of others."

The Colonel rubbed his chin, "So they will have muskets?"

"Yes sir, and that gives them an edge. Dragoons can fire from the back of a horse or, if they wish, they can form ranks and act as infantry. They can mount and dismount as quickly as any horsemen I know, sir."

"Then let us be circumspect and obey our orders. We are here to discourage them." He turned to Troop Sergeant Seymour, "Send a rider back to the column and ask Captain Lutyens to join us!"

"Sir! Bland, you heard the colonel!"

"Yes, Troop Sergeant!"

"Troop, forward march!"

The colonel led us along the north bank of the small river. It was easily fordable, but the spring rains had made the banks slippery and it would act as a very effective barrier. The French rode towards the southern bank and we stopped about one hundred and twenty paces from one another. Who would blink first?

"A Troop, draw carbines!"

I had already loaded my Baker as had Sharp. If this came to a shooting match, then the Dragoons were in for a shock. There were fifty of our carbines against forty or so muskets. The Colonel was testing the resolve of the French. Would the Dragoons dismount, leaving one man in four as a horse holder, and form up as infantry? If they did then they would present a bigger target but, equally, they would cause more casualties amongst our men. I saw that the Major who led them was a Chasseur. Chasseurs did not understand muskets!

I primed my Baker. The Chasseur Major was one hundred and fifty yards from us. The forty Dragoons still formed his front rank and I heard him order them to draw muskets. He was going to order them to try their muskets from the backs of their horses.

The Colonel shouted, "Prime!" While they had a much shorter range the carbine was easier to fire and fired well could be more accurate.

I said, "Do you mind if Sharp and I upset them a little first, sir?"

"Go ahead, Matthews, I have heard much about your weapon and your skill with it."

"Sharp, take the Dragoon sergeant!"

"Sir!"

I aimed my gun at the Chasseur Major. I rested my arm on Donna's neck and controlled my breath. I aimed at the centre of his chest. The carbine rifle was accurate, but the wind still had an effect. The ball hit his shoulder and a moment later the Dragoon Sergeant was thrown from his horse. The Major was wounded but he had not fallen. Before he could order his men to fire Colonel Cummins had shouted, "Fire!" The French fired barely a moment later and the shallow river disappeared in a sea of smoke. Both sides were ordered to reload. I was still doing so when I saw that we had emptied some saddles and three of our men had been hit. I suppose that we could have fired again but we were pre-empted by the sound of a bugle as Captain Lutyens brought up his troop.

The French Captain ordered the retreat although, to be fair to the French cavalrymen, they put their wounded and their dead on their horses. They had lost three men killed and I could not tell how many wounded. However, with just four of our men wounded we had the moral victory. Light Dragoons always had a couple of men who knew first aid and they went to the injured men. Sharp, who was an expert, joined them.

Captain Lutyens looked disappointed, "It looks like we missed all the fun, sir."

"Don't worry, Lutyens. Two troops a day will be doing this. You never know the French may be foolish enough to try it again! Although if they see Major Matthews and Sergeant Sharp they may decide to withdraw. Those were two damned fine shots, Major."

"They are good weapons and we have had lots of practice."

We continued our patrol and rode as far as the south bank of the Guadiana. By the time we returned to the scene of the skirmish the rest of the regiment were in sight and I could see General Graham's men. The French were now cut off from help from the south,

General Graham then turned to take his men further south; we had the fortress cut off and with General Graham and his men to the south watching for Marshal Soult then we had time to reduce the fortress. We had just a day to wait before Viscount Wellington appeared to the north of us with the bulk of the army and the enormous siege train. Unlike Ciudad Rodrigo, we would not need to clear a fort before work could begin on the trenches. As soon as the general arrived the work began on the sixteenth and I was not needed again for a day or two as the Colonel wished all of the officers and troopers to become familiar with the town. On the seventeenth, Captain Dunbar fetched me. I was needed by Viscount Wellington once more.

As we rode to the new headquarters I asked, "What is it this time, John?"

"Sir Richard has asked for you and Sergeant Sharp."

"Bodyguards eh?"

"Partly sir, but you do seem to know the fortress better than anyone else."

This time the infantry digging the trenches knew what to expect and already had the first parallel in place and the guns, more than twice what we had had at Ciudad Rodrigo, were being hauled into place. The Russian naval guns looked strange, but Alexander Dickson looked happier than he had been at Ciudad Rodrigo. The men digging the trenches would, largely, be the ones assaulting the walls and this time they would be viewing the enormous walls with slightly more interest than the first time. While Sharp took Donna and our gear to our tent, I walked with Sir Richard to view the earthworks.

"Tell me, Robbie, did you get the chance to inspect those forts when you were here?"

I shook my head, "No, I saw them from the walls, and they looked formidable, even from that side."

"Then we shall have to work at night for I wish to have a trench less than two hundred yards from the fort." He looked up at the sky for it had begun to rain. "A little rain will not be too bad but if this becomes a quagmire then all of our calculations go by the board!"

I nodded, "Sir, you will stay as far away from trouble as you can this time, won't you?"

He smiled, "I shall try but the plans which Viscount Wellington has devised have also been created by me. I need to see how they progress."

I sighed. I was not in for an easy time.

As we walked, I saw that General Phillipon had not been idle since my visit. Even as we watched more embrasures were being created in the walls. Badajoz made Ciudad Rodrigo look like a beach hut! The defences were formidable and the walls bristled with guns, both cannons and muskets. As we would be digging at night Sharp and I ate and then slept in our tent, which leaked! We rose with Sir Richard so that he could supervise the men at the works. Even with our cloaks wrapped tightly around us, we were both cold and wet but the sound of the storm managed to prevent the French in Fort Picurina from hearing us and when we left with the night shift to have some hot food, I knew that Sir Richard was more than happy with the progress. We had a parallel six hundred yards long and a communication trench four thousand feet long. We had done the hard work and men could walk to the parallel without being seen and continue to dig!

When I woke it was to heavy rain but the men working at the trenches had added four hundred and fifty yards to the trench. A worried Sir Richard joined Sharp and I, "The soil here and the rain mean that instead of making a rampart of soil before the ditch the rain is making a muddy slurry. This will not do!" He was an engineer and knew that against nature we were helpless. Although Ciudad Rodrigo had been besieged in the depths of winter there had been little rain. At Badajoz, it was as though we were in a permanent tropical rainstorm.

We joined the men who were working and I noticed that, even when the rain ceased, the soil refused to make a neat mound into which cannon and musket balls would lodge. We had our cloaks about us, but I saw that the men had taken off their red tunics. The colour tended to run, and they worked in their shirt sleeves. I had no idea how they would manage to dry them! The veterans would have their dry clothes and muskets inside their tents despite the standing orders to stack muskets neatly outside the tents. A damp musket would not work.

On the nineteenth of March, we were watching the work, grateful that the rain had at least stopped albeit temporarily when we were surprised by the French. There was a line of defences on this side of the inundation. They ran from Fort Picurina to a small redoubt at San Roque. The French had wooden walkways across the water. If we managed to take the defences then the walkways could easily be removed. Unbeknown to us the French had massed a force of men behind them. Without warning fifteen hundred infantry and the remains of the cavalry the 11th had trounced, suddenly appeared before us. It was an attack similar to the one at Ciudad Rodrigo but on a much grander scale. As the bugle sounded out the alarm, Sharp and I primed our Baker rifles and stood before Sir Richard who had drawn a pistol. He had learned from us. The three of us were standing on a small mound to better see the work and so we had a good view of the attack.

Some of the diggers used their tools as weapons whilst others ran. The similar attack at Ciudad Rodrigo had meant that Viscount Wellington had put in place a system of relief. I knew that horsemen would be racing to our aid but, in the meantime, it was clear that these men were intent on two things: destroying the trenches and taking away the tools. I saw a Chasseur raise his sabre to strike down on the unprotected head of a digger. He was close enough for me to hit with a musket, but the more accurate Baker rifle punched a hole in his chest and knocked him from his horse. I dropped the now useless weapon and drew a pistol and my sword. Over the years I had become as accurate using my left hand as my right.

Sir Richard cursed, something I had never yet heard him do, "Damn their eyes! We take three steps forward and two back!" He raised his pistol and shot a Dragoon in the arm.

The horsemen were bigger targets and the handful of armed guards we had hit were enough for the others to return to the other side of the fort. I saw that, as they ran, they grabbed weapons. We learned after the siege had ended that the cunning General Phillipon offered a bounty for every tool that they brought back to him. The French had men with muskets and pistols, and they turned their attention to us. It was as Sharp and I emptied our pistols that Sir Richard was shot. The musket ball came from below us and hit him in the groin. Eager French soldiers ran at us. Dropping my pistol and wrapping my cloak about my left arm, I shouted, "Sharp see to him!" Running down the small slope I hoped to slow down the attack of the five light infantrymen until help arrived.

Perhaps they did not expect an attack, or it may have been that they saw just a single man but when I charged, I caused confusion. The officer who led them was young and instead of slashing at me as I ran at them, he lunged, and I used my cloak covered arm to knock the sword to the side. His sword struck my oiled cloak but not my flesh. I brought my sword down diagonally to hack into his neck above the collar on his tunic. Even as the dying officer fell I was aware of a bayonet coming at my side and I pirouetted on the slippery mud so that the bayonet merely slid along my tunic and I punched the light infantryman in the side of the head with the basket hilt of my sword. The light went from his eyes and he fell. There were three of them advancing now and they would not be taken in so easily. I saw that German Hussars were arriving and that meant that the French were fleeing but I still had three men who had lost an officer and tent mate. They wanted vengeance. Suddenly a pistol cracked from behind me and as one of the men dropped his musket and clutched his arm I lunged, and my sword pierced the eye of one of the other two. I withdrew the tip and swung the blade at the head of the last man standing. My sword hit his head. The three wounded men turned and ran. They did not get far as a German Hussar, presented with an easy target of three injured men fleeing him, finished them all off with two blows and the hooves of his rearing horse.

I turned and saw Sir Richard with his breeches around his ankles and a smoking pistol in his hand. Sharp was tending to the wound and I heard him shout, "Medical orderly!"

I retained my sword and ran to Sir Richard, "Thank you, sir!"

"I did little. I do not doubt that even without my lucky shot you would have despatched them."

I looked down and expected to see a great deal of blood. Wounds in the groin were normally bloody and fatal but there appeared to be little blood. Sharp looked up and grinned, "Sir Richard, you are the luckiest man I have ever met. The musket ball struck the pocket of your frock coat and has driven a silver dollar into the wound. It prevented it from penetrating too deeply."

Sir Richard laughed, "Perhaps I should take up gambling, eh?"

Two medical orderlies ran up, "We will take over now, sir!"

Sharp and I rose and saw that more men had arrived, and we joined them to drive the French from our position. The ones we caught were shown no mercy. There were no prisoners taken for the men saw the destruction that the French had caused. Half a day of work had been undone and countless tools were taken. When the recall was sounded Sharp and I ran back to where we had left Sir Richard and our rifles.

While Sharp reloaded the Bakers, I went to speak with Viscount Wellington to tell him of the disaster. While the damage to the earthworks could be remedied, how could Sir Richard be replaced? The area behind the siege works was like a disturbed ants' nest for some of the French horsemen had penetrated as far as the park and they had caused mischief. Luckily none of the guns had been damaged. I found Viscount Wellington who was busy sending aides hither and thither with orders. He looked up at me; his initial reaction was of annoyance but when he saw that I was alone and that my uniform was covered in blood he put two and two together. "Sir Richard?"

"A ball in the groin, sir, but he is lucky, it did not penetrate."

Viscount Wellington shook a fist at the skies for rain had begun to fall again. "If it is not the land it is the weather and if it is not the weather then it is this cunning Frenchman! You were right in your assessment of him, Matthews, and I will not underestimate him again! Thank you for watching over Sir Richard for me."

I returned to Sharp and took my Baker. Already the men were beavering away to repair the damage. The bodies of the dead Frenchmen were used to make ramparts which would not be washed away. We wasted nothing, not even the enemy dead.

The wound to Sir Richard was serious but not life-threatening. However, it meant that he could no longer be at the trenches and so

Viscount Wellington took to meeting with him each day at the field hospital to give a report. Sharp and I were no longer bodyguards and we became, once more, Viscount Wellington's aides.

The rain became our worst enemy and three days after the attack the rain was so heavy that all work on the trenches ceased. We stood with Viscount Wellington sheltering in an engineer's tent and I saw that he was as depressed and down as I had ever seen him. I had been with Viscount Wellington so long that he often confided in me knowing that I was discreet. "You know, Matthews, we may have to abandon this siege. Soult is probing from the south and I know that Marshal Marmont will not wish Badajoz to fall. We cannot prosecute the siege and fight a battle at the same time. We do not have enough men. If this rain continues unabated then I fear that I will fail, once more, to take Badajoz."

There was little that I could say for I knew he was right. However, I had been speaking with some of the men in the trenches. I was well known enough for them to wish to speak with me and my reputation as a soldier meant that they were, generally, honest with me. "You know sir, the men can't wait to attack the walls."

"Really? I would have thought that after Ciudad Rodrigo they would have feared such an assault."

"No sir, the British soldier is a funny creature. He knows that men will die when they go into battle, but they always believe that it will be their neighbour who falls and sad while that might be, they will win through. They are all superstitious and have routines before they go into battle and good luck charms that they carry. Not one of them think that they will die when they attack for some always make the walls. They also think that man for man, they are better than the French. They would rather fight hand to hand than stand in a line firing a musket. This is the kind of street fighting they like!" I did not say that it was exactly the same in the French army; they had the same self-belief.

Viscount Wellington had never been an ordinary soldier. He had begun life as an officer and that gave him a different view of war. He smiled, "Then that gives me hope. If we can have a day or so without rain, then we can get the guns into position. We have enough heavy guns for once, and when we have rid ourselves of the annoyance of these two forts then we can begin the real work and destroy the walls. Hopefully, that will be before Marmont or Soult arrive."

Chapter 10

Two days later the rain did stop long enough to bring up the batteries and to begin to pound Fort Picurina. The French artillery in the fort responded until silenced by the heavier siege guns and then the gunners began to destroy the walls. Viscount Wellington had me bring Major General Kempt so that he could give him his orders.

"Have five hundred men from the Light Division and the 3rd Division attack at nine p.m. this evening. I want the fort in our hands before dawn."

"Sir."

"I will have some engineers guide your men there."

"Viscount Wellington, it would help if we had an officer who knew what the fort was like close up." He pointedly looked at me.

"Major Matthews is too valuable to lose at this point in the siege."

Seeing the disappointment on the face of the Major General I said, "I will lead them, sir, and then hang back when they assault. The Major General is right. Thanks to my work with Sir Richard I know the defences better than anyone."

"Very well but be very careful!"

The commander of the assault was Major Shaw of the 74th. I knew him from Ciudad Rodrigo. His men were tough fighters and I recognised Captain Oates of the 88th, the Connaughts. The Major General was taking no chances and was sending in his best troops.

He briefed his officers before we attacked, "We go in hard, gentlemen, and we go in fast. Make no mistake they will defend this fort well and although their artillery is no more, they have muskets and enough of the fort remains intact to ensure that they have men within. We know the mettle of our enemy! Major Matthews and the Royal Engineers will guide us in. Is there anything you wish to add, Major?"

"They will not fire until we are almost at the walls and that means a wall of lead which will scythe through our ranks. If there is cover close up then the men ought to try to use it."

With that sombre thought, we joined the men who would attack. They were unencumbered by packs and I saw that many of those who had assaulted Ciudad, the 74th and the 88th now carried a second bayonet in their belts. There had been plenty to recover from the battlefield. I had two pistols and my sword as well as a dagger in each boot. I would go in bareheaded. Sharp was similarly attired and armed and he would be two men behind me in case I fell. He would take over.

At nine p.m. when it was as dark as it was going to get, I led my detachment; they were half a company of the 88th and a company of the 74th led by Major Shaw. We moved across the muddy ground towards the ditch. The miners and sappers carried axes and digging tools to get through the palisade. Unlike a building built of stone, the guns we had used merely shattered the outer palisade and the balls were buried in the earth behind. A fort like Picurina needed men to reduce it. One advantage I had over the others I led was that I had fought with the French army and I had attacked at night many times before. I knew the mind of the Frenchmen who defended the fort. French musketry was abysmal and whoever commanded would wait until the perfect moment to fire. They would wait until we reached the edge of the ditch for if we made the ditch, we would have some shelter from the muskets. Besides, I was listening and as we neared the ditch, I heard muskets being prepared. I hissed, "Down!" The two hundred men I led obeyed me and the wall of blazing muskets sent balls over our heads. Some of those, at the rear, caught musket balls but they only hit the backs of their legs. The screams and shouts from around us told us that the other two parties had not been so lucky.

Major Shaw shouted, "Stand! Fire!" This would be the only volley we would be able to send for the men would have no time to reload and would be reliant upon their bayonets. The volley caught some of the defenders and as Captain Oates laid ladders across the ditch to make improvised bridges the defenders fired at us. Men fell, some men were hit by four or five musket balls and they would not survive. Others were hit by spent balls and they would only require attention after the battle. With sword and pistol in hand, I followed Captain Oates and his sergeant across the improvised bridge of ladders.

Some of the sappers had made it with us and they began to hack at the wooden palisades. There were fewer of them than we had intended, and the work was painfully slow. The first grenade dropped from above killed two of them. I stepped away from the protection of the palisade and looked up. I saw the fizzing fuse and I fired at the white face of the Frenchman who was about to hurl the grenade down. The fuse and face disappeared and then I heard an explosion. Sharp emulated me but other grenades managed to kill men. In the confined space of the ditch, the pieces of metal from the exploding grenades scythed through men's flesh causing terrible and bloody wounds. I emptied my second pistol and was rewarded by another internal explosion. In the light of the explosion, I saw that a piece of the palisade at the embrasure had been destroyed. I saw a chance and I shouted, "Captain Oates, follow me with some of your men."

Holstering my pistol and sheathing my sword I ran along the wall past what seemed like a sea of mangled and bloody bodies. I clambered over the corpses of four Irishmen. I had to use two hands to haul myself up and the grinning light infantryman who raised his musket to bayonet me must have thought he had an easy victim. The pistol ball from Sharp actually singed my face but it destroyed the Frenchman's and, pulling myself inside, I reached down, grabbed the primed Charleville musket and waited for the others to join me. Before me I saw the bodies killed by the exploding French grenade. They were like the dead redcoats the other side and some were barely recognisable as men. When Captain Oates and his sergeant stood behind me, I shouted, "Charge!"

The French soldier Sharp had killed had been the only one to spot the danger we represented, and the rest were still firing over the parapet and lighting grenades. I bayoneted the first French soldier who was firing through an embrasure. Captain Oates slashed and hacked with his sword at other French soldiers who were completely taken by surprise while the sergeant wielded two bayonets like some circus performer. I threw the musket at another Frenchman and then drew my sword. The confined space of the fort was no place for a bayonet at the end of a musket. This is where the French defenders were hampered for they had muskets while the men we led had knives, axes and bayonets. It was not war it was a street fight and men were butchered.

I recognised Colonel Thierry and I shouted, "Colonel, you have lost the fort! Surrender and save bloodshed!"

As a young lieutenant standing just before him had his head split by an Irishman wielding an axe the colonel nodded, "We surrender!"

Major Shaw shouted, "Cease fire! We have them!"

The Colonel did not recognise me, and I did not remind him of our meeting. I turned and saw a grinning Sharp, "I am in your debt, Sergeant!"

"Aye sir, but then you would have done the same for me."

Leaving Major Shaw to see to the prisoners and the fort we made our way back out of the charnel house that was the fort to Viscount Wellington who was still awake and nervously waiting for news. When I told him what had happened he looked relieved. "But you say the defences were still largely intact?"

"Yes, sir. The artillery was destroyed but they had earth between the outer and inner palisades and that absorbed the impact and the cannonballs. Howitzers might have been better."

He nodded, "Hindsight, Matthews, is always perfect."

Major Shaw arrived at dawn and he had with him the butcher's bill. Sir Arthur shook his head, "In the two regiments we have four officers and fifty men killed, and fifteen officers and two hundred and fifty men wounded. Those two hundred defenders hurt us."

Sharp and I went to get some food and sleep. We were not there when the French began to pound their own fort. It took some time for the artillery to silence those guns and then begin the real work and destroy the walls. The engineers spent a day placing batteries 7, 8 and 9 where the former fort had been. Less than five hundred yards from the imposing walls of Badajoz their job was to reduce the Trinidad bastion. The next day we went, with Viscount Wellington, to view the new batteries.

The battering from the huge siege guns appeared to have had very little effect on the walls and Viscount Wellington could not hide his disappointment, "I had hoped that being this close we would have been able to see an effect immediately.

Alexander Dickson was with us and he seemed happy enough and, as he patted one of the barrels, he said, "Don't worry, Viscount Wellington, these ladies will keep battering and the walls will fall."

"Yes Dickson, but there are two French armies to consider! Time is not on our side and already we have taken longer here than at Ciudad Rodrigo."

"Ciudad Rodrigo was nothing, sir, this is a real fortress!"

Viscount Wellington's face darkened, "Tell that to Generals Craufurd and Mackinnon and all the brave men who fell there." It was still a raw wound for Sir Arthur.

The Master Gunner recoiled.

We walked the complete circuit of the defences and Captain Dunbar took notes for the general who was planning for the assault. I could see the plan for the attack forming as we walked and as he spoke. While the guns blasted away at Trinidad and Santa Maria bastions, Viscount Wellington, with me as his constant companion, met with generals to plan, with Sir Richard to report on the progress of the bombardment, and then to sit up until it was almost dawn writing the twenty-seven paragraphs of the plan. I did not stay up with him all night. Sharp and I took it in turns but it meant that we were both privy to the master plan concocted by Viscount Wellington for the attack which would, hopefully, finally take Badajoz. Between the first of April and the fifth, the guns battered away until a clear breach could be seen. Then we had bad news; Daddy Hill, who was protecting our southern flank, had had to fall back before Soult's army which was now just seventy miles away and so Viscount Wellington sent Captain Dunbar to bring General Graham and his men to reinforce us and give us his extra men. It was

Sir Arthur's worst fear that we fight a siege and an army at the same time.

The assault was planned for the fifth of April, but Viscount Wellington realised that the curtain wall was still in place and so every gun was ordered to blast holes in it. It worked and so the assault was delayed until the next day. It should have been at half-past seven in the morning but none of the assault parties was ready and so it was delayed for a disastrous two and a half hours during which time the defenders, knowing that an attack was coming, repaired some of the breaches and added defences to the two wrecked bastions.

Viscount Wellington had given me my orders the day before. Sharp and I were attached to Sir Thomas Picton and our job was to liaise with Viscount Wellington. I felt sorry for Lieutenant Dolan, the youngest of Sir Arthur's aides, who was attached to the Light Division attacking the Santa Maria breach with the Light Division. I was flattered and surprised that Sir Thomas had asked for me by name. Apparently, he thought I was like him and not a gentleman! Although the 3rd Division, with my old comrade in arms Major Henry Ridge, had to climb the walls using ladders I doubted that they had expected us to attack there. Major General Leith would attack the San Vincente fort, also using ladders, while another force would attack the San Roque lunette. The final assault would be made by the Portuguese who would make a false attack on the San Cristobal fort. The two Forlorn Hopes were going to be the ones to attack the two bastions. As I passed them on my way to the castle wall, they were almost unrecognisable as British soldiers. Most had discarded their hats and some their jackets. I even saw some going barefoot. Many were carrying grass bags: huge sacks filled with grass and intended to cushion their fall when they threw them in to the rock and trap-filled ditches!

As I marched with Picton's men we were able to watch the two assaults on the bastions for they started their attack first. The Forlorn Hopes charged forward screaming curses fuelled as they were by rum. At first, they made good progress as the men with muskets supporting them fired at the walls. It was an illusion. Some of the Forlorn Hope missed the ditch in the dark and threw their bags filled with grass into the water by mistake and some drowned. Then as they began to climb the breach the French opened fire. The Forlorn Hopes fell to a man and their places were taken by fresh men eager to get to grips with the French. Suddenly a lighted carcass was thrown into the breach illuminating the red-coated troops clambering up. They were bloodily swept away by muskets, grapeshot and grenades. The ditch, even in the darkness, resembled an abattoir! The corner where we would turn to march to the castle walls could not come quickly enough for me as it turned my stomach to see the lives of so many men ended so horribly. The last image I had was of the mines the French exploded in the breaches. In the delay, they had had time to bury the charges and as a mass of men clambered up the rubble from the breaches they were exploded, and bodies were thrown and tossed into the air like rag dolls. The pieces of flesh which fell to earth did not resemble bodies. Then we turned the corner of the fortress and I no longer had to watch the scene from Hell.

Our own Hell was awaiting us. Here we had huge, undamaged walls to scale and the defenders within had not had to fire their muskets nor light their grenades. They were ready and eager to butcher us. As we attacked, we could hear the cries, explosions and musket fire from the two breaches as the men attacked the two bastions more than forty times. Even now I cannot believe that men did this and yet I was there, and I can attest that they did. We had ladders but I could see that they would not be long enough to reach the top. In many ways, our attack, like Leith's, was supposed to be a feint to draw men from the breaches and, in theory, it did not matter if we failed. However, the breaches were failing and that changed the situation dramatically. We reached our walls but we discovered later that Leith's men lost their way and the diversion did not begin until after eleven.

We had no Forlorn Hope and it was the grenadiers who placed the ladders against the walls and began to ascend. Muskets were fired and grenades were thrown but they hit few men. Muskets, especially at night, were very inaccurate. The grenades struck the bottom of the ladders and although they caused wounds few were fatal, but they did destroy ladders. Then someone on the walls hurled down a lighted barrel of gunpowder, a dangerous thing to do, but as it exploded the shards of wood scythed through our men waiting to climb. Even though many of our best troops were either dead or wounded I saw the first men reach the top. They could not reach the parapet, and so men climbed on the shoulders of those on the top rung. It was all too easy for the French defenders to ram a bayonet or a pike into their faces. Often the top man would bring down the second and the third. Then a lucky shot from the walls wounded Sir Thomas in the foot and he had to be taken away.

I turned to Sergeant Sharp, "Get to Viscount Wellington and tell him that Sir Thomas has been wounded and the ladders are not long enough."

"Yes sir, but you keep your feet on the ground, sir! We are here to liaise and not to attack!"

"Go, Sergeant."

Major General Kempt took over and Sir Thomas' curses and blasphemy were replaced by words of encouragement. More men fell as every soldier in the division tried to get to grips with the Frenchmen on the walls. I looked along the walls and thought I saw something we could use to our advantage. I looked around for a familiar face and I saw Major Ridge with the men of the 5th Foot as they prepared to ascend. As I looked over to him, I said, "Major, it seems to me that the wall over there is marginally lower and less well defended."

His eyes lit up when he spotted the section of wall that I had identified, "It is! Sergeant, move the men further down the wall." Just at that moment Major General Kempt fell wounded and I sensed that the men were losing heart. Colonel Winspear took over and he began to exhort his men to greater deeds.

I saw Major Ridge begin to ascend the ladder and that it was against the top of the wall. He would have no circus tricks to perform. Then I saw a second ladder thrust against it and a young Lieutenant began to climb it. In his eagerness, he did not wait for the others and with just four men on the ladder, the French were able to put a forked pole on the top rung and push it away. The unfortunate Lieutenant was impaled on a chevaux-de-frise as he fell. Despite my promise to Sharp and the Viscount, I could not simply stand and watch men die. To hell with being the liaison! British soldiers were dying, and I was just watching!

I shouted to the sergeant of the 5th who had, thankfully, just fallen a couple of feet. "Sergeant, get a dozen of the biggest men you can find and fetch the ladder. I will lead you up."

"Sir!"

I saw Major Ridge struggling, "Major, go more slowly and pack the ladder with men! Make it too heavy for the French to push it away!" He waved his acknowledgement. I took off my tunic and grabbed and primed a pistol. I wanted my men to see the white shirt and to follow it.

"Ready sir!"

"Place it as close to the Major's as you can. We can support each other."

"Sir!"

I had been seen from the walls and a musket ball plucked at my white shirt. "Sergeant, we get up the first ten rungs as quickly as we can and then have the men as close together as you can. Tell them to drop their muskets and just take their bayonets. They will be easier to use and we can take muskets from the French when we reach the top."

"Yes, sir! You heard the officer and we are doing this for Lieutenant Samuels, poor little bugger!"

I grasped the rough rung of the crudely made ladder. I kept my pistol jammed in my belt for I wanted to shift up the ladder as quickly as I could. I pressed myself into the ladder to make it harder for them to push it away. I heard and felt musket balls as the French fired at us, but a musket is inaccurate and many of the badly loaded balls simply rolled from the barrel and dropped on to us.

I could hear the French officer exhorting his men to kill me and it spurred me on. I saw a face appear and the fizzing fuse. I drew my pistol and as the hand appeared fired at it. The hand was less than five feet from me and the double shotted pistol almost severed the arm. The lighted grenade fell, and I heard the officer shouting for his men to clear it. Dropping my pistol, I almost ran up the ladder using both hands to do so. Had there been anyone on the fighting platform then I was a sitting duck but the explosion from the grenade cleared those around the top of the wall. Major Ridge made the top a heartbeat before I did. I drew my sword and ran to my right while Major Ridge ran to the left. I saw the French officer, who drew his sword and ran at me. I reach down and took the stiletto from my boot. This was not a place for honour.

He shouted at me, in French, "You have the luck of the Devil!"

I answered in French, "In my experience, a man makes his own luck!"

I had spoken in French to put him off his guard and it worked for he hesitated, and I did not. I swept my sword over the top of the embrasure and he had to bring his sword across his body to block the blow. I lunged with my stiletto and rammed it through his eye and into his brain. He fell to the ground. Below me was what used to be called the inner bailey or courtyard of the old castle and I saw the stairs leading from the battlements. The fighting platform was littered with fallen muskets and I saw that General Phillipon had been prepared for in the courtyard were more stacks of muskets. I saw soldiers racing to form ranks. I recognised them as the elite Hesse D'Armstadt regiment, more of Bonaparte's Confederation of Germany allies. They would be able to clear the others from the fighting platform. Already Colonel Winspear's men were making the battlements but as they had to climb over each other to do so it would take time.

"Major Ridge, we need to get down to the courtyard and clear it before the others come!"

He waved his acknowledgement, "Sergeant Major get the men down."

The sergeant who had followed me pointed to the gate. I saw senior officers, including General Phillipon and Colonel Lamare running from the castle towards the town. The castle was now lost but I guessed that men were still fighting at the breaches.

"Forget them, get as many men with you as you can and follow me to the courtyard." The dead French officer had a pistol in his belt. It had been primed. He could have killed me had he wished but he wanted the honour of killing me with a sword! Foolishness! I took it and ran down the ancient stone steps. The German soldiers of the Hesse D'Armstadt regiment wasted musket balls trying to hit me and the others. Although they hit a couple they then had to reload. I had only commanded infantry a couple of times before and I was glad that Major Ridge was with me. He had shown at El Bodón that he was a good officer.

I nodded to him as he joined me just a hundred paces from the German soldiers. They were busily reloading. "This is your show, Major! I am just a spectator."

"You have done a fine job," he grinned, "for a cavalryman!" Turning to his men he shouted, "Fetch the French muskets, powder and ball. I want two ranks here. One kneeling and one standing. Major Matthews if you would be so good as to command the second rank."

"My honour, sir!"

We managed to cobble together some thirty men all of whom had muskets although they had never fired a Charleville musket. The Germans fired a volley at the men on the walls and this time were rewarded by a dozen soldiers falling from the walls. It was, of course, a double mistake. It enraged the British soldiers and they should have fired at us. However, Major Ridge had cleverly used the shadows of the castle keep to hide us and perhaps they had not seen us.

The Sergeant Major had not been idle and he shouted, "Find a musket and fall in next to the others!"

It was only a matter of time before we were seen. Major Ridge decided that the range was too great for unfamiliar weapons. "The 5th will advance twenty paces!" The men who were kneeling stood and their old training took over. They carried their borrowed muskets at the high port. This time we were seen but having just fired the Germans were busy reloading and we had time to make the required paces. "Halt." We stopped. "Present! Fire! Kneel!" His front rank fired and then knelt.

It was my turn, "Present. Fire!" We did not need to kneel for we could fire over the heads of the front rank.

Just then the Germans fired. They outnumbered us but even as we reloaded, I could see that the 5th were better and more efficient. Then their balls struck. I saw Major Ridge stagger a little. His voice sounded strained as he shouted, "Front rank! Present! Fire! Kneel!"

We had more men joining our line and so rather than diminishing our numbers, we were growing. "Present. Fire!"

This time our muskets thinned their ranks. Even as Major Ridge gave the order to fire another German volley hit us and I saw Major Ridge fall, a bloody stain filling his tunic. I raised my sword, "The 5th! Let us avenge our dead! Charge!" The men were eager, and we raced across the courtyard screaming and cursing. I aimed my pistol at a large moustachioed sergeant and gave him the coup de grace with my sword. The battlements were now in our hands and Colonel Winspear brought the reinforcements over to us. It was butchery as men who had had to endure the horror of the escalade were now let loose to chase a defeated enemy. The losses ascending the walls and now the death of Major Ridge meant that none of the Germans was spared. They were simply massacred. I saw the gate to the town slammed shut and realised that we had missed a trick. We would now have to beat down the door.

"Sergeant Major, find some axes and break down the gate. We have a town to take!"

Colonel Winspear looked at the body of Major Ridge, "He was a damned fine officer."

"I know sir."

"Thanks for lending a hand, Major Matthews. Unusual to find an aide who is also a proper soldier." He turned, "Captain, have the wounded tended to and then ask Captain Waring to bring all of the men who have survived the escalade here. I have no idea what is happening in the rest of the town and we may be the only ones who have reached their objective. I want as many men as we can muster and relieve the pressure on those poor chaps at the breaches!"

The Sergeant Major had the men who had followed me hacking at the door for they were all big men. I still had my sergeant. "Keep your men with me, eh, sergeant."

He nodded, "We'll have to, sir. Our officers, Major Ridge and Lieutenant Samuels are both dead."

"Form up in a column of fours. We will give them hard steel!"

As the door crashed open the Colonel led the remains of his company and they charged through the castle entrance. We followed them. As we did so I saw General Phillipon and his aides. They were making for the Las Palmas gate and trying to escape. As much as I admired the man, I knew that Viscount Wellington would want him a prisoner and not free to defend another town. While the Colonel headed to the breaches I said, "That is the commander of this fortress. He and the others are our targets."

"Right, lads, skirmish order!"

Even as the gates opened, French soldiers ran down from the gatehouse to join them. We would have to fight our way through them if we were to capture the General. I had too few men and there were too many of the French trying to escape for me to capture the General, but I did my best. The fighting was savage. The men of the 5th were ruthless as they used the French bayonets to stab and skewer their enemies who were massing in the gate. The French General and his staff had raced across the bridge and were aided by men who came from the small fort and fought off the Portuguese. I used my dagger and sword to fight my way through the fleeing French. Some hurled themselves in the river. I did not try to kill anyone for my aim was to capture the General but, inevitably, men died. I had just reached the bridgehead and the Portuguese who were attacking there when I saw the gates of the fort slam shut. General Phillipon was safe inside the fort of San Cristobal.

I spoke with the Portuguese Captain who sheathed his sword as the last Frenchman surrendered. "I am Major Matthews of General Wellesley's staff. I would have your men surround the fort. Do not risk yourselves but I do not want the men inside to escape."

The fact that I spoke to him in Portuguese impressed him and he nodded, "Of course, sir."

As I crossed back across the bridge, I saw the sergeant and the men I had led robbing the dead. If he expected censure, then I disappointed him. I tossed him the French officer's pistol, "Here you are sergeant, back in England you can tell them that you captured this pistol from General Phillipon himself. If asked I will give you the provenance."

He deftly caught and nodded his thanks, "Major Ridge was right about you, sir. You are a good 'un. I would serve under you any day." He gave me a salute and I walked back into Badajoz feeling ten feet tall. A compliment like that from a fighting sergeant was worth more than any medal I could be given! My good feelings lasted until I headed through Badajoz which, thanks to the 3rd Division had finally fallen. We had won but the wild men who had bled their way into the town were now on a rampage. It made Ciudad Rodrigo look like a Sunday School picnic!

I actually felt in fear of my life for drunken soldiers were threatening anyone and everyone. I saw a lieutenant from the 44th regiment who had been beaten badly and was being helped away by two of his regiment. There were soldiers who three hours earlier had been saluting and smiling were now looting, robbing and raping. I had to get to Viscount Wellington and the quickest way would be through the breach. I almost made it safely but as I neared the huge mound of bodies which marked the fiercest fighting, a half dozen soldiers emerged from a wrecked tavern, and I could smell the drink on them. The leader was a huge man, who when he spoke had a clear London accent.

"What do we have here? From the sword and the boots, it must be an officer, but he has no jacket! I reckon he's a deserter. Let's do old Nosey a favour and hang the bastard!

Three of the others laughed but one of them said, "I have seen him, Lofty, he is one of Old Nosey's aides. Best let him get on his way!"

Lofty whirled on the man and backhanded him so hard that he rendered him unconscious, "When I want your opinion then I will give it to you! All the more reason to hang the stuck up bastard. While we were climbing the walls, he was just watching."

It would have done me little good to argue and tell him he was wrong. I drew my sword and my stiletto, "Back off and go on your way. You are drunk and I do not want to hurt you."

He laughed and pulled the axe he had been hiding behind his back, "Hurt us? There are five of us and, my friend, I will have both those boots and that fine sword." He swung his axe at me, but his reactions were off for I had been right and he was too drunk. I stepped aside and slashed my sword across his middle. I did not cut deeply but deep enough for him to drop his axe and clutch his stomach. "Get him! I want his bollocks for my tea."

Two of them were game and came on. Both had bayonets. I deflected one with my sword and ducked beneath the bayonet to hack across his wrist with my stiletto. He dropped the bayonet. I punched the other in the face with the hilt of the sword. I thought it was over but Lofty picked up his axe and ran at me. The ball from the Baker rifle hit him square between the eyes. Sergeant Sharp was standing atop the breach and he picked up his carbine. "I am in a killing mood. I will count to three and then shoot. One, two…" They fled.

He rushed up to me, "Sir, what part of stay out of trouble do you not understand? The General has had men looking all over for you!"

"I am safe, but the populace of Badajoz is not. We have taken the town, but we risk losing an army."

I was whisked away to safety, but the rampaging redcoats would not be stopped. It was not hours but days before order could be restored. This time Viscount Wellington had to erect a gallows and threaten to hang every man in Badajoz before order was restored. It is a sad fact that almost as many men died after Badajoz was in British hands as when the fortress was taken and that deeply upset Viscount Wellington.

It was Lord Fitzroy Somerset who accepted the surrender of General Phillipon. The French survivors fared better than the populace and I knew that Viscount Wellington was apoplectic with rage. His opinion of the British soldier reached its nadir that April. As for me? I was feted as one of the heroes, but I did not feel like one. John Ridge had been a hero and I had merely been lucky.

We did not have long to recover. Just a few days after the town surrendered, we received news that Marshal Marmont was threatening Ciudad Rodrigo and so we headed north once more leaving behind the bloody bodies as they were cleared from Badajoz.

Part 3

Salamanca

Chapter 11

I ached all the way north. Although I had not been wounded as such, the assault had injured me, and I was no longer a young man. Sergeant Sharp was perceptive, and he commented on my silence. "You came out of this well, sir, and you survived. We both know how unusual that is!" Sergeant Sharp had a dry and wry sense of humour and I smiled.

"It was the waste, Alan. John Ridge was a good officer and, if he had been promoted, then he would have been a good colonel or even a general. We have seen too many bad ones, have we not?"

"That we have, Major Matthews, but Nosey has surrounded himself with some good generals and officers, sir. I like Sir Thomas and both General Anson and General Alten know how to lead. We will be alright. You should be a general!"

I laughed, "You know how to raise my spirits by making me laugh!"

When we stopped each night we were not under canvas, but we had a roof for we travelled with Viscount Wellington. Poor Alan often had to make do with stables but he did not mind for, as he told me, it was warm and always dry! I often had to share a room with Captain Dunbar and Lieutenant Hogg. It was John Dunbar who told me Lieutenant Dolan had died in the breaches. I thought it had been wrong of Viscount Wellington to risk the young untried officer there. You survived war by serving an apprenticeship. There you could learn without, hopefully, not too much risk. I know that when I had been in the Chasseurs I had been protected. I had tried to do the same with Alan when he was but a trooper. He also brought me some good news, not only did we had reinforcements, we had heavy cavalry! Three regiments of British Dragoons and Dragoon Guards had arrived in Portugal along with two regiments of German Dragoons. Up until now we had always been not only outnumbered in terms of cavalry but outclassed for the French had many Dragoons. I just hoped that we had a good commander for them. Heavy cavalry needed a different hand on the reins than light horse!

Sharp had been right, Viscount Wellington was surrounding himself with good officers; Lord Fitzroy, William Ponsonby, Edward Pakenham and Stapleton Cotton. When Captain Dunbar told me that Major General John Gaspard Le Marchant was to command the cavalry then my spirits soared.

John Dunbar said, "I have not heard of him, sir. I thought he was a newcomer."

"And that is because you are not a cavalryman. General Le Marchant devised the sabre which our light horsemen use. He has written a fine manual on sword drill and established a college for officers. All that might be for nothing except that I know he has a good reputation amongst cavalrymen who have served under him. I served with Lord Paget, the Earl of Uxbridge and he spoke highly of the man. Let us say, John, that the news that he is to take command of the cavalry fills me with hope."

Other reinforcements were heading north to join us. As well as more line regiments there were two battalions of guards as well as more rifles and light infantry including the Brunswick Oels who were desperate to fight against the men who had taken their country. We had lost many men, almost five thousand dead and wounded. That had been almost three times the number the French had lost. Some, like Sir Thomas Picton, would be able to fight against Marmont but many would need hospitalisation while some would never fight again. Fresh blood was needed.

Sir Richard would not be needed for a while and so, when we reached Ciudad Rodrigo, Viscount Wellington sent him back to Lisbon with the one task of using his engineers to repair the roads between Lisbon and Ciudad Rodrigo and Lisbon and Badajoz so that supplies and reinforcements could reach our troops quickly and easily. Sharp and I were sent to escort him back to Lisbon and to deliver some despatches for London. Sir Richard had been chastened by his wound as well as the losses he had witnessed. We spoke at length on the way south to Lisbon. When he had built the defences at Torres Vedras, it had almost been an intellectual exercise and he had never been in any real danger. Ciudad Rodrigo and Badajoz had been different, and he determined to be a better engineer. We parted in Lisbon and Sharp and I went to the house we always used. We were always made welcome. I left Sharp to go to the house for I knew that he was anxious to speak with Maria and her son Juan. I knew my way around Lisbon and when I reached the military headquarters with the despatches I was not only given letters to take north, including some for me, I was also told that the *'Black*

Prince' was in port but about to sail and that I should take Viscount Wellington's documents to her for she was being used as a mail packet.

This was fate for I knew Lieutenant Commander Jonathan Teer very well and considered him a good friend. The letter I had for Emily would be delivered far more quickly if I gave it to him. As we reached the quayside, I saw that the sloop was preparing to leave port. Luckily, we were recognised by the crew and allowed on board.

"Robbie, what a pleasant surprise! You wish a passage home to England?"

"Would that were true but I work for Viscount Wellington now and these are despatches which must get to London!" I handed him the sealed packet. "And I have a favour to ask."

"Ask away. I miss your little jaunts behind enemy lines! Now my sloop delivers letters. I enliven our lives by seeking prizes when we sail."

I took out the letter to Emily and handed it to him. "I am now married, and my wife lives on my farm near Tottenham Court. When you reach England, I would be grateful if you would send this to her." I took out a coin.

He waved it away, "You insult me, my friend! Firstly, congratulations and secondly, I must see the lovely lady who has stolen the heart of this cavalier! I shall sail to your farm and deliver it personally!"

"Can you do that?"

He gave me a sly grin, "The winds can be precocious at this time of year and damage can occur. I may well have to put in, albeit briefly, at the docks at Tilbury which are not too far from Tottenham Court."

"Then I am in your debt. Tell Emily that..." I was lost for words.

He smiled, "I will tell her and the fact that you are whole will, I have no doubt, be the best news that she could hear. And now, I fear, that I must ask you to leave. Time and tide!"

We clasped arms and, not for the first time, I thanked the Fates who had thrown us together all those years ago. As the gangplank was raised the crew shouted their farewells to me and the '***Black Prince'*** sped down the Tagus towards the sea. Emily would have the letter within days and not weeks. She would not have to endure the uncertainty when she read of the casualties at Badajoz.

That night, as I read her letters, I realised that she did not know if I had survived Ciudad Rodrigo! My letter home and Jonathan's testimonial that I lived would ease her heart. After I had finished reading them Sharp and I ate in the dining room. Paulo had told Alan that Maria had made herself useful and was a good cook. He was happy to have them share the house. Donna Maria had chosen good people. Alan was full of talk about Maria and I suspected that he had feelings for her and I reflected on my position. I had thought to ask for a leave, but I saw now that was impossible. The only way I would be granted one would be if I was wounded. Of course, if we were successful against Marmont and had no winter campaign then Viscount Wellington might grant my request for a leave but as I knew the French were gathering their two hundred and thirty thousand men to bring their full weight to bear on Viscount Wellington's sixty thousand then it was unlikely that we would be successful. I doubted that Viscount Wellington could field more than fifty thousand men. His task was gigantic!

Before we left, I formalised the arrangements for Maria and her son. They were to be paid from the same funds which were used for the upkeep of the house and Paulo. Maria and her son were happy for, as we left, she dropped to her knees and kissed my hand. Her parting from Alan was tenderer. There were mutual feelings there.

"So, Alan, you and Maria?"

He blushed, "I don't know, sir. I mean I am a soldier and that is all that I know."

"And she is the widow of a soldier." Emily's letters were still in my head. "I know what a difference it has made to my life now that I am wed. Think about it."

Maria and her son were still in our heads when we reached Torres Vedras. We heard that the Marquis had left the town and disappeared. It seems he had accepted money from the Portuguese Army and not delivered. I suspected that he would no longer be in Portugal, but I put him from my mind. He could no longer hurt Maria and Sharp and I could not cure all of the ills in the world.

By the time we reached Ciudad Rodrigo it was the end of April and Viscount Wellington was eager for news from London and so we were welcomed with a smile when he saw the despatches. The threat from Marmont had not materialised as the guerrillas had been emboldened by our victory at Badajoz and increased their activity. A day after our return Viscount Wellington sent for me. He tapped a letter, "Your friend, Colonel Selkirk, has been busy! He has discovered a plan to make me the piece of English beef between two pieces of French bread!" His confused metaphor told me that he was in good humour. "Marshal Soult and Marshal Marmont have a plan to join each other and to destroy us here with a combined army of over eighty thousand men! There is but one bridge over the Tagus which Soult can use to bring his army north. It is at Almarez."

"I remember crossing it, sir. It is not far from Plascencia. I was there before Talavera."

He smiled, "I know, and you made some contact with the guerrillas there. I wish you to take a troop from the 11th and join Major General Hill." He folded and sealed a letter. "Here are his orders. He is to render the bridge over the river unusable. You are to aid him in any way you can and if you can use the guerrillas then so much the better. They can stop the French from escaping north of the river when General Hill attacks and takes the fort and the bridge. When the bridge has been destroyed then you will return here. It is imperative that we keep Soult in the south. General Hill has enough men to make life hard so long as he is south of the Tagus."

I did not think that Colonel Cummings would thank me for his men had just ridden from Badajoz and now they would have to return there to meet with General Rowland Hill and his ten thousand British and Portuguese troops. As we headed for their encampment, I wondered just how I would contact Juan. I knew he lived around the La Calzada de Béjar area, but I had no direct means of communicating with him. The bridge at Almarez had to be attacked from the south for that was where General Hill and his troops were encamped and Juan lived north of the Tagus. I would have to find Juan first before delivering my orders to General Hill. The shortest route for a couple of riders to take was the direct one, through La Calzada de Béjar and Plascencia. I had my plans already in my head when I met with the colonel. I explained what I needed and gave him my suggestion that the troop take the long route and I take the shorter one.

He shook his head, "I thank you, Major, for your consideration, but our troopers must learn every skill if we are to win this war. Cavalrymen need to learn how to swim a river."

"But sir, the Tagus?"

He smiled, "Can you do it, Major?"

"Of course, sir, and we have done so on a number of occasions."

"Then Brevet Major Austen and his troopers will learn under your tutelage!"

And so we left for a ride through, what I hoped would be, a deserted part of Spain. The road from Talavera to Madrid was heavily patrolled but King Joseph commanded that region and he was a cautious general. He would not stir unless he had to and I doubted that he would have patrols as far west as Almarez.

I explained to Percy and Lieutenant Harper as well as Troop Sergeant Seymour who had recently been moved to A Troop, not only what we would be doing with General Hill but the role the guerrillas would play. "We will probably not see them for they are the masters in the art of being hidden in plain sight. Your men must keep their hands away from their guns and swords. "I pointed to the new shakos which had been issued. "They are new and make you look like Chasseurs. I am hoping that they will recognise me. Teach your men the Spanish for I am English. Don't worry about the accent. That will identify them as English as quickly as anything."

"Sir, do we really need the guerrillas? I mean their armies are not that good."

"Never say that in front of a Spaniard for it is wrong. The Spanish soldier is good when led well and these guerrillas, whilst few in number, are tying down thousands of French soldiers. We face sixty thousand men under Marshal Marmont. If there were no guerrillas, then it would be more than twice that number." I think I made them understand.

Much had changed in this part of the world since Sharp and I had first scouted it before Talavera. That battle had been a real shock for the French. Before then this part of Spain was patrolled by French Dragoons and was regarded as their fiefdom. Now it was empty, and the Spanish were reclaiming their land. I led the troop, all fifty of them, through La Calzada de Béjar. There was a water trough which we used. I gave the headman some coins for its use and said, "If you see Juan the guerrilla then tell him that milord with the rifle wishes to speak with him."

He gave me a blank look, but I knew he had understood me, and I hoped my crudely coded words would get through to him. We rode on and I halted just six miles from the village. The site I had chosen was familiar as Sharp and I had used it when we had scouted. It was just off the road to Plasencia with water, some graze and was bowl-shaped. It could be defended, and we were sheltered from winds. The troopers went about their business happily enough but Sergeant Sharp and I kept our eyes on the hills around us.

Darkness had fallen and we were eating when Percy said, "This land is fairly empty, sir. Viscount Wellington could retake it easily."

"And what would be the point of that, Percy? Think of Spain as a chessboard. Viscount Wellington is trying to control the key access points. He has castles at Badajoz and Ciudad Rodrigo. The only other place the French can attack Lisbon is by coming through Portugal and Marshal Masséna was taught a lesson about that at Torres Vedras. Viscount Wellington needs to take Salamanca and then Madrid."

"Madrid! That is impossible, sir, I have not been in Spain long but even I know that."

"After Talavera, Percy, we were very close to Madrid. We did not have a large army but if we had had just a few more men then we could have taken Madrid." I let him take that in and then smiled, "Of course, that would have brought the wrath of Bonaparte upon us. Luckily the Emperor is now in Russia."

"Russia? Will he win?"

"When Sharp and I were in Lisbon we heard that he had made great gains and had the support of the Polish army. I am guessing that he will do well until Russia's greatest weapon is used."

"What weapon is that, sir?"

"Winter!"

A movement caught my eye. We had sentries watching the horses and the road, but the movement was not one of our men. Without turning around, I said, in Spanish, "Good evening, Juan. I see you received my message."

The guerrilla and three of his men stepped into the light and he laughed, "I wondered how long it would take you to spot us, milord."

I saw the sentries raising their carbines, "Stand easy, troopers, these are friends. Join us, Juan."

We shuffled along the rock we used as a seat and a surprised Major Austen stood to allow the guerrilla leader to sit next to me.

"What is it you want of us, milord? As you can see the French have learned to avoid this part of Spain. You were lucky that I was visiting my home for I am often found around Talavera where the French have learned to fear us."

I knew Juan appreciated brevity and so I got to the point quickly, "The general is sending men to attack the last bridge over the Tagus."

He nodded as soon as I mentioned the bridge for it was clear that he knew it, "Almarez. There is a fort, you know, and they have guns." He went into detail about the garrison. It was clear that he had scouted it.

"The numbers are immaterial for General Hill has more than five thousand men."

"Then he might just be able to destroy it. And what is it that you wish of us?"

"Cut it off. We will be attacking from the south for that is where General Hill and his men are camped. We would wish you to stop men coming from Talavera or Madrid. The aim is to stop Soult from attacking Viscount Wellington when he goes to fight Marshal Marmont. We need the messenger the French might send for help to be intercepted."

He beamed, "Then consider it done. If the French flee, they will be easy targets and we will have even more weapons for my men."

Inside I shuddered for I knew what would happen to the French who survived and fled. The guerrillas would capture and torture them. Their best hope would be to surrender to General Hill.

"Thank you."

"And you, milord, are you not a general yet?"

I laughed, "No, I am still just a major but happy enough in that."

He stood and offered me his hand. "It has been good to see you. We are both alive and that is reason to celebrate. When this war is over then come to my village and I will show you the real Spain."

"Thank you, Juan."

They disappeared and Percy, who had not understood a word, returned to my side. "Sir, how do they do that? Appear from nowhere."

"Practise, Percy and that is why this land is empty of French. Had they wished to then they could have slit the throats of all of your sentries and then killed us as we slept." I saw him looking around and taking that in. He was learning what war was like here in Spain.

Two days later we rode into General Rowland Hill's camp. He was a popular general and his men referred to him as Daddy. I liked him too.

"Ah Matthews, I take it this is not a social visit?"

"No sir," I handed him the sealed orders, "these are from Viscount Wellington."

"Take a seat and pour yourself some wine. One of the few benefits of fighting in this country is the availability of fairly decent wine."

I poured myself some of the wine while he read. That done he put the orders down and folded his hands. "And Viscount Wellington could have sent any rider with these orders. Why, even the officer commanding the cavalry could have delivered them so why you, Matthews?"

I smiled. For all his affability General Hill had a razor-sharp mind. "I have made contact with the local guerrillas. They will seal off the bridge and the fort from the south. When you have the fort then, before you destroy the bridge, I will ride north to deliver the news to Viscount Wellington. Your action will determine his next move."

Satisfied he smiled, "Good! I like things to be clear, eh? Then we will begin on the morrow. I take it you will be with the 11th?"

I shook my head, "Brevet Major Austen needs to learn how to lead his troop over here. The regiment is relatively new to the Peninsula. I shall stay with you, sir. Use me as you will."

That pleased him even more, "Good. Now, what can you tell me about the garrison?"

"There are two small battalions in the complex of forts. One is Prussian and the other is light infantry. They have gunners and sappers and eighteen guns. One fort dominates the bridge and the river. The guerrillas said that it is hard to approach it unseen. In fact, it is not just one fort. Fort Napoleon is the main defence but at the bridgehead, on the north side of the river is Fort Ragusa and there is also an old castle, Mirabete, which protects one side of Fort Napoleon. In addition, there is a small fort north of the river. It is why he is using your division, sir. It will take coordination. The 11th is here to keep the French from getting messages out or reinforcements arriving."

He nodded and sipped his wine while he doodled a plan, "Then the one thousand defenders are spread out as, I assume, are their guns. I think we will use a three-pronged attack. I will send the 28th, 34th and some Portuguese under Brigadier Chowne to take the castle. The 6th and 18th Portuguese line can support them and I will take Brigadier Howard's men to attack Fort Napoleon itself. Your Major can cut off the road to Trujillo." He looked at me, "Your guerrilla friends will stop reinforcements from the north?"

"Fort Ragusa will not be getting any help, sir."

"Good. Then it will take most of tomorrow to get close and we can make a night attack."

"Do you not wish to scout it out, sir?"

He shook his head. "As soon as the French see your horsemen, they will know what is coming. We make a surprise attack!"

I gave Percy his instructions. He seemed disappointed. "You mean we are not to attack, sir?"

"Percy, this is a mountainous country. The Portuguese Caçadores and the light infantry were made for this. Just give me one trooper and then as soon as we take the forts, I can send for you as your horses may well be needed to swim the river and help to force the garrison of Fort Ragusa to surrender."

"Sir."

The plan seemed simple enough but this was Spain and although we reached the starting point easily enough it was when we began to climb to the two forts that things went awry. Had we had locals or if we had scouted it out then we would not have become lost and had to retrace our steps. When it became obvious that we would not be able to make a night attack General Hill decided to concentrate his men on Fort Napoleon. As dawn broke, we found ourselves half a mile from the fort. We knew that Brigadier Chowne had had similar problems for, as the 50th prepared to attack, we heard our guns open fire on the castle at Mirabete. We heard the drums inside both Fort Napoleon and Fort Ragusa as the garrisons were summoned to the walls.

Daddy Hill said, "Well that takes away the element of surprise then."

Just then the guns of Fort Ragusa began to fire from across the river and some of the 50th, advancing up the steep slope, were hit. Luckily the men with the ladders were not amongst them. Brigadier Howard was leading the 50th and General Hill said, "Matthews, get the 71st to support the 50th eh?"

The Glasgow Light Infantry was a good regiment and I knew that they would be eager to join in. I found Colonel MacGregor and said, "General Hill's compliments, sir, and would you care to lead your men to attack the fort too?"

He grinned and rubbed his hands, "Just waiting for the chance laddie! Right you band of villains, pick up your muskets and follow me."

We could hear the pop of muskets from the walls and the cannons from Fort Ragusa still swept the hillside below Fort Napoleon but as the 50th were in open order there were few casualties. I watched the leading company use their ladders to climb the first scarp and then, after securing them, throw down ropes so that their fellows could climb. They then used their ladders to scale the second rocky scarp which gave them access to the walls. The first man to reach the walls was Captain Chandler and I heard him shout, "Come on the Dirty Half Hundred!" before he was shot and bayoneted. The Dirty Half Hundred was the nickname for the 50th.

The Colonel led the Scottish Light Infantry in a wild charge and, mindful of what had happened when the 74th and the 88th had been let loose in Badajoz and Ciudad Rodrigo, I drew my sword and followed them. I turned to the trooper and said, "I think you can fetch Major Austen and ask him to secure the bridge for us!"

Pleased to be doing something he raced off to the main camp where his horse was tied.

"Come along, Sergeant Sharp, let us see what we can do."

We did not follow the Colonel but ran obliquely to the corner of the star-shaped fort where Captain Chandler had fallen. We reached the ropes despite the occasional cannonball which whizzed across the river from Fort Ragusa. The French were wasting ball and powder! After pulling ourselves up the ropes we reached the ladders and I led Sharp up the nearest roughly made ladder. We followed a couple of the 50th. I could hear the fighting within the fort. The muskets had been fired and now it was the brutal hand to hand fighting which filled the small fort. The defenders would outnumber the 50th but it would only be for a short time as the Glaswegian battalion was coming to their aid.

I stepped over the body of Captain Chandler and drew my sword and pistol. One of the sergeants from the 50th was using his pike to deadly effect. Now that the fighting was in the heart of the fort, he was able to cause terrible wounds as his weapon was longer than the French muskets. I saw a French officer racing towards him, and I lifted my pistol and shot him in the shoulder. Holstering my pistol and with Sharp at my side, we began to clear the French from the side of the sergeant. Suddenly there was a wild Gaelic cheer as the Scotsmen who had followed us poured into the fort. The defenders were the Prussians and they fought ferociously with no quarter sought nor given.

Within five minutes of their arrival, the Prussians were completely destroyed, and the French survivors fled out of the fort down towards the bridgehead and the tower which was there. I saw a French colonel, I assumed he was the commander of the fort, and he and his men fought on until the sergeant with the pike ran him through.

"71st! With me!"

I ran from the star-shaped fort down the slope to the bridgehead fort. I thought at first that the French would make it and then I heard hooves and saw Brevet Major Austen leading his troop. They caught the fleeing French in the open and there is no better target for a horseman. I led the wild Scotsman down to the bridgehead. The troopers could cut the French to ribbons when they were in the open, but they could not do so if they were behind wooden walls. The mistake the French made was to keep the gates open just a heartbeat too long. Two Scottish sergeants who towered over me threw their not inconsiderable weight against the gates which had not been barred and they burst open. There were just five of us in the gateway but the sight of the Scots pouring down the hill and the cavalry sabring those outside made them surrender.

Fort Ragusa continued to fire and so I sent a runner to order the 50th to turn the guns of Fort Napoleon on to Fort Ragusa. Then I went with Sharp along the pontoon bridge of boats and saw that the French had removed the middle two. Turning, I spied a couple of boats tied next to the bridgehead fort and I pointed to four of the 71st who had joined us. "You boys take those boats and find the pontoons the French removed."

"Aye, sir!"

They had just gone when I saw the first muzzle flash from Fort Napoleon as my orders were obeyed. It took just a few cannonballs for the men to get the range. I saw General Hill and the men who had taken the castle marching down the slope to join us. It was then that the garrison of Fort Ragusa decided that they had had enough, and they fled. If they thought they would escape then they were in for a shock. I could not see them, but I knew that Juan and his men would hunt them down and they would all die. The lucky ones were the ones who were already dead!

By the time the pontoon was repaired then Fort Ragusa was empty. General Hill himself ordered its destruction. As the eager soldiers obeyed him, he said, "Thank you, Matthews. When you and your troopers have crossed the pontoon bridge then I will have it destroyed as well as Fort Napoleon. A nice piece of work. It is a shame that the 50th lost so many men!"

The attack had only cost us thirty-three men killed but twenty-eight had been from the 50th.

"Right sir. It was an honour to serve with you."

"Aye, well, tell Viscount Wellington we will watch his back for him!"

We were just three miles north of Fort Ragusa when we found the first of the French who had fled. Perhaps they thought they could reach the hills and disappear, or it may have been that they thought the larger numbers would attract pursuit. Whatever the reason the three naked and mutilated bodies lay next to the road, a sure sign that the guerrillas had found them.

Troop Sergeant Seymour said, "I know they are the enemy, sir, but that isn't right. I will have the lads bury them."

He started to dismount, and I shook my head, "Joe, leave them. The guerrillas did this and they might take offence if we interfered. They will leave the bodies there as a warning to any other French soldiers. The guerrillas do not play at war."

He nodded and remounted, "Aye sir, you might well be right."

Despite our victory, the three corpses had a sobering effect and there was neither banter nor jokes for the next few hours.

Chapter 12

We reached Viscount Wellington three days later and it was clear that he had put his plans into place. He was eager to hear my news for we had ridden as fast as any messenger would have done.

"Well, Matthews? Is my southern flank protected?"

"Yes, sir. The Tagus cannot be crossed, and General Hill has eighteen thousand troops stationed between Badajoz and Elvas."

The general looked relieved. "Then we will try out this new marshal and move towards Salamanca. From what you have reported to me it is not as strong as either Ciudad Rodrigo or Badajoz and now that we have the Dragoons and Dragoon Guards then we can meet his cavalry eh?"

"Yes, sir."

"I want you and Sergeant Sharp to ride east and then north to see if there are any new defences and cavalry patrols. Take no risks for this is the beginning of a long campaign. I want a battlefield where I can hide my numbers and draw in the French." I already had an idea of a perfect place between the villages of Carbajposa and Las Torres but if Viscount Wellington was thinking of using my selection then it had to be right. He suddenly pounced, "You know of such a place!"

"Perhaps, Viscount Wellington, but as we were fleeing from lancers at the time my judgement might be a trifle coloured."

"Then when you have ascertained that the French are still in Salamanca that task becomes your priority!"

Sharp and I made certain that we had both Baker rifles and carbines with us for the lesson of the lancers had been learned. We left at the end of the first week of June and both of us felt the full force of the sun for this was Spain in summer and we would have to husband our horses! The first part was relatively easy. We boldly rode up the main road to Salamanca knowing that Miguel and his guerrillas would be watching the road. As with Juan, it was the guerrillas who came to us before we had seen them.

Miguel and his men gave us valuable intelligence. "The French only have thirty thousand men in Salamanca, and they have done nothing to strengthen the defences. Our men in the north are attacking Bilbao and I do not think that the French can reinforce from there. Your general comes to attack?"

I smiled, "He comes to attack!"

"Good, then soon this part of Spain will be free!"

The next morning, we rose early, and Miguel took us to view the small fort of Santa Maria. Satisfied that we could take it easily for it was like Fort Napoleon but without the natural advantages of the scarp and the river, we headed down the road and I saw that the land was undulating. If we held Salamanca, then the River Tormes would guard our left flank. We reached the village of Las Torres and spoke with the locals who, when they discovered that we were English, could not do enough for us.

Sebastian, the headman, and his son took us to a piece of high ground just a mile or so east of the village. He told us it was called the Lesser Arapil and pointing further south he showed us another piece of high ground, slightly larger, called the Greater Arapil. "I was a soldier in my youth and I would think that guns on there would sweep the French from before them."

I thought that it would be hard to get artillery there, but infantry could make it a killing ground. I saw that behind both of the patches of upland there was dead ground in which infantry could shelter from artillery shot. To the east, the ground rolled away, and it meant that any advancing French army would be coming uphill. I made a sketch of it for the General. The trick would be to get Marshal Marmont to oblige and fight us there!

When I reported back to Viscount Wellington, I don't think I had ever seen him as happy. He patted me on the back and told me to take some time off! I am not sure what he thought I would do with the time, but I returned to the 11th. The attack on Almarez had been their coming of age and I was proud of them. I joined them for dinner and was able to tell Colonel Cummings of the progress they had made.

"The proof of the pudding, Major Matthews, will be when we face French cavalry in a pitched battle. Up until now, we have been on the periphery of this war. The test of this regiment is when we fight sabre to sabre. I am grateful to you for the work you have done. They can now act as Light Cavalry and use their carbines, but the other role is when we charge the French and that, as I am sure you know, is a totally different matter."

He was right as Major Wilkinson had so disastrously demonstrated. "And what do you intend for the regiment, sir?"

"Back to basics and have Sergeant Major Jones put them through their paces."

I did not think that Jack Jones would ever have to go to war again and it was doubtful that he had ever had to fight from the back of a horse but what he did know were the drills which were necessary to give the troopers the tools they would need to survive on the battlefield.

The only others not taking part in the drills were the Colonel, Corporal Dunne, Sergeant Sharp and myself. We watched while Sergeant Major Jones bellowed out his orders. Even the officers were not spared his criticism.

"Lieutenant Pope, were you given the order to draw sabre? You could take an eye out with it. Leave it sheathed until you are given the order!"

"Trooper Atkinson! Has Corporal Wade upset you in some way? Boot to boot, if you please and not wandering all over the place like a drunken maypole dancer!"

And so it went on. The regiment was keen to impress but they lacked the precision which they needed. When they were not being drilled the Colonel had them grooming their horses and ensuring that their equipment was in good condition. This was not for dress, as Major Wilkinson had tried, but for efficiency. The Colonel had seen the value of the carbine and the regiment was also put through their paces. Now that Major General Le Marchant was in Spain the drill book for swords which he had written was reissued and was in constant use. In the end, we had just five days to train and to sharpen up the troopers and then the army began to move. The guerrillas had continued to send Viscount Wellington valuable intelligence about the French dispositions and they also sent the coded orders which they had captured. Captain Scovell was an aide who, when I first arrived in Spain, appeared not to have too much to do. It had taken me some time to realise that he was the one who could decipher the French codes. All the information which had been gathered meant that Viscount Wellington was sure that we outnumbered the French and we crossed the Agueda.

Although I rode with General Anson's Brigade and the 11th I was not attached to them. I was Viscount Wellington's eyes and ears. There were French piquets south of Salamanca, but they quickly moved back to the city when the brigade of cavalry appeared. As horsemen, we could have reached Salamanca in a day but we moved at the speed of the infantry, many of whom were new to Spain and the Spanish sun. The newcomers could all be identified by their increasingly red skin. The veterans had tanned!

On the 17th of June, we entered Salamanca. Most of the French army had gone but, to my dismay, as I rode towards the Salamanca forts bordering the river I was fired upon. I returned immediately to the General, "Viscount Wellington, while Salamanca is ours the French have left a garrison in the forts and it is as I told you, sir, they are heavily fortified."

"Then I fear we have another siege and I have no Sir Richard for advice!" He nodded and waved forward Major General Clinton. "Clinton, have your division reduce the forts."

"Sir."

Captain Dunbar said, "We only have three eighteen pounder cannons, Viscount Wellington. The rest are still on their way north from Badajoz!"

"Do the best you can. Matthews, find Marshal Marmont for me!"

Sharp and I galloped through the town and left by the same gate we had when we had scouted out the town for Viscount Wellington. Before we passed through the village of San Cristobal, three miles from Salamanca, we were able to see the French in the distance. The ground dropped away to the village and a huge plain opened up before us. I could see the rearguard of the French. We could, I suppose, have returned to the General and reported that we had found them, but I knew that Viscount Wellington would wish to know where they were camped. We would follow.

Although the French Army was a larger target than we presented, I knew that we would be visible and so we rode with our weapons loaded, if not primed, and we rode on opposite sides of the road. Such tricks had saved us before. We were twenty miles from Salamanca when we were attacked. A half troop of Chasseurs suddenly turned and galloped down the road towards us. Even as we turned and headed back down the road to Salamanca, I knew that the French must be preparing to camp. The French cavalrymen were eager to get to us and they galloped hard, eating up the ground. We were trying to conserve our mounts as, at that moment, I still intended to find out the French plans. Glancing behind I saw that there were less than twenty of them but that was still too many for us to handle and they were less than forty yards behind us.

"Sergeant Sharp, we will return to the General and then ride out again tomorrow but use the parallel road. Let us lose them!"

As soon as I dug my heels into Donna's flanks she responded and within just half a mile we had lost the French. Nor did we have far to go to find Viscount Wellington. He had the bulk of his army camped on the heights above the village of San Cristobal. I could hear, from Salamanca, the sound of muskets and cannon fire as General Clinton's division began to attack the forts.

"Well, Matthews? Where is Marshal Marmont?"

"At the moment he is twenty miles up the road."

"And numbers?"

"We have not had time to ascertain them accurately yet, sir. Some French cavalry decided to make a nuisance of themselves. We will ride out again tomorrow."

I could tell that he was disappointed, but he nodded and said, "Very well. You were right about this country, Matthews. Lots of places to hide my men!" He waved a hand at the dead ground and I could see that the vast majority of our troops were well hidden.

We did not ride our own horses the next day. This was high summer, and they had been ridden hard. I still had the lancer's horse and Sharp had one we had captured from the Dragoons. We left before the sun had risen for I wished to be able to rest during the heat of the day. Neither of us were dressed as Light Dragoons and we left our Bakers with the 11th. I planned to ride the road which was parallel to the one the French had taken so that we could view them from the rear. We passed refugees who had fled Salamanca. At first suspicious of us, once we spoke to them in Spanish then they became mines of information and it was clear that the French had stopped the previous day so that they could form a new line of defence. When we stopped, I estimated that we were level with the French who were some way to the east of us. We rested in a small village where I paid for food and the water our horses drank. A local farmer told us of a path which led to the next road and when the sun began to lose some of its heat, we headed along it. I deduced that if we could get north of the French army we would be less likely to be spotted.

The land through which we travelled was undulating and that brought many inherent dangers. When we crested a rise, we did not know if we would suddenly see our enemies. As luck would have it, the path we took managed to pass through a stand of trees. They were scrubby ones and windswept, but they afforded some cover. I saw the main road from the north below us and it was empty. I wondered in which direction the French were camped when we heard hoofbeats and I saw a pair of riders galloping from the north. They were French despatch riders; I recognised the leather bags on one of the horses.

"I am guessing the French are down this road. Let us see if we can take these two and read Marmont's news before he does."

We rode at an angle to cut them off and they saw us. Perhaps they had been riding for longer or had to escape guerrillas but whatever the reason their horses were slower than ours and it became clear that we would cut them off. As we neared them one made a mistake, in his case, a fatal one. He took out a pistol and tried to fire at us. His pistol fired but the spark from the priming pan made the other horse rear in fright and the rider, not expecting the reaction, was thrown to the ground. We were just thirty yards from them but even at that distance I still heard the crack of his skull as he hit the ground.

I shouted, in French, "Surrender for there is no escape!"

The despatch rider, as his attempt to shoot us had shown us, was a brave man and would not go without a fight. In answer, he threw his pistol at Sharp who managed to jerk his reins and move out of the way. The rider then drew his sword and rode at me. I barely had time to draw my sword and deflect his blow. The movement allowed him to gain five yards on me as he whipped his tired horse's head around. I did not want to kill him, but I had to have the despatches he carried. They could give us valuable intelligence. My lancer horse ate up the ground and I rode at the Frenchman's left side so that he would find it hard to ride and use his sword.

Once more I shouted, "Surrender!"

"Never!"

I slashed at his leg to wound him. My sword was sharp enough to shave with and it tore through his breeches and into his leg. He jerked the reins and he, too, began to fall from his horse. The animal was weary, and the weight of the man pulled the horse over. The weight of the animal, added to the fall, crushed the man. I reined in my horse and arrived back just as Sharp had helped the horse to its feet and confirmed that he was dead.

I went to the leather satchel containing the documents. To my great relief, they were neither sealed nor coded and were from General Caffarelli and the army of the north. They informed Marshal Marmont that thanks to an attack by Sir Home Popham on Bilbao and the continued guerrilla attacks he would not be sending the eight thousand men who had been requested. In addition, it said that King Joseph was also short of men and reinforcements would not be forthcoming. The other documents were just information about the successful Russian campaign and the Emperor's victories. Bonaparte was never shy about telling his marshals how good he was. One reason Sir Arthur liked to use me was because I was quick-witted.

"Sharp put the dead man back on his horse." I replaced the despatches and then primed my two pistols. "Prime yours and then fire them in the air!" He fired and then I fired mine together. "Now mount your horse and lead the dead Frenchman's. Ride as though the devil is behind us!"

Sharp merely nodded and did as he was ordered. I knew that there would be piquets ahead and would have heard the first pistol shot fired by the Frenchman. One would not unduly worry them, but four shots suggested a fight and they would come. I wanted them anxious and to gallop to discover the problem. Half a mile later ten troopers of the Chasseurs rode towards us.

I reined in and pointed behind us, "We found the guerrillas attacking this despatch rider and his companion. I think the other rider was thrown from his horse, but we managed to save this man although I fear he is dead."

The Captain rode next to the man and put his fingers on his neck. "You are right. We will escort you back to the camp."

"Are you not going to find the guerrillas?"

He laughed, "With ten men? I will ride back with you and we will take a squadron to recover the body!" As we rode, he asked, "Who are you and how did you happen upon them?"

I reverted to the identity I had used at Badajoz and Ciudad Rodrigo. All the senior officers who had met me were either dead or were prisoners. "I am Colonel Fouquet and I work for the Ministry of Police." The title was enough to silence the Captain.

Marshal Marmont had his headquarters at Fuente Sauco. As we had ridden through the camp, I had recognised the standards and eagles of a number of regiments. From the tone of the letter from General Caffarelli, the eight thousand men he had been going to send were vital and I could see that Viscount Wellington's army outnumbered the French or it would once General Clinton's division captured the forts and rejoined the army. The Captain was relieved to hand me over to the Gendarmerie. I repeated my story and the Major took the despatches then led us to the Headquarters. I recognised some of the generals, Clausel, Foy and Ferey, I had seen them on the battlefield. Dismounting I handed the reins of my horse to Sharp. I had my forged document in my tunic, but I hoped that I would not have to use it.

The Gendarme Major handed the document case to Marshal Marmont. Auguste Marmont had been an aide to Napoleon Bonaparte but that had been after I had left the French army and I had never met him. Although he had commanded the army for a year, he had yet to fight a battle. He read the documents and I saw the disappointment on his face.

"I understand, Colonel Fouquet, that you work for the Ministry of Police although the major here has never heard of you."

I sneered as I spoke, "I am not used to guarding camps. I have more serious matters to resolve for the Emperor."

The Major flushed and Marshal Marmont said, "And how did you happen to chance upon these despatches?"

"My assistant and I heard firing and found guerrillas attacking the despatch riders."

The Major said, "He could be a spy!"

The Marshal laughed, "And if he was then he would not have brought the despatches here, would he?" Turning to me he said, "So, Colonel, we thank you for your intervention but I am at a loss to understand why such an important man as yourself is riding with just one companion in a land which is filled with guerrillas."

"I was heading to Madrid. I have a message for King Joseph, but I intended to ride via Salamanca. It seems it has fallen and so we will now risk the land to the south and east of us."

Seemingly satisfied the Marshal said, "I would offer you an escort but as you can see, we are woefully short of cavalrymen. However, if you dine with us this evening, I can promise better fare than on the road."

"Of course."

"And in return, you can deliver a letter to King Joseph for me. It is now imperative that he sends me some of his troops."

I gave him a silky smile, "I will guarantee that the letter gets into the right hands!"

The Marshal evicted one of his aides so that Sharp and I had a room. As they could not guarantee that we would not be captured by guerrillas once we left him the Marshal and his officers were guarded about their plans. However, they could not disguise the fact that the Marshal intended to relieve the siege of his forts which still held out. It told me that he had spies and riders who had access to the forts, and I guessed that they were using the river. As was our usual strategy Sharp and I kept in role when we spoke for who knew who was listening?

The next day we headed out of the village and rode south and east. We took the Avila road but turned west once we were out of sight of the French.

It was almost night when we wearily rode into the camp above San Cristobal. Leaving Sharp to look after the horses I went towards the tent with the light shining from within. I knew that it would be the general's and Lieutenant Hogg confirmed it. He beamed, "The General will be pleased to see you, sir." He lowered his voice. "A bad day, sir, we still have not taken the forts. General Bowes died leading one of the attacks."

Viscount Wellington's irritated voice snapped out, "Hogg, stop gossiping and find me some bread and ham! You can do that, can you not?"

"Sir!"

I stepped inside the tent and he looked up, "Tell me you have good news, Matthews."

I nodded and smiled, "I hope it is but if it is not, I am quite happy to take the reprimand!"

He shook his head, "Sometimes, Matthews, you are too impertinent for words. Sit and tell all!"

"Sir Home Popham has attack near to Bilbao and the reinforcements Marmont sought are not forthcoming." I dropped Marshal Marmont's letter to King Joseph on the table. "He asks Madrid for more men." I smiled, "Of course as I was the one commissioned to deliver the letter then the request will not be made."

He beamed, "Your impertinence is forgiven for you are a magician. And is there more?"

"Yes sir, you are matched in numbers, bearing in mind that General Clinton's division is occupied and Marshal Marmont intends to come and relieve the siege of the forts!"

"Better and better! Then he will come soon?"

"My guess is tomorrow or the day after at the latest for he must have spies feeding him information and he knows that they are holding out and fears that we will make it fall."

"Then we have him. I will show him a token force on the high ground and invite him to attack." Hogg returned, "This, Lieutenant Hogg, is a real aide who actually delivers useful intelligence! He is no glorified waiter! Watch him and learn!"

"Yes, sir."

"Will you join me, Matthews?"

Having witnessed his unfair treatment of the aide I said, "No sir. Sergeant Sharp will have something for me."

"Your loss!" He was unperturbed at my refusal to join him.

Sharp had indeed foraged and foraged well. I sat on the camp stool and hungrily wolfed down the bread and the rough stew. I had just washed it down with a rough but welcome red wine when Lieutenant Hogg appeared.

"Off duty, Lieutenant?"

"Yes, sir. I began before dawn. How does the general do it?"

"The first thing you should learn about Viscount Wellington is that he is not human and the second is that he is never satisfied!"

"He is pleased with the news you brought him. He speaks highly of you." I heard the envy in his voice.

"And he also berates me at every opportunity. I do not let it worry me and nor should you."

"How do I get to be like you, sir?"

I sighed, "I did not begin my military career as an aide. First, I served my apprenticeship as a soldier and learned how to fight. That gave me an innate sense of survival and that helps me in what I, we, do. Last night I dined with a French Marshal and I took a great risk. It paid off but, equally, Sergeant Sharp and I could now be prisoners."

His eyes widened, "Tell me what you did, sir."

I nodded to a packing case, "Take a seat. Alan, get the Lieutenant a drink!" I then told him how we had succeeded. I did not glorify it and I was honest in my description of the deaths of the two riders. I regretted it and I wanted him to know that.

When I had finished, he said, "Your skill with languages helps you, sir. I can speak French, but it would not fool a Frenchman."

Sharp said, affably, "Sounds like me, sir! I tend to keep my mouth shut and say as little as possible and the Major blinds them with his words!"

Although I was exhausted, I took the time to talk to Lieutenant Hogg for there were many ambitious officers like him and, often, they would make a poor decision in the hope of attracting a senior officer's eye.

I was roused before dawn to join the General. He had the Durham Infantry placed in the village of Moriscos as our only advanced troops and the rest, about a quarter of the infantry with artillery, were arrayed on the top of the high ground. As I had suggested Marshal Marmont brought his army; there were just twenty-five thousand of them. One thing I had learned in the French Camp was that Bonnet's division of twelve battalions was still on its way from the Asturias and when they reached Marmont then he would have the superior numbers. All of Viscount Wellington's aides were ordered to bring horses to further tempt the French to attack. I used the French horse. I would not risk Donna!

Viscount Wellington had his telescope out and was viewing the advancing French. "You were right, Matthews. Now let us hope that he makes a concerted attack."

Some Dragoons headed towards our left flank and the River Tormes. I wondered if that was where their spy was hidden. The Allied infantry there stood to. In the town of Salamanca, we heard the sound of the eighteen pounders bombarding the forts. It was an unreal situation for in the town there was a battle and here, where there were the majority of soldiers we were watching each other. It took most of the morning for the French guns to be placed. During that time there was skirmishing from the horsemen and our infantry but there were no losses. They were probing only. Then the French cannon began to fire and they aimed at the ridge. As soon as they fired Viscount Wellington ordered the men to lie down.

After seven or eight cannonades, Captain Dunbar said, "Should I order the artillery to open fire, sir?"

"Whatever for? Have the French hit anything, yet?"

"No sir, but…"

"Then they are wasting powder and ball. This is just Marshal Marmont testing our resolve and our discipline. He has yet to fight me and we shall keep him guessing as to our intentions."

The French did make an attack in the afternoon and they sent two battalions of their light infantry to attack Moriscos. The village was close enough for us to witness the attack. The understrength 68th defending the village were not a large battalion but they were one of the best and had served at Badajoz. With them, they had a company of Brunswick Oels and so had rifles to pick off enemy officers. As I knew from the battle of Fuentes de Oñoro, fighting in a village was not for the faint hearted. The Brunswick Oels began the skirmish firing at officers and sergeants. As the French Light Infantry danced their way across the open ground so the Durham Regiment began to add the fire of their muskets. There was little point in firing volleys at light infantry but the Durhams managed to thin the ranks a little. Then, when the French reached the houses we could hear the fighting in the village, and we saw some of the casualties being carried back to our main line.

Viscount Wellington allowed this to continue for an hour or so and then said, "Matthews, the village is not worth the loss of a battalion. Tell them to withdraw."

"Sir." I mounted my horse.

"Lieutenant Hogg, ask General Anson to send a squadron of light horse to support the infantry as they withdraw."

"Sir!"

He was far too eager. I said, "Sergeant Sharp, go with him!"

"Sir!" I knew that Sergeant Sharp was not happy, but he would obey. I saw Viscount Wellington shaking his head. He never did understand such things.

I galloped down the road towards the 68th. Although they had been at Badajoz, they had not had to do much fighting. From the sounds emanating from the village, they were giving a good account of themselves, especially as they were down to two hundred and seventy men before the attack by the French. When I reached the rear of the village, I saw a very confused scene. The Brunswick regiment were now at a disadvantage and were having to use their sword bayonets rather than their rifles for they did not have time to load. I dismounted and tied the reins of the horse to the wooden rail of a small corral. I drew my sword and took out the pistol I had already primed before I

145

began the ride. I needed to find the commanding officer quickly. At the entrance to a small house, I saw a sergeant with a pike. He was keeping four Frenchmen at bay but even as I watched a bayonet sliced into his cheek. I lifted my pistol and fired it into the side of the head of one of the Frenchmen while I lunged at a second, stabbing him in the leg. The pistol ball punched a hole in the man's head and showered the others with bone and brains. The sergeant took advantage of the distraction and gutted a third. The fourth grabbed his wounded comrade and ran.

"Thank you kindly, sir." He gestured inside where I saw a doctor and an orderly dealing with an officer. "Captain Mackay, the bastards bayonetted him twenty-two times."

"Get him out, doctor. The battalion is ordered to fall back." I saw that there were another three wounded men. "All of you get out! Are you alright to continue, Sergeant?"

He gestured at the wound, "This? Nowt sir. I have had worse wounds shaving after too much rum!"

"Then let's find the bugler and your commanding officer."

"That would be Major Heywood, sir. I think he was in the centre of the village."

Each group of men we found we told the same thing, "Pull back in an orderly fashion." The fact that few did so willingly speaks volumes for their spirit and their courage. When we heard the staccato sounds of muskets and pistols then we knew we were close to the main action. I had holstered the pistol I had used, and I would have to rely on my sword, but the stout sergeant and his pike were reassuring. I saw the hatless Major. He was exhorting his men to hold on and laying about him with his sword which had already bent.

I shouted, "Major Heywood, General Wellesley asks that you withdraw the battalion to safety."

He flailed his sword to make the French soldier he was fighting reel back and then turned, "Major Matthews isn't it?" I nodded. "Corporal Dickson, sound disengage and fall back!"

The Frenchman who had been fighting the major saw his chance and lunged forward with his bayonet. He was fast but I was faster. My long and heavy sword smashed down on the Charleville musket driving the bayonet into a wooden gate post. I then punched him hard in the face with the basket hilt of my sword.

We were in the narrow entrance to the tiny street and the Major had been holding up the French advance. Major Heywood turned to the Sergeant Major and said, "Get eight men here and have them load their muskets."

The French had heard the bugle and were now renewing their efforts as they saw their chance to win. The sergeant with the pike and I were well placed, and we faced the line of light infantrymen who ran at us. I managed to grab one musket behind the bayonet of one Frenchman as I slashed across the arm of another. The pike kept the others at bay. As I pulled the musket forward, I swung my sword at the side of the light infantryman's head. When he tumbled to the ground, I used the butt of his own musket to render him unconscious.

Major Heywood's voice sounded very calm, "Major Matthews, Colour Sergeant Gilliland, if you would be so good as to fall back now!"

We stepped through the line of men with loaded muskets. The Sergeant Major shouted, "Present! Fire!" There were just eight muskets, but they acted as a giant shotgun and stopped the Frenchmen, quite literally, dead. None of us needed any urging and we raced towards the safety of the rear of the village. The hard part would come when they struggled up the slope with the eager Frenchmen behind them. Major Heywood, the Sergeant Major, Sergeant Gilliland and myself were the last ones out of the village.

I mounted my horse and, after sheathing my sword, drew my two loaded saddle pistols and primed them. "Off you go. I will follow!"

I waited until I saw blue and then emptied my pistols. Holstering them I turned and galloped after the Durhams. I heard a bugle from my right and saw troopers of the 12th with Lieutenant Hogg and Sergeant Sharp. As they appeared the French who had emerged from the village halted. It was one thing to chase fleeing soldiers but quite another to do so in open order with cavalry around. We made the crest unmolested and the Durham Foot and the Brunswick Oels were cheered as they passed the battalions lined there.

We reported to Viscount Wellington who looked inordinately pleased because one of his weaker battalions had seen off two larger French ones. He took Hogg and me along with his generals to view the French lines as the sun began to set. It was as the light from the west illuminated us and Viscount Wellington was pointing out to his generals what he wanted to do that the French in Moriscos and their artillery began to fire at us for we were a tempting target and worth the powder and ball.

Viscount Wellington smiled, "I think, gentlemen, that we will continue this briefing where we do not annoy our neighbours!"

To my relief, we moved back to his command tent.

Chapter 13

Later that night, as Sharp and I sat outside our tents with a fire to keep the flies away, Lieutenant Hogg strolled by. He was ecstatic still following the action at Moriscos. Alan had told me how the young Lieutenant had insisted upon leading the Light Dragoons and that he had been desperate to use his sword and actually fight.

I smiled as he sat on the packing case chair. "Well Lieutenant, what was your first action like?"

"Exciting! I had thought that facing cannons and muskets would be more dangerous, but none came close."

I shook my head. "That is because we were not facing the serried ranks and artillery of a French attack. Then it is a lottery. The men on either side of you can be cut down and you survive. There appears to be no sense in it. "

He looked a little crestfallen.

Sergeant Sharp said, "I have suggested that the Lieutenant acquires a brace of pistols, sir."

The young officer looked a little shamefaced, "I am not a very good shot, sir!"

I smiled, "Could you hit me with one now?"

"Why yes, sir, for it is only six feet between us!"

"And the length of a musket with a bayonet is five feet; a man with a sword less than four feet. If you can stop them with a pistol ball, then you have more chance of survival and that is what combat is about. It means doing whatever you can to survive."

I saw realisation dawn and it was the beginning of a change in the General's aide.

The next day the General's plan was put into action. He planned on attacking a small knoll which overlooked Moriscos. He intended using a small force: the 51st, the depleted 68th and skirmishers from the Light Brigade. He had General Graham and the whole of the 1st Division hidden to intervene when the French counterattacked. If the French would not oblige us by a full attack, then he would bite chunks out of their army.

The 68th were buoyed by the fact that their Captain Mackay, who had suffered twenty-two bayonet wounds had survived the night and looked likely, against the odds, to recover. As the 68th marched past us, some of those with whom I had fought cheered and waved. Colour Sergeant Gilliland raised and waved his pike as he passed. General

Wellesley said, wryly, "I see you have made friends amongst our northern cousins, Matthews!"

"Yes, sir, they are stout fellows."

Nodding, Viscount Wellington said, "Aye, but we need more of them!"

The fighting retreat had given our troops more confidence and they charged up the small hill and quickly dispersed the French who fled to Moriscos. General Graham and his 1st Division were not needed, and our troops began to fortify the knoll.

Viscount Wellington turned to Sir John Marchant who had joined us, "Damned tempting! I have a great mind to attack 'em!"

It was clear that Moriscos would be untenable and Viscount Wellington began to plan to take it the next day and, perhaps, make it a wider advance. I believe the only reason he did not organize an attack there and then was the fact that the Salamanca forts still held out and Clinton's men still bled upon the walls.

We awoke the next morning to see that the French had gone. Moriscos had been abandoned. The French artillery, cavalry and infantry had all decamped. Viscount Wellington summoned General Anson, "Have your Light Dragoons find them, eh? They are up to something!"

"Yes, sir." Eager for something to do after just watching the infantry fight, the general hurried to order the 11th and 12th into action.

"Matthews, I do not doubt that General Anson will find them, but I want your eyes on them and try to determine what they will do!"

Donna had had some days of rest and so I took her, and we had our rifles and carbines with us. The French would have piquets out and their Dragoons would be keen to capture solitary riders. It took longer for the Light Dragoons to begin their search and it was Sharp and I who rode through Moriscos. I saw the crude grave markers where the French Light Infantry had buried their dead. The French trail was easy to follow as they had discarded damaged equipment while they had marched. We found their main camp and I saw that there were graves there too. They had not died in battle; there were other killers in this land, disease and the heat. The French were heading east and an hour after leaving the deserted French camp we saw the village of Aldea Rubia where the dust and the dark blue uniforms confirmed that the French were there. We could have turned around and ridden back to Viscount Wellington, but I knew that he would not be happy with a half-completed report. However, we were not fools and we primed our carbines and pistols before moving closer.

Our caution was justified when we were attacked. The French horsemen had used a wrecked house for cover. There was no roof but the house walls and the low wall around what must have been a vegetable garden hid what looked to be a half a dozen troopers. Luckily for us, they opened fire too soon and the Dragoon's muskets just made fog and the musket balls zipped harmlessly overhead. Rather than running we both raised our carbines and waited for the smoke to clear a little. Reloading a musket meant a Dragoon had to stand. My musket ball struck the hand and musket of one while Sharp's hit the wall and sent chips of stone into the face of another. I heard a voice order them to mount but we still did not flee for I could now see that there had been just six and two were incapacitated. I drew a pistol as the four unwounded men mounted and came at us. I waited until the nearest rider was five paces from me and sent a ball into his arm. Sharp had his pistol levelled and was about to fire when I heard a bugle behind me. It was the 12th Light Dragoons and the three remaining Dragoons turned to flee. Sharp hit one in the back of his shoulder as he galloped away. I turned and saw the troop of Light Dragoons galloping towards us and we reloaded our weapons.

"Lieutenant Gaines, sir, D Troop, 12th Light Dragoons. Shall we chase after them?"

"I think not, Lieutenant, but the General would like us to take a closer look and your troop can ride thirty paces behind us. If the French, try to get at us then have your chaps use their carbines."

"Carbines sir?"

The blank look on his face told me that the 12th had not practised that drill too often. "Just have them take them out and point them at the French. Make them think that you know how to use them."

Leaving the bemused Lieutenant, we rode closer to the French camp. Bugles and drums sounded as the wounded Dragoons returned to their camp with the news that British cavalry were around. Hanging my carbine from its sling I took out my telescope and saw that Marshal Marmont had stopped to make a new camp. I also saw that the divisions of Foy and Thomières had now reinforced Marshal Marmont and I estimated that, until the forts fell then Viscount Wellington would have a marginal numerical advantage. I saw that they had an artillery park and that meant they were not digging in but what was their plan? Sharp and I needed to stay close by and watch Marmont to see where he went. We were both experienced enough to survive on what we had with us for we always carried some food and plenty of water.

Even as those thoughts raced through my mind, the French made our decision for us. They sent a full troop of Chasseurs after us. "Sharp, follow my lead. Wait until they are a hundred and fifty paces from us then fire at the leading riders. We will then ride back to the Light Dragoons."

He shook his head, "It looks like the Lieutenant has decided to join us."

I turned and saw that the Lieutenant had ordered his men to draw sabres and not carbines. The French were rapidly closing with us. I shouted, "Lieutenant, have your men sheath their sabres and draw their carbines. That is an order!" I then aimed at the French sergeant riding next to the officer and, when I fired, was rewarded by the sight of the sergeant clutching his leg. Sharp's shot was even better, and he knocked the bugler from his saddle. "Present Carbines!" A ragged line appeared next to us and the carbines were raised. "Fire!" Only ten were actually primed and loaded. The effect was ragged and although it did no damage that we could see the smoke and the noise made the French halt. "Retreat! We ride back to Viscount Wellington."

"But sir!"

"But nothing! Do as you are ordered. Troop Sergeant, if Lieutenant Gaines does not obey my order then arrest him and take command."

"Sir! Right lads, move!"

I rode next to the sergeant and Lieutenant Gaines and spoke as we rode. "Get back to the general and tell him that Marshal Marmont is camped at Aldea Rubia. I will shadow him and see where he goes. Clear?"

"Sir!"

I glanced over my shoulder and saw that we had a two-hundred-yard lead. "Right Sharp, let us make these Chasseurs think that we are afraid of them. Gentlemen, we will leave you!"

I dug my heels into Donna, and she leapt forward. We had a lead of fifty yards in a very short time. I knew that the Troop behind us would disguise our movement and I waited until the ground dropped a little and then turned Donna to ride to the east along a shallow stream which twisted and turned. When I saw that I could no longer see the road I stopped, and we let our panting horses recover. I heard the Light Dragoons gallop by and then the Chasseurs. It was then I allowed the horses to go to the stream and drink.

"We will camp here until dark and then get closer to the French so that we can follow them tomorrow. If they move."

Sharp disappeared and I thought he had gone to make water, but he reappeared a short while later, "Sir, I have found a better place to wait. There is an animal shelter and some trees. I am worried that the French might come down here."

"Good thinking."

We did not mount but walked our horses just five hundred paces to what looked like an improvised animal pen. In more peaceful times shepherds might have brought their flock here where there was grazing and water to mark them or simply examine them. For us it was perfect. We took the saddles off the horses and then reloaded our weapons. In the distance, I heard the French horses return but they did not stop at our trail. We rested while we could but did not sleep. Donna would let us know if the French were close. As I lay, with my eyes closed but my ears listening, I wondered where the guerrillas were. It struck me that they would be close to the French army and looking to pick off lone riders. The French were getting wise to that.

As the afternoon wore on, we saddled our horses and made our way up the man-made trail which led to the shepherds' corral. I reasoned that it would join a road or reach a house some time and it headed in the right direction, east. We walked our horses and I knew that it would make it hard for French piquets to see us. We walked until I could smell the French; it was a mixture of wood fire, human sweat, dung and horses. The trail we had followed undulated, twisted and turned following the natural contours of the land. It meant we could not see them but when I heard French we stopped, and we dropped our horses' reins. They were both well trained and would not move. I took off my hat and cloak and we ghosted up to the top. It looked like we were at the northern extreme of the camp. This was the furthest point from the allied lines. We managed to get within twenty paces of the two sentries smoking their pipes.

Their conversation was the usual one from sentries on campaign; they moaned. They were not fed enough, they had limited access to wine, they did not like the duty and the generals had no idea what they were doing. Both sentries were convinced that if they were allowed to attack then the British would be swept back into the sea.

Their moans were silenced when the duty sergeant who must have wandered up unseen suddenly shouted, "And if I had been a pair of guerrillas then you two would have your throats cut but I would be rid of two of the most useless excuses for soldiers it has ever been my misfortune to command. Put those pipes out!"

"Sarge! There is no one within a mile of us, listen!"

"How have you lived this long in such a God-forsaken country? They are out there so you keep watch!"

The other soldier spoke, "Sarge, are we just going to keep marching around Salamanca? We can take these roast beefs!"

I heard the smile in the sergeant's voice, "Don't you worry about that. I heard today that we are going to cross the Tormes at Huerta and catch this Englishman with his breeches around his ankles! The cavalry will keep the Roast Beefs guessing and we will relieve Salamanca! Now, you keep watch for tomorrow we have a long march south!"

I waited until the sergeant had gone and the two men had relit their pipes. Their conversation told me that they had already decided to ignore the sergeant and Sharp and I were able to retreat down the slope to our horses. We led them all the way back to the corral where we could talk. "I think we have heard enough to warn Viscount Wellington."

"That is a long ride back in the dark, sir."

"Can you think of a better time? We will take it steadily. By my calculation, we are only ten miles or so from our camp. We will be there before reveille."

Our hooves would have been heard on the road but the last thing the French would do, especially at night, was investigate, as any soldiers who left the encampment would be unlikely to return. The empty road helped us for it meant that we would be able to hear any other rider on the road. It was fortunate that I had been seen at Viscount Wellington's side for the sentries were especially jumpy. We passed through three sets of piquets before we arrived at the main camp. For once we reached San Cristobal before he was awake, but the cooks were already preparing food. Sharp and I had that rare pleasure, hot fried ham between two slices of bread and washed down with hot sweet tea.

"Alan, get your head down. I won't be long. I suspect the General will want to see us in action again soon."

Dawn was just breaking when he emerged from his tent, and he looked up in surprise as he saw me approach. "Successful foray, Matthews?"

"Yes sir, I think that Marshal Marmont is going to try to cross the Tormes at the Huerta ford. He will use his cavalry to try to confuse us."

He smiled, "I am getting the measure of this man. Hogg!" He went to his map and began to pore over it. At times like this, we were all forgotten.

A bleary-eyed Lieutenant Hogg appeared, "Sir?"

"Get dressed, man, and take this message to Major General Graham." Lieutenant Hogg disappeared, "Captain Dunbar!" The Captain had served Viscount Wellington for a long time and he was dressed and ready. "Have Brigadier Stapleton Cotton take his Cavalry Brigade and manoeuvre before the French. I want them to think that we mean to attack."

"Will you divide our forces, sir?"

"Dunbar, you are a good chap, but you do not know me at all do you? Until the siege is over then I squat here! I want Marshal Marmont to do the running around. Once the forts are taken then we can begin our offensive!"

"Sorry, sir."

"Well don't stand there with that hangdog expression!" As the embarrassed officer fled Viscount Wellington turned to me. "I don't know how you find out this sort of information, but I am grateful. Just wait while I write out this order and then we can examine the map."

By the time he had scribbled away Lieutenant Hogg had returned, and I leaned over, "Have you bought a pistol yet?"

"No, sir, I have had no time."

"Then make time. Here," I unbuckled my holsters and handed them to him, "use these."

Viscount Wellington folded and sealed the orders and said, "Lieutenant, heed the Major's words. I say this about few officers, but he knows what he is doing. Now make sure that you don't leave before the General has read them. He must place himself so that he can intercept whoever the French send to the Huerta ford. When you are sure that he has understood then return here."

The two of us pored over the map for some time as Viscount Wellington used my knowledge of the land allied to his grasp of strategy. "What I cannot understand Matthews is why he has not gone towards Madrid. King Joseph has a large army there."

"Perhaps not, sir. The threat in the south comes from Marshal Soult in Estremadura. Even when we were at Almarez there was no threat from Talavera nor Madrid. Perhaps Marshal Marmont's reinforcements are coming from the north."

"Hmn, then so long as we keep him from Salamanca, we frustrate him. I wish Clinton would get on with it! I need his men!"

The sentry outside coughed and said, "Sir, there is an officer here says he is to report to you."

"What?" He put his hand to his head, "Of course, Captain Deardon." He shook his head, "You have relatives, Matthews?" Without waiting for me to answer he continued, "One of my wife's relatives, probably the idiot son of some backwater vicar, asked to be an aide. Send him in."

Viscount Wellington had not been quiet and when the officer came in, I could see that he was flushed and red in the face having heard the scathing attack on him. "Viscount Wellington, Captain Reginald Deardon of the 78th Foot, reporting for duty."

Viscount Wellington frowned, "The 78th? I have not heard of them. Where are they based?"

"They are a Suffolk regiment, sir, but they sailed for the West Indies three months ago."

Viscount Wellington and I shared a look. The West Indies was often a death sentence for British regiments and Captain Deardon had sought an easier posting. He must have thought that being an aide to a senior general would be an easy posting. He was in for a rude shock. "I hate to impose upon you, Matthews. I know you need your sleep but if you could just explain the Captain's duties to him before you get your head down."

"Of course, Viscount Wellington."

"Captain, report to me at noon; your duties will begin then!"

Once outside he said, "Is he always that grumpy sir?"

I smiled, "For Viscount Wellington that was what we called a good mood. I fear, Captain, that this posting will prove to be as hard and as dangerous as any West Indies duty." I looked around. "Do you have a horse?"

"I left him somewhere."

I shook my head. I did not need this distraction. "Captain, your horse is as important out here as your sword! Go and find it and keep it close! Your first lesson is this, Viscount Wellington gives orders and you might have to travel to the other side of the camp to carry them out! You need a good horse!"

"Sorry, sir!"

He scurried away and I sighed. I could do without this task. The horse he brought looked to be a good horse for hunting to hounds, but she was not what we called a warhorse. For a start, she looked to be just fourteen hands and while she looked to have a pleasant nature she also looked as though she had not been schooled properly. She pranced and was a little skittish when a battery of guns was dragged by. I guessed that she was the captain's horse from England. She would have been dismissed out of hand had someone tried to sell her to the 11th. I could do little about that.

"And where is your tent?"

"Tent, sir?"

I nodded, "You know, the place where you sleep?"

"Sorry sir, I thought I would be staying in the same quarters as the General." He suddenly looked around and saw that he was in a sea of tents. "Oh, I see."

This was going to be even harder than I had expected. "And have you a servant?"

He looked more comfortable with that question, "The chap I had was sent to the West Indies. I thought I could find some chap here."

I would see the doctors. There were often soldiers who, because of a wound they had received were unable to fight. They would by and large be discharged upon reaching England. I would find a suitable soldier who would be able to continue to earn while the army was in Spain. He would be fed, and I would persuade the Captain to pay him more. "Leave that with me. Fetch your horse and we will go to my tent." I would have to wake Sharp and get him to use his foraging skills to find a tent.

With Donna, I would just have dropped her reins and she would have grazed happily. I picked up a captured French musket and when we reached my tent, I drove it bayonet first into the ground and tied her to it.

"Sit down, Captain." He looked with disdain at the bully beef packing case we used. "Get used to it, Captain, this is life on campaign!" He brushed away what he took to be dirt and sat. "Your job will be to rise before the general does, and he rises early. You will present yourself to him and await orders. Sometimes, if you are lucky, then you will not be needed and can breakfast. At other times he may wish you to find him food. He does not tell you where to find it. You are an aide and you have to learn where to find the food and drink he likes. You will need to know where all of the regiments, battalions and generals are quartered. He expects you to know that. He might send an oral message or a written one. If it is an oral one, then you have to give it exactly the way he tells you down to the last syllable and inflexion." I could see that this was not what he expected. "He will tell you when he is finished with you. As Lieutenant Hogg will tell you, sometimes he only gets a couple of hours sleep at night. Until you came, the Lieutenant was the one who drew such duties."

"But I am a Captain!"

"And that makes no difference whatsoever!"

Sergeant Sharp put his head out of his tent, "Do you sirs fancy a brew?"

"Have you had enough sleep, Sharp?" I knew he had been woken by our conversation and being quick-witted had worked out that I needed some help.

"I reckon I have taken the edge off it."

"Good, then when you have put some water on see if you can find a tent for the General's new aide."

"Righto sir, will do."

He went off whistling cheerfully. He knew that we would not be needed for the rest of the day and he would have a goodnight's sleep at the end of it.

"The duties I have just mentioned are the easy ones. When we fight then the General's aides are sent into the thickest of the fighting. General Wellesley often puts himself where the fighting is the hardest and you are just as likely to be sent into the middle of a skirmish to tell a unit that their orders have changed." By the time I had finished the captain was due to report to the general. He stood and began to walk off, "Captain?"

"Yes, sir?" I nodded at his horse and he untied it and walked through the camp. He had not had a good morning.

Sharp returned with a tent and said, "Where should I put it, sir? I am assuming that the officer will not know how to do it."

"No, Alan, and much as I dislike the idea, we had better put him close to us. I will go to the hospital and see if I can find a servant for him although it seems unfair to lumber an invalid with an officer who has no idea what he is doing."

In the end, I found a compromise. Captain Mackay would recover from his wounds but it would take some time and his servant, Private Gourlay had also been slightly wounded. He agreed to be Captain Deardon's servant for a month. I was fairly certain that he would tire of the arrangement long before that, but I had other duties to perform.

The unfortunate aide did not return until it was pitch black. He led his exhausted horse and looked ready to drop. "Captain, until you can find your own servant, Private Gourlay, here, will tend to you. I told him you would pay him sixpence a day for his trouble." I winked at the private who nodded his thanks.

"Of course. Er, is that my tent, Private Gourlay?"

"Yes, sir."

"Sergeant Sharp will see to your horse for now but tomorrow you put in a full shift, Captain!"

Lieutenant Hogg came before reveille to rouse us. "Is the new chap near here, sir?"

"The tent next door. His horse is by the horse lines. When you fetch yours, you will recognise it." He nodded. "Did you successfully deliver your orders?"

He grinned, "And I managed to take my time getting back. I had almost six hours of sleep last night."

"Make the most of it as I am guessing that we will be kept busy this day."

I was proved right for Viscount Wellington mobilised almost half of the army and we played a giant game of chess with Marshal Marmont. The French Marshal moved his men and his cavalry in an attempt to cross the Tormes and get around our flank and Viscount Wellington used our shorter lines of communication to thwart him at every turn. There was no fighting and our two sides often faced each other and then withdrew. All of that changed at the end of June when the forts finally fell. They had taken longer to reduce than we had expected but now Viscount Wellington had General Clinton's brigade. I know not how they were communicating but, on the day the forts fell, the French army began to withdraw, not towards Madrid as we had expected, but Valladolid on the far side of the Douro. That, in itself, was a victory, as Marshal Marmont was admitting that he could not beat Viscount Wellington with the men at his disposal.

Chapter 14

We followed the French and this time it was our cavalry who kept their eyes on the French for it was clear what they were doing; they took every opportunity to try to get around our flank. It became a test of horsemanship as much as anything. We won the duel for we thwarted them and once they reached the Douro we stopped and camped on what became the new border. We faced each other across the river. It was a strange couple of weeks for both armies regularly bathed in the river, often at the same time. It was almost as though there was a gentleman's agreement not to fight. That, of course, was not true, and I was sent, with Sergeant Sharp, across the Douro to watch for reinforcements coming from the south. Captain Dunbar and Lieutenant Hogg performed the same task to the north leaving poor Captain Deardon to bear the brunt of the fetching and carrying for Viscount Wellington.

Sharp and I rode well to the east of the Douro and found ourselves somewhere we could watch the roads from the south-east and the north-east. Juan and his guerrillas now had a stranglehold on the land around Talavera and they sent regular reports of troop movements. I knew the way the French thought and they would do all that they could to avoid being seen. They had been in the country for some years and they knew every road and trail. They would avoid main roads if they could. The letter given to me by Marmont had not reached King Joseph, but he might have sent another. Who knew how many Frenchmen were marching to join Marshal Marmont?

We saw riders hurrying up and down the road. We watched for four days and there was a temptation to intercept them for we knew that they would have despatches. However, the French had learned valuable lessons and each rider was accompanied by half a troop of horsemen. On the fifth day, we saw not a half troop but a squadron of horsemen and behind them, there were twelve battalions and a battery of artillery. It was a fresh division of troops for Marmont. From our place of hiding, we watched them march north to the Douro. We waited until the road was clear and headed west. After five days of sleeping in the open and enduring the hot summer sun, we were keen to reach our camp and sleep on a camp bed and eat hot food. Perhaps those thoughts made us careless but whatever the reason a half troop of cavalry spotted us as we headed on the road to Castrillo. We were in the open and there was not a sign of cover anywhere. There were too many for us to fight and so we would have to race them.

We were confident in our horses and understood the pace that they could maintain. We had a lead on the French, and we tried to maintain that steady gait. It was when we crossed the River Guarena that they almost caught us for the Chasseurs had carbines too and we were just fortunate that their weapons were not as good as ours. The musket balls zipped across the water and one of them caught Sharp's horse. It merely hurt Mary, but the effect was to make her rear and throw Sharp into the river. Although he hung on to the reins and would be able to either remount or swim the fall helped the French to close with us. I whipped up my primed carbine and cocked and fired it in one move. I hit a horse which fell into the river and dragged its rider with it. It forced the Chasseurs to spread out and Sharp managed to remount. As we clambered out of the river, I saw that the Chasseurs were spread out and a handful were just forty paces back. They would press on for we were tantalisingly close.

Although not badly wounded Sharp's horse was in some pain and was slower than she normally was. By my estimate, we were still at least ten miles from safety. Sharp said, "Leave me, Major. My horse cannot keep up this speed and I will not kill her."

"We stay together." I risked a glance behind me and saw that the line of troopers had spread out and now covered more than a hundred and twenty yards, yet I could see no hope. What was worse was that the land began to rise and that sapped energy from our horses' legs. I drew a pistol and I was ready to turn and slow down the pursuit by hitting one of the Chasseurs. Donna still had enough energy left to be able to catch Sharp. I decided to wait until just before we crested the rise. As we neared it, I turned and saw the young trooper who followed me was just four horse's lengths from me. I fired and missed and regretted giving Lieutenant Hogg my old pistols. Fate favoured me as the Chasseur's horse was spooked by the flash and reared. It allowed me to make the rise where I saw Captain Lutyens and his troop of Light Dragoons. Sharp had already reined in and I joined him.

The Captain saluted with his sword as he passed me and shouted, "Sound the charge!"

The bugle sounded just as the first Chasseurs crested the rise. Captain Lutyens sword hacked across the leading Chasseur's chest and I heard the French bugle sound the retreat. Sharp and I had the time to see to his horse's wound and head, at a more sedate pace, back to our lines.

The troop caught up with us as we neared the British piquets. They had with them four prisoners and three spare horses. The captain and his men were naturally elated.

"Thank you, Captain!"

"We were about to head back when we heard your Baker, sir. It makes a very distinctive sound. It was a pleasure to be able to come to your assistance!"

The general was disappointed with my news." I should have attacked him when he came to San Cristobal, that was a chance missed and now he is reinforced by a fresh division. No point worrying about that. It is in the past and that we cannot change; the future, however, is another matter."

We now had every troop of cavalry watching the French. This was no longer a task for a single aide. It was not minor movements we needed to observe but larger ones and on the sixteenth of July, the Division I had seen marching from the south joined General Foy's and moved across the Douro to Toro which lay on our left flank. The bulk of his army appeared to be remaining at Tordesillas and it seemed they were trying to flank us with the increased numbers they now had. Viscount Wellington anticipated a move from Toro and so he moved some divisions to Fuente la Pena and Canizal.

"Matthews, let us be cautious about this move. Ride to the 4th Division and the Light Division. Have them wait at Castrejon and ask General Anson to support them with his brigade of light horse."

I was quite happy for the duty as it would give me a chance to speak with the 11th. I had not seen the Colonel and Sergeant major Jones for some time. General Anson was not there but Brigadier Stapleton Cotton was, and he nodded when I gave him his orders. "Viscount Wellington is wise. We have witnessed some manoeuvring and moves across the river which are not consistent with Johnny Frenchman sitting on his arse! If they come, then we shall be ready! I shall have piquets further north and I have asked the horse artillery to prepare a defensive position here."

I found Colonel Cummings and saw that Sergeant Major Jones was with him. I gave him a questioning look and the oldest soldier in the regiment shrugged and said, "Couldn't sit in camp while the lads were fighting a battle, sir. Besides, it is good for the circulation."

Colonel Cummings smiled, "The Sergeant Major keeps us all on our toes. I am not surprised that my uncle spoke so highly of him. So, Major, do we see action this day?"

"If not today then soon, sir. Marshal Marmont has been reinforced and General Wellesley thinks they are up to something. I had better return to the General. Good luck, sir."

Viscount Wellington kept all of his aides with him. After he had briefed his generals on the evening of the sixteenth, he gathered us in his tent.

"Marshal Marmont is up to something, gentlemen, and all of you," he glowered at Captain Deardon and Lieutenant Hogg, "will need to be on your toes and as sharp as a razor. When I give an order, I will not repeat it nor qualify it. You will deliver my message as quickly as possible and then return to me. I want you all back here, breakfasted and ready to ride at three o'clock, before the sun has even thought about rising." I smiled at the look on Captain Deardon's face; the West Indies was looking like a much better prospect.

Sharp and I did not need much sleep and we were the first to arrive at the General's tent having eaten with the 68th who remembered my service at Moriscos. Captain Deardon was the last to arrive and it was after the appointed time. The look he received from Sir Arthur almost turned the Captain to stone. "Captain Dunbar, I wish you to ride to Toro and report on the movements of Bonnet and Foy. Major Matthews, return to the rearguard and report on the French movements there. The rest can remain here with me."

Sharp and I rode ready for war and reached the outpost not long after the sun had risen. Our men at Castrejon were now isolated from the rest of the army which had pulled back between Castrillo and Canizal. I saw that General Campbell and General Alten had their men in a defensive position and the cavalry squadrons were preparing to ride even as I arrived. I reported to Lieutenant General Stapleton Cotton, Viscount Combermere, the cavalry commander. He was a good man and I knew him from Porto and Talavera. He was known as the Lion of Gold for he was always immaculately turned out. He reminded me of Murat, without the arrogance.

He had his telescope out and was scanning the north, "Something wrong, sir?"

"Could be. The last patrols who returned from the north, last night, reported hearing movement. Probably nothing but I sent Major Austen and his troop to investigate."

"I had better join them, sir. The General is worried and that is never a good thing. He will want to know immediately about any problems which we encounter."

We headed up the road towards Alaejos. We were just a mile beyond it when we spied the troop. They were in skirmish order. We both drew our carbines and primed them. Percy saluted us and pointed north. French Dragoons were advancing and behind them, a column of blue uniforms snaked back to the Douro. Tordesillas was fifteen miles from Alaejos. "We spotted them a couple of hours ago. We thought, at first, that it was just a cavalry patrol, but it soon became clear that it was at least a division."

I took out my telescope and stood in my stirrups. I could see now that it was at least three divisions and that two cavalry brigades were guarding the flanks. This was more than had been seen at Toro. Was that a feint to make us pull back to avoid being outflanked? If so, then the rearguard was in great danger and Viscount Wellington was in danger from an attack he had not anticipated. I sat and put my glass away. "Sergeant Sharp, ride to Lieutenant General Cotton and tell him that the French are heading down the road to him and then go to Viscount Wellington and repeat the message."

"Sir, and what will you be doing, sir?"

"Staying alive, mother!"

He galloped off. The orders for the rearguard were quite clear. Their task was to delay any enemy attack, but Viscount Wellington had anticipated an attack by two divisions and not most of the army. I guessed that Captain Dunbar would report that Bonnet and Foy were also heading for Alaejos and that Marmont would soon have almost forty thousand men which was more than enough to defeat the men we had here at Castrejon. The rearguard had to be pulled out but only Viscount Wellington could issue that order. I took out my watch. It was now gone noon and we were seven miles from the main body. We had to delay the advance so that Viscount Wellington could reorganise and the rearguard could prepare defences.

"Major Austen, we will buy the rearguard some time. I propose to annoy the French. We will wait here until they are one hundred paces from us. We will make it appear as though we are charging by sounding the bugle when, in fact, we will halt fifty yards from them, fire a volley and then fall back a quarter of a mile where we will reload."

Percy grinned, "Sounds like fun. Troop Sergeant Seymour, tell the troopers exactly what they are to do. We want no mistakes now!"

"Sir!" Joe Seymour used his own choice language to ensure that they all knew what they were doing.

Once ready I had the bugle sounded and we began to gallop towards the French. As I expected the infantry went into square and the French cavalry changed formation from column to line. All of that took time and, by then, we had halted and raised our carbines.

I gave the command and used the voice I had had when a French sergeant! "Fire! Fall back!"

The smoke from the carbines prevented us from seeing the results but even if we had not hit a single man, we had halted the French. It takes time to change formation and the whole of the French army would have been stopped. By the time the head of the column was moving again, the rear would be stopping. The French army would become extended. We repeated the manoeuvre twice more before the French Brigadier in command of the cavalry realised what we were doing and sent two squadrons to rid himself of the annoyance. This time I waited until they were forty paces from us and then fired a last volley before ordering the retreat. By that time it was late afternoon. The French cavalry reorganised and charged after us. I saw that Lieutenant General Cotton was ready and just north of the village of Castillo. He had the river for protection, although it could be forded by cavalry and light infantry, and he had his guns in the centre backed by infantry with the 11th on one flank and the 12th on another. The French realised the futility of attack and they withdrew.

I reported to the Lieutenant-General, "It looks like the main French army is heading down this road, sir."

He nodded, "A Captain Dunbar rode in just after your Sergeant to warn me that two more French divisions were heading here from the direction of Toro. You have done well to slow them, Matthews." He turned his horse, "Come let us put our heads together and see if we can come up with a plan, just in case Viscount Wellington decides to leave us here."

"Well, gentlemen, we need to do as Major Matthews did and slow down the French until we receive orders from Viscount Wellington. We do not have enough artillery to defeat the French and so we must use other means."

General Alten said, "We can use my Light Division as skirmishers across the river. We have two battalions of riflemen and we can cause them a great deal of trouble. The river can be swum but if there are French cavalry then I do not want my lads left out there."

"Quite. I like that plan. We will deploy the Light Division on both sides of the road. I will be with the cavalry in the centre and we will have the artillery on the other side of the road. The rest of the two divisions will be ready to head back down the road but will stand to in case they are needed to support the Light Division." The officers all nodded their understanding. The orders were quite clear. "Major Matthews, you can have the rest of the evening to yourself. You look all in. Well done for today. That a troop of Light Dragoons held up the French Army is no mean feat! It bodes well for the rest of the campaign."

I headed for the camp of the 11th which was on the west side of the river. I would be able to warn them that they would be up before dawn

164

and in position blocking the road. The cooks were preparing food and, after recovering my carbine, I found one of the camp stools and began to clean and load it. As the sun set and the night piquets were set the bulk of the regiment returned. Only A Troop had actually fought and that was obvious from their manner when they walked their horses in. They had fought and they had won. What was more they had not lost a single man! The other troopers trudged in having been sat in the sun all day listening to the fighting north of them.

Colonel Cummings came over to me along with his officers. "Do you think Viscount Wellington will pull us back, Major?"

I nodded, "I don't understand why he hasn't done so already but as Sergeant Sharp has still to return there may be other issues. Major Austen and A Troop did well today. It is not often that a single troop of Light Dragoons can hold up an army!"

Percy beamed, "It was hard though, sir. I mean the chaps began a charge and did not complete it. The troopers do not like that and their blood was up."

"I think it showed how far they have come, Percy. They obeyed orders and that is sometimes a rarity. The 11th has come of age."

It was the right thing to say not least because it was true but also because it improved their spirit and that was never a bad thing. Sergeant Sharp arrived just as we were preparing for a brief sleep. "Viscount Wellington will be along in the morning, sir. He wanted to see the French for himself. He has Marshal Beresford with him. I think he thinks we can bring Marshal Marmont to battle."

It always felt better having Sergeant Sharp close to me. He was not only reassuring he was the best soldier I knew. We both rose when it was dark and ate a quick breakfast before saddling our horses and heading across the bridge to the other side. Thanks to their successful day the 11th were in position long before the 12th. I was able to observe our position more clearly than I had the previous night. The French would advance from the east and the river here ran north to south. As we would discover later on it generally ran east to west, but a geographical anomaly made it a barrier that we could use. The skirmishers nodded to us as they took their places on the eastern side of the river. The 95th deployed in pairs of men one would fire and the other reload. The 43rd were also in their open formation. It would be the rifles of the 95th who were called into action first. We heard the French as they marched towards us with their drummers giving them the beat. The Colonel ordered the bugle to be sounded and we heard it repeated in the main camp. Thanks to the Lieutenant General's orders the whole camp was already moving into position. As the sun rose the Lieutenant

General and General Anson joined us with their aides. The two colonels were also present, and it was they who were addressed, "If you gentlemen would send a couple of squadrons forward and discourage the French horsemen, eh? We don't want them to set their guns up."

"Sir." I heard the rifles begin to bark as the 95th attempted to shoot the cavalry officers.

"Right Squadron! Move to the right and ensure that the French do not set up a battery. Major Mathews would you lead the squadron please?"

"Certainly, sir! Sound, *'form two lines'*."

We had just formed the lines when I saw General Wellesley, Marshal Beresford and the rest of his staff arrive at the bridge. He was, indeed, coming to see for himself.

"Right Squadron will advance, walk, march!"

I had my carbine ready and I was pleased to see that the rest of the squadron did too. I watched the 12th as they moved forward. Suddenly the French Dragoons sounded the charge and I watched the Light Division fire one more round each and then make for the river. The last thing that they wanted was to be caught in the open even though there were two squadrons of light horses close by. The Dragoons were still not at full speed and so I shouted, "Right Squadron, halt. Present!"

Just at that moment, I heard the clash of steel as French Dragoons charged the 12th. I concentrated upon our action. The Dragoons were just eighty paces from us when I shouted, "Fire!" A number of things happened all at once. The smoke obscured the Dragoons who were charging us but we heard the cries of men and horses as they were hit and then the 12th, fleeing the French, charged into our left flank and disorganised us.

"Reform!" We were in great danger of losing not only large numbers of men but our position. Whoever commanded the 12th had lost control and the Dragoons we had beaten back were now reforming. At that moment Captain Deardon galloped up, "General Wellesley orders the cavalry to move west, now!"

It was the wrong order and Viscount Wellington would never have issued it. Unfortunately, I heard an order from the major leading the 12th, "Fall back to the bridge!" The bridge lay to the west of us.

It was a disastrous order for Viscount Wellington and all his staff were on the east side of the bridge and the 12th, already shaken, rode back without any order at all and they allowed the French Dragoons to get close to them. Viscount Wellington and the other senior officers were in danger. I took a chance and disobeyed what I knew to be the wrong order. "The 11th will draw sabres and charge the Dragoons."

I heard the sabres drawn as our gunners and some of the 12th fled over the bridge. I saw Viscount Wellington draw his sword. Without waiting for my command, Sergeant Sharp left my side and galloped to go to his aid.

"Charge!" We had already turned to obey the wrong order and were facing north. It meant we could plough into the flank of the Dragoons. We were in two lines and they were a disorganised mess.

I brought my sword across the left shoulder of a Dragoon and being the first blow of the day, my blade was as sharp as it was ever going to be, and it hacked through cloth, cotton, flesh, muscle and bone. Donna barged her way into the enemy ranks. She was the best horse in the regiment, and she acted like an arrow for the rest. At my side, Troop Sergeant Seymour slashed and swiped with his sabre as did Major Austen on the other side. The three of us cleaved a path through the French Dragoons.

I heard Colonel Cummings shout, "The 11th will charge!" Normally he would have just said charge but as the debacle of the wrong order had demonstrated we needed clarity.

It helped us that we were charging the left-hand side of the Dragoons and they were weaponless on that side but even if we had charged their right, we would have defeated them. The men's blood was up and with the commanding general watching they were keen to impress. I saw that we had beaten those who were close to the General and his staff and so I began to wheel Donna to drive the French Dragoons back and to allow Colonel Cummings to bring into play the rest of the regiment. In theory, there should have been a second squadron from the 12th but I could not see them.

Some of the French Dragoons were fighting back and we were no longer able to force our way through the green jacketed Dragoons. French Dragoon swords were, generally, longer than ours but I was the exception and added to my height, not to mention the skills taught to me by my French aristocrat father, there were few men, especially on horseback, who could defeat me. The Dragoon captain who tried to fence me thought that he had the skill and certainly he knew the moves, but I had the experience. I riposted and deflected every blow and then I used the longer, straighter sword I wielded to slide my sword over his hilt and into his side. I twisted as I withdrew my sword, widening the entry hole and guaranteeing more blood. He dropped his sword as he tried to stem the bleeding and I allowed him to turn his horse and gallop off. It was not simply mercy which made me do so, his flight made some of his troop follow him and that allowed the men around me to drive a deeper wedge into the heart of the Dragoons.

Troop Sergeant Seymour's sword was notched and nicked. He was a fighter and did not use his sword as skilfully as I did but when he struck the Dragoon's shoulder his skill did not matter for it was as though he had battered the Dragoon with an iron bar. The corporal fell from his horse and if he was not dead already, as our horses trampled over him, he certainly died soon after. The French call to retreat meant that many of the French Dragoons withdrew but a handful fought bravely on. It was for honour more than anything.

"Dunne, order the halt and reform!"

As the notes rang out, I looked around and saw that the French had been stopped. Viscount Wellington and his staff all looked to have survived and I saw Sergeant Sharp next to General Wellesley. Lieutenant Hogg rode up to us, "Viscount Wellington's compliments, Major Matthews and you can bring the regiment back."

I nodded towards Colonel Cummings, "Thank you, Lieutenant, but Colonel Cummings commands."

"Right sir." He rode over and repeated the order.

"The 11th will retire!"

Lieutenant Hogg rode next to me, "Magnificent, sir." He nodded towards the General who was also withdrawing with his staff, "Captain Deardon is in such trouble."

"He gave the order wrong?"

"Yes, sir. He was supposed to order you to charge the Dragoons who were north of your position, but the river confused him. I am glad it was not me."

I smiled, "Lieutenant, you would not have made such a mistake for you have learned to keep your head in the heat of battle."

Alan Sharp was waiting for us at the bridge, "Thanks for going to the general's aid, Sergeant."

He nodded, "I know that you can look after yourself, sir, but Viscount Wellington? He is not a young man anymore."

"Don't make the mistake of telling him that."

As we neared the village, I heard orders shouted out; the camp was being struck. The rearguard was going to join the main army. Viscount Wellington had almost miscalculated. Leaving the 11th to pack up their camp I rode towards the General's horse. He was inside the house which Sir Stapleton Cotton had used and I saw John Dunbar outside. I dismounted and he shook his head and put his finger to his lips.

I heard the reason as Viscount Wellington tore into the unfortunate Captain, "You sir, are incompetent. In a line officer that is bad enough but in an aide to a general it is indefensible. You almost lost me not only the battle but two regiments of cavalry not to mention the lives of the senior officers."

"But sir, they didn't do what I meant them to do!"

"You fool! I have been told what you said, and you ordered them to ride towards the bridge! You asked them to move west and not north as I had intended. Pack your gear, you are dismissed. Find your own way back to England for I have done with you. I gave you a chance for my wife's sake but when men begin to die because of it then I have no choice."

The unfortunate and stunned Captain came out. I agreed with Viscount Wellington as did all those around me. He walked past us as though in a daze. It was not until we returned to Ciudad Rodrigo that I discovered his fate. His body was found in the Portuguese mountains along with his horse. It seems he had lost his way and fallen down a ravine. The Peninsula was unforgiving, and failure was savagely punished either by our enemies or the land.

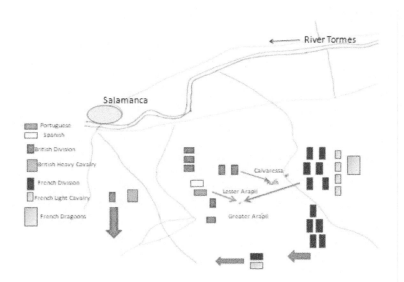

The Battle of Salamanca
Author's Map

Chapter 15

The next four days were the most bizarre I had ever experienced. It was as though the two generals were playing a game of ducks and drakes on a draughts board as they tried to outwit each other. This was not the place for a battle and both generals were trying to get to the best battlefield for their armies. Marmont kept trying to turn our left flank. For the first day, the two armies marched south sometimes just a few hundred yards apart. We camped almost within sight of each other and both armies had little sleep for we both feared a night attack. With Captain Deardon now departed the rest of his aides, as well as the light cavalry, were kept busy as we tried to keep watch on the French. Their light horsemen were doing the same. It never came to blows and not a shot was fired which struck me as strange but each day, as the two armies marched south, sometimes within musket range, we watched our opposite numbers and looked for the sudden move which might preface an attack.

When we reached Cantalpino, Viscount Wellington and his senior generals held a meeting. I was invited but only because I knew the ground to the south of Salamanca while Captain Dunbar was there to take notes.

"Gentlemen, it seems obvious to me that Marshal Marmont is heading for Salamanca. The fact that he has been attempting to turn our left flank indicates to me that he wishes to attack on the north side of the Tormes. I intend, during the early hours of the morning, to slip away due west and return to San Cristobal. I now regret the fact that I did not bring him to battle there for it was perfect ground and so we will await him there." He looked at me. "However, it may well be that Marshal Marmont does not come west. He seems to me to be an awkward sort of chap who does not do that which I want!" His generals smiled. Had Black Bob been there it would have been more of a scowl than a smile. "Major Matthews, you know the French better than any save Colonel Selkirk, what is your opinion? Where do you think he will attack?"

I took a deep breath for the eyes of all the general staff were upon me. I saw a wry smile on John Dunbar's face. The best policy was always honesty. "I believe, sir that he will head south and cross the Tormes at the Huerta Ford. He tried that once before and you thwarted him with Major General Graham's men. He will be hoping to take us unawares. His march from Tordesillas was at night and was intended to catch us with our attention diverted to Toro. I believe he will do the same here."

"Hmm, something of my skill must be rubbing off on you Matthews for that was my thinking too. I would have you take the squadron from the 11th, the ones who acquitted themselves so well the other day and watch the ford." I nodded and he smiled, "Major Matthews has also found me another battlefield which may suit just south of Salamanca. If Marshal Marmont does not play my first game, then we shall have to try another! Warn your commanders that if we have to move it will be south towards the Lesser Arapiles!" Before I left, Viscount Wellington added, "Take Lieutenant Hogg with you as I wish to be kept informed about every action Marmont takes!"

"Sir!"

I wondered how Percy Austen and Lieutenant Hogg would feel about these honours being heaped upon them! In the event, they were both delighted, especially the Lieutenant who had only seen the cavalry in action and now he hoped he would be part of it. Although Huerta was just five or six miles from San Cristobal, we would need to be on the south side of the river to spot the French army. We left immediately and rode hard for the ford. Galloping through it I saw no sign of large numbers of men having crossed. We headed up to Babila Fuente a small village less than a mile from the ford. Firstly, we had shelter from the sun and secondly, I was able to talk to the villagers and from them, I discovered that French scouts had been in the village the previous day and, after inspecting the ford, had returned north.

I sent an unhappy Lieutenant Hogg back to warn Viscount Wellington of the scouts. "Return here immediately. Use a different horse to make the best speed!"

It was late in the afternoon when the piquets we had had up the road, Trooper Harrison and Trooper Bates, galloped in, "Sir, there are French cavalry coming down the road and I think they have the French army with them!"

"Major Austen, mount your men and have them prepare their carbines." I turned to Sharp, "Come with me, Sergeant!"

I was not blaming the troopers, but they had little experience in identifying French formations. I knew the signs to look for. With our carbines loaded and primed and held across our saddles, we rode north. We spotted the French within a mile of the village. I took out my glass and looked up the road. The blue snake was long enough for me to realise that it was Marshal Marmont and he had brought his whole army to attempt to get around our flank. The half troop of Dragoons spurred their horses. We both lifted our carbines and fired. The smoke obscured the result, but it would have the effect of making them wary. Then we turned and galloped back to the squadron. Of course, the two shots had alerted Percy, as we had intended, and as we galloped through the skirmish line the volley A Troop fired emptied some saddles and sent the rest back up the road.

"Well done Major, now back to the ford. Sergeant Sharp ride to the General and confirm the report I sent with Hogg; add that it is the whole of the French army."

"Sir!"

We reached the ford and waited on the north bank. I had the men spread out to make us look like a regiment rather than a squadron and we waited with primed weapons. When the Dragoons arrived they had been reinforced but, strangely, they did not try to force the ford. They just watched. Some of them dismounted and tried a few desultory musket balls but they were wasting powder for we were too far away. When one of the French troopers was ordered to move towards the ford, I lifted my Baker Carbine and fired at him. The ball hit his shako and he retired.

The French halted and brought up some artillery. I was watching the sky. It was getting on to late afternoon and the sky was filling with ominously black clouds. I would not risk the troopers and I was just waiting until they had the three guns set up before I gave the order. "Present!" I had loaded my Baker carbine and I lifted mine too. "Fire!" Even as I dropped my Baker to hang from its swivel I shouted, "Dunne, sound the retreat!" I planned on riding to Calvarassa de Abajo which lay half a mile from Santa Maria which we had fortified. I was counting on making a camp but Marshal Marmont had proved to be a little unpredictable and we might just have to sleep by our horses.

As darkness fell, I saw that the French had camped but it was to the south of us. We camped in the village, but I went with Troop Sergeant Seymour for we needed to find the camp. We found it two miles to the south of us. The French were heading for Calvarassa de Arriba. I had no idea what Marshal Marmont was planning and I felt a little out of my depth. When we reached the village Hogg and Sharp had both returned. Sergeant Sharp was riding the lancer horse and Lieutenant Hogg the other French horse we had captured.

"The General has set the army off, sir. He has the majority with him, but he has sent a second column to Aldea Tejada in case the French try to outflank us." I was relieved. The General knew his business and I thanked God for that.

The clouds had been gathering all day but that night thunder and a rainstorm began which had the villagers terrified. I was just glad that most of the horses were in barns and not in the open. Even so, most were absolutely terrified. The storm lasted hours and rain lashed the ground. Both armies would have suffered, and I knew that it would slow down any soldiers who were not on the roads. Who would be affected the most? The thunder stopped in the middle of the night but the rain continued until just before dawn when we saddled our horses and left our nocturnal sanctuary. We left the village and headed south across soaked and muddy fields. We spotted the French as they headed down the road to Calvarassa de Arriba.

"Lieutenant, ride to the General and tell him that Marshal Marmont is coming and he is headed for Las Torres. We will confirm that is the direction and then follow you to rejoin the army."

"Sir!"

It soon became as clear as the blue sky above us that Marshal Marmont had chosen his route and we hurried west to rejoin the army. We met Viscount Wellington at Santa Maria. He was heading south. The storm the previous night had cleared every cloud from the sky and already it was hot. I could see the soaked ground drying even as we approached. He said to Major Austen, "Thank you for your service, Major, be so good as to join General Anson and the cavalry at Las Torres."

"Sir!" He saluted and then turned to me, "Thank you again, Major, for another invaluable lesson in how to handle cavalry!"

As they rode off many of the troopers, sergeants and officers either waved or shouted their farewells. General Wellesley shook his head. If you are quite finished, Matthews. You have done good work thus far, but all will be wasted unless we can win this battle." As we continued to ride south, he elaborated, "Marshal Marmont has been quite obliging and has allowed me to use ground which is even better than San Cristobal." He pointed to the low hill called Lesser Arapil, "I shall place some men there and occupy the eye and mind of my opponent."

"Sir, there is another a little to the south-west. If you recall I said that there were two hills and the locals called them brothers."

He nodded, "I vaguely remember something about that. Well, we shall see when we reach the first hill. I shall put a brigade on the top with two divisions behind it. That shall anchor our right while the 1st and the Light Division will guard the rest and the 5th, 6th and 7th can remain hidden in that fold of ground." He pointed to his right where I could see the mighty 3rd Division marching. "The 3rd Division has two brigades of cavalry and they shall march, unseen, to outflank Marshal Marmont. I tell you all this because you are a clever officer and need to see the whole picture and to use my mind." He smiled, "Who knows,

Matthews, this day we may see that rarity, a battle decided by your beloved cavalry! Now I want you and these two," he gestured behind him to Captain Dunbar and Lieutenant Hogg, "close by me. Your fellow, Sharp, is a useful sort of chap and he can act as an aide today!"

I knew that Sharp would not be happy about that as he liked to see himself as my bodyguard. We dropped back to join the other two as Viscount Wellington waved forward some of his generals.

I rode next to the other two. "From what I have seen the armies are roughly the same size. Today will be interesting. I think Marshal Marmont has been fooled into thinking that we are weaker than we are and intends to stop us from falling back to Portugal."

Just then we heard some firing from the left side of the British line. It sounded like it was coming from the ruined chapel close to Calvarassa de Arriba. Viscount Wellington stopped and took out his telescope. "Sergeant, be so good as to ride to the 68th and the 3rd Caçadores. Ask them to retake the chapel and hold until relieved eh?" I heard him say to one of the generals with him, "Can't have them occupying that. They might see all of my tricks eh, what?"

Sharp rode off and so began the fighting on what was to be a very long day. It was clear Viscount Wellington was heading for the hill called San Miguel where a farmhouse afforded a good view of the whole battlefield. When we were there, he took out his telescope and snapped it shut, "Matthews, is that the other hill you spoke of?"

"Yes sir, the Greater Arapil."

"It is bigger than the other and we need it. Be so good as to ride to the 7th Caçadores and ask them to take it!"

As we had been riding, I had been working out where the various units were and I recognised the Caçadores. They were British led and good light infantry. I galloped up to the Major who led them. "General Wellesley's compliments, Major, and could your battalion take and hold that hill, yonder."

He looked and said, "You mean the one those French infantry are racing towards?"

"Yes Major!"

He wasted no time and his Portuguese ran towards the hill. I saw that it was a footrace and it became obvious who would win, the French for they had begun the race first. I waited to watch the outcome so that I could give a good report to the general. I was right and the defeated Portuguese, seeing that their target was beyond them, fell back and I returned to Viscount Wellington. First blood to the French!

He nodded, "I saw. Let us hope that is my only mistake this day. At least we have the ruined chapel in our hands. Now let us see what our opponent does."

It was now noon with the sun burning the ground and drying the earth so much that I could see, to the north, the dust raised by the 3rd Division and the four brigades of cavalry as they moved to protect our right flank. Would Marshal Marmont think that we were retreating to Ciudad Rodrigo?

"Dunbar, tell General Leith to move to support the right side of the Lesser Arapil and have Generals Clinton and Hope move closer to the hill."

"Sir!"

"Lieutenant Hogg, have the light company of the Foot Guards occupy the village of Los Arapiles."

"Sir!"

"Matthews. Take yourself off for a ride. Get as close to the French as you can without getting yourself shot. Take your sergeant with you. It will take time for the divisions to move into position and I will have a spot of lunch while I wait. Off you go!" He waved for his camp chair and he sat as though on Hampstead Heath in England.

I knew why he sent me. I would recognise some of the commanders and the units. Dunbar and Hogg would just say French infantry, guns or cavalry and give rough numbers. I would recognise the eagles, standards and what Sergeant Sharp called the 'Jingling Johnnies'. They were, in fact, a musical instrument with metal crescents and other shapes hung with bells and metal jingling objects, and often covered by horsetails. I headed for the Greater Arapil and saw that it was a half battalion of skirmishers who occupied it but that Marmont and his staff were also there using its elevation to observe our movements. There was musket fire from the ruined chapel as skirmishing took place between the piquets. They had their own private battle and would carry on all day no matter what happened on the rest of the battlefield. That was in the nature of battles. Only the generals saw the whole picture. For the rank and file, it was a personal battle with whoever was in musket range! I headed for the river and saw Foy's Division.

As I turned to head south and view the main force, I reflected that I had seen no cavalry as yet. We rode to within just four hundred yards from the French, but we were safe. No gunner would waste a cannonball on two riders and the French did not employ rifles. The worst that could happen would be that they would send cavalry and we could easily make the Allied lines. It meant I did not need a telescope to identify the units. Next to Foy was Ferey and his division and behind them were the entire corps of French cavalry! It was as I headed south that I saw five divisions, who were marching south too, and as I neared them I saw that they were intending to move around our right flank. Marmont was shifting men away from the main Allied divisions in the centre. Before I turned, I headed south and west and saw an even juicier prize. Thomières Division and a brigade of French cavalry were heading due west. If they were trying to outflank us too then they were too far ahead of the five divisions of Maucune and the others for they were almost two miles behind them. There was a gap between them which could be exploited and the five flanking divisions would not be able to get to Thomières and his isolated men.

I had seen enough, and we galloped hard for the farmhouse. When Donna slithered to a stop on the cobbles I saw that Viscount Wellington had given up his seat and was pacing around eating a chicken leg. Without dismounting I pointed over my shoulder, "Viscount Wellington, there is a French Division supported by a brigade of cavalry. They are a couple of miles from their comrades and appear to be heading due west!"

Viscount Wellington tossed the chicken leg over his shoulder and said, "The devil they are! Give me the glass quickly!" Lieutenant Hogg handed it to him, and he turned to look. He rested his arm on the low wall and said, "By God! That will do!" Then he turned to General Alava, his Spanish liaison officer and said, 'Mon cher Alava, Marmont est perdu!" He ran to his horse and mounted. "Matthews, Sharp, with me. Marshal Beresford keep your eye on the French."

Viscount Wellington was a good horseman and the three of us were soon galloping to Aldea Tejad where the 3rd Division and D'Urban's cavalry were awaiting orders. They were completely hidden from the French by the low hills which shielded them from enemy eyes. It was a wild three-mile ride and we reached the division at 3.45 in the afternoon. The 3rd Division, following Sir Thomas' wound, was now commanded by Sir Arthur's brother in law, Edward Pakenham, and Viscount Wellington began without preamble, "Edward, move with the 3rd Division, take those heights to your front and drive everything before you!"

"I will my Lord." They shook hands.

We then rode to Leith's 5th Division and repeated the order. As we headed back to the farm he said, "I know I could have sent you, Matthews, but after that half-wit, Deardon, almost lost me two regiments my confidence in my aides is somewhat shattered."

"I quite understand, Viscount Wellington, and we enjoyed the ride!"

"And now you two can deliver some messages for me; Sergeant Sharp ride to General Arenstchildt and ask him to use his horsemen to join D'Urban. Matthews, ask Lieutenant General Cotton, General Bradford and General de Espana to support General Leith and his 5th Division."

"Sir." That meant that the 11th and the 12th would be in action soon enough.

After I had delivered the messages, I rode back to the farmhouse aware that all the troops I could see moving were hidden from the French. I also heard the crack of artillery which told me that the French were now in range of our guns. The French had been firing for some time and our red-coated divisions were suffering. As I dismounted Donna and let her drink from the water trough, I found somewhere I could watch the battle unfold and still be close enough to hear orders from Viscount Wellington. I saw Marshal Marmont suddenly leap to his horse. I was not on the Lesser Arapil, but I knew what he had seen. He had seen that Thomières was isolated and was doing as Viscount Wellington had done and riding to deliver his message personally. He was unlucky in that, as he raced down the hill to get to his horse, a shell exploded close to him. When I saw him being carried away, I knew that not only had the French lost its leader but that there was now no one to stop Thomières' disastrous march.

"Sir, Marshal Marmont has been hit."

"I hope the fellow is not too seriously hurt. War is damned dangerous enough without its leaders being killed!"

I watched the 3rd division marching in columns towards the wooded hills. Sir Edward was a good general and his approach meant that when they reached the hillside the division would merely have to turn, and they could bring all of their muskets to bear on the isolated Frenchmen. However, it was the sight of the allied cavalry which met Thomières first and he ordered twenty guns to be brought up. It was too little and too late for by the time the troops were in position the 3rd had opened fire. Belatedly the French cavalry accompanying the French Division came into action, but they were outnumbered by the German and British cavalry. At first, the French were holding their own and then I saw Sir Edward's arm slice down with his sword and the whole British line, led by my old friends, the 88th Connaught Rangers fell upon the French division with bayonets. It was as though someone had put a red-hot knife on a slab of butter. The ground was littered with the blue uniforms of the French dead and the survivors were flooding back towards Maucune's division.

I moved my telescope aware that little time had elapsed since the order had been given to attack and yet the French left had crumbled already. At 4.15 the men of the 5th Division rose and prepared to advance, pleased, no doubt, not to have to endure the cannonballs which had been striking them. I saw Le Marchant's heavy cavalry, splendid in their red uniforms with glistening helmets, moving forward. Viscount Wellington must have ordered them to advance while I had been delivering my messages. The 5th Division also marched towards the French. There were eight battalions and two companies of rifles. They advanced despite the cannon fire they had to endure and the skirmishers before them. The battle of the skirmishers was decided in our favour and as soon as that was won then the whole of the French line began to withdraw. It was ever so when a British line met a French one. I saw a piece of dead ground and the French made for it. Then to my surprise, I saw the French form squares. They must have feared General Le Marchant and his three British heavy cavalry regiments would fall upon them. I watched the 5th Division reach the ridge and, still largely intact, open fire at a range of fifty yards. The French managed one volley before the whole of the 5th Division fell upon them. The squares meant that although protected from cavalry the British volley had almost wiped out one edge of each square and when the redcoats charged into the demoralised squares some of those in them had their backs to the bayonets. It was at this time that the survivors of Thomières' division made the disaster worse by trying to get inside the crumbling squares. General Bradford and his Portuguese had managed to avoid the French fire and his brigade, having advanced unseen and without losing a single man, fell upon the survivors of the French Division. Suddenly, in the space of a few minutes, two divisions had been almost completely destroyed.

It was then, at 4.45, that the most terrible spectacle unfolded before me. The one thousand red-coated heavy cavalry led by General Le Marchant poured over the hill and swept around the flank of Bradford's Portuguese. The thick musket smoke hid them from the French but I knew that the enemy would have heard the thundering of the hooves of those mighty horses. The French were still trying to keep some semblance of squares, but I saw one French battalion completely annihilated by the deadly long straight Dragoon swords and the hooves of their huge horses and once broken could not be reformed. The heavy cavalry swept all before them and the survivors of the French divisions, pursued by the cavalry fled towards some woods in the hope that they might escape. It was a futile hope.

The battle was almost won, and Viscount Wellington had not had to amend one order so well had his orders been obeyed. Then things began to go wrong. Sir Lowery Cole's Division, the 4th, advanced to attack Clausel's Division. At the same time, General Pack's Portuguese began their attack on the Greater Arapil. He had seen General Cole's men were in danger of being outflanked and he moved to support them. They were doing well until, and I watched all of this through my telescope, they had to drop their muskets to begin to climb the rocky slopes of the steep scarp. A French battalion suddenly appeared above them and fired a volley which swept them from their precarious perches. The Portuguese were broken and fell back. General Cole's Division suddenly found itself attacked from the front and the flank.

Viscount Wellington stirred himself, "Major Matthews, ask General Clinton to bring forward his 6th Division and engage the French to his front."

I knew what he intended, and I mounted a rested Donna and galloped towards the 6th Division who had yet to fight. As I reached them all of the officers turned towards me expectantly. I was the Viscount's aide and having watched others having success they were keen to emulate them. "General Clinton, his lordship wishes you to engage General Clausel's Division. They are giving rough treatment to the 4th Division."

"Of course. If you would just point us in the right direction, Major. In this damn smoke, we might find ourselves attacking the wrong place."

"Of course, sir."

I drew my sword for I might yet need it and I rode with the Major General who saw, as we neared the remains of the 4th Division, the French who were firing into the red coats and the Portuguese who had been so badly handled.

The General calmly formed his men into lines and, hidden by the smoke, ordered five volleys. The French counterattack ended there and then for the five volleys rolled on and scythed through Ferey's men. Two French Divisions were broken. I had done that which I was asked and saluting the General rode back to Viscount Wellington who looked pleased. I saw that Captain Dunbar was not there and I saw him galloping towards the, as yet unused, 1st Division.

"Well, Matthews. We may be able to head to Madrid tomorrow. With the Tormes held by the Spanish, we can capture this whole army."

Just at that moment, when victory seemed complete, a Dragoon Guard rode in, "Sir, Sir Stapleton Cotton sent me. Sir John Le Marchant is dead. He was shot and killed in the woods."

Viscount Wellington's face told me how upset he was, but I knew that he would save his grief and mourning for later, "My compliments to Lord Combermere and he is to take command of the cavalry. Ask him to keep pushing the French to the Tormes." That was a mighty blow. We might have won the day but the loss of so gifted and charismatic a leader was as bad as the day we had lost Black Bob at Ciudad Rodrigo. To say the edge was taken off the victory was an understatement, but equally, bad news had yet to reach us.

It was only after darkness had fallen that the messengers reached us and told Sir Arthur that the Spanish General had abandoned his position and the French had all escaped. We still had the victory, but it was not the complete one he had hoped. The French still had their cavalry largely intact and enough infantry to fight us when they were reinforced. He turned his wrath upon General Alava the liaison officer who had the good grace to take it all without complaint. He knew that we had had the chance to change the face of Spain. The numbers of dead and wounded were brought to the General throughout the evening. Over five thousand allied soldiers had been casualties but only seven hundred of our men had been killed. Not only had the French lost fourteen thousand men, we had captured twenty guns, six colours and two Imperial eagles. By any measurement, it was a great victory, but the Spanish had stopped it being complete and the General's staff were deflated rather than euphoric.

Chapter 16

It was too late for us to push on, but General Wellesley wrote orders out for his cavalry. His aides were to deliver them. "I want you with the cavalry, Matthews, take Sergeant Sharp and Lieutenant Hogg with you. I shall make do with Dunbar. The orders are quite clear but, in case they are misinterpreted, you should know that I want the cavalry to keep their sabres in the backs of the French. The enemy will have to rest tonight, and we should catch their rearguard. The Light Division and the 1st Division will be there to support you if they dig in but if you are able then I want the cavalry to destroy them. General Le Marchant showed us what can be done by well-led and disciplined cavalry."

"Sir."

We rode to the cavalry camp and I delivered the orders. Viscount Wellington had decided to have the 11th, 12th, 14th and 16th Light Dragoons ride to Garcia Hernandez, while the heavy cavalry, two regiments of British Dragoons and three regiments of the King's German Legion, would take the road to Penaranda. The Light Brigade would carry on after Garcia Hernandez and pursue with the Heavy Brigade. I let Lieutenant Hogg ride with the Heavy Brigade. He had seen their charge the previous day and was keen to be part of it should it be repeated.

I spoke with Brigadier Anson before I went to see the 11th. "The Viscount stressed, sir, that we were to prosecute this pursuit with energy and vigour."

He smiled, "I know, and we are all annoyed that we were let down by our allies. Our men who die tomorrow will die needlessly. We had won, not just the battle, but the war! Now many men will escape!" I nodded for I endorsed his sentiments. "I am glad that you are with us on the morrow."

Sharp had our billet sorted out and I joined the officers of the 11th. Captain Lutyens was full of the battle. "The heavies broke a square! That is unheard of, is it not, Major?"

They all looked at me as I had the most experience. "I have heard of it happening but never against a French square. Normally, we just stay eighty yards from the square to keep them in square and wait for the infantry and the guns to join us. At anything more than thirty or forty yards the French have little chance of unhorsing a rider." I smiled, "And your sabres are not long enough to hurt them."

Percy said, "But yours is, sir."

"It is indeed and if you can find one on a battlefield or have one made when you are in London then I would do so. I saw Joe Seymour's sabre bent and buckled the other day. It is a good job that he is as strong as a blacksmith and was able to bludgeon them to death or he might have been in trouble." Although they laughed, I saw some of the younger officers looking at their own weapons. Some had very fancy, well-decorated blades which they had been given when they were commissioned. Well-meaning family members would go for artistry rather than functionality. Mine was unadorned and plain but as solid as they come. It was functional rather than beautiful. I stood, "Anyway, we shall have an early start and remember there are some German Chasseurs still with the French. They will not be happy about having run today and they may well decide to take it out on us. Do not let your troopers think this is all over. Tomorrow, it will be as though we have not fought today. We start afresh!"

I was awake and ready to ride even as the sun was rising. The four squadrons were all keen and ready to go. To my surprise, Viscount Wellington and Captain Dunbar joined us. "I thought I would see for myself where the French had got to. Don't mind me. I am not a cavalryman!"

General Anson was as thrilled as I was at the presence of the commander in chief. We set off down the road from the bridge at Alba de Tormes. Sir Arthur appeared to be enjoying himself. Perhaps the ride the previous day had given him an appetite for it. I saw, a little behind us and to our left, the Heavy Brigade as they came down the other road. I spied the village ahead of us and, beyond it, the stream. The French drums and bugles told us that we had been seen and that they were preparing to receive us. I saw them when we neared the village. They were on the far side of the stream and a battery of guns was being loaded. Curto's Chasseurs were formed up as the infantry made a rapid retreat down the road. I saw a troop of French Dragoons with them.

Despite the Viscount's promise, Sir Arthur could not help himself, "Anson, take four squadrons and shift those Chasseurs eh? I will ride to the Heavy Brigade and see what they can do!" He and the Captain rode off.

I formed up with Right Squadron and we made two lines with a troop from each regiment as a reserve. As soon as we formed up the artillery limbered up and moved towards the road. The stream was not deep and as the alternative was to cross the bridge in fours and risk a counter charge by the Chasseurs, we risked a soaking and we forded the water. Once on the other side we lost momentum and had to form up. The result was that the German Dragoons and Dragoon Guards were in a line and charging the Chasseurs even as we were forming up. I saw Sir Arthur urge them forward and they charged. There was no way that the Chasseurs and the troop of French Dragoons were going to endure an attack by three regiments of heavy cavalry, and they turned tail and ran. The heavies were not going to give up easily and, as they gamely galloped, they failed to see a French regiment in square, to their side. The French fired a volley at a range of eighty yards. Even at that range, saddles were emptied but the Germans merely turned and charged the square.

General Anson saw the danger for the French cavalry had halted and saw a chance to charge the disorganised German Dragoons. He ordered us to turn and support the Germans whilst watching the Chasseurs.

The French opened fire again at a range of twenty yards and this time they had more of an effect. I recognised the officer leading one of the squadrons as I had met him at the horse lines. It was a Captain von Decken and he was a fine officer. I saw that he was hit even as he charged the square and when the second volley rang out and shrouded him in smoke he and his horse were mortally wounded. I saw them both begin to fall. It was a disaster for the French 76th regiment for the horse and rider crashed into the front rank and created a hole through which the angry Germans poured.

The Chasseurs looked ready to go to the aid of the stricken square and General Anson shouted, "The Light Brigade will charge!"

This time the French squadrons could not run away as they were committed to riding to the aid of the infantry. We only had two hundred yards to go and we would not be at full speed when we hit them, but we all rode bigger horses and we had not lost the previous day. At fifty yards we drew our swords and then we smashed into their flank. My heavy sword smashed down and split the shako of one Chasseur before slicing open his cheek and then tearing into his shoulder. Our charge meant that I could no longer see the German Dragoons and the broken square. We had our own battle to fight and although we were winning, we were fighting superior numbers.

The French Dragoons charged at us and I recognised them. We had fought them at El Bodón and when a French voice shouted out, "You! You are a traitor! And I shall have vengeance for my friend Jacques!"

The angry Captain with the scarred face galloped at me. He was reckless and he was angry. The red mist descended and that is never a good way to fight. His troopers were equally angry and ready for vengeance. All around me the 11th showed how far they had come by fighting coolly and dispassionately. I jinked Donna away from the scything Dragoon's blade which struck fresh air and I hacked my sword at his side. It bit into his arm and as I pulled the sword back felt it grate against bone. He swung at my head and I reacted by bringing up my own sword to block the blow. His left arm was badly wounded, and his fingers lost their grip on his reins. His terrified horse tried to escape but was hemmed in by the horse on the other side and it reared. The Dragoon Captain was unable to hold on to his reins and I gave him a merciful death by slashing across his throat. Had he fallen he would have been trampled to death. I looked around for more enemies but the hot-blooded Dragoons had been defeated and I urged Donna on through the riderless horses, wounded Dragoons and Frenchmen whose hands were in the air.

And then, just as suddenly as we had hit them, I found myself in the open on the other side. I saw a pile of blue uniforms which marked the end of the 76th Regiment. That there were at least fifty prisoners surprised me for I was sure that the angry German Dragoons would have butchered all of them. Then I saw another regiment, a light one had tried to make the high ground and were attempting to form a square. A second German regiment of Dragoon Guards was attacking it and I saw three squadrons of Chasseurs and Hussars racing from our fight to attack the Germans in the rear.

"Right Squadron! On me!"

Major Austen and his men obeyed my strident call and I pointed my sword at the enemy horsemen. This time we had even less opportunity to get up to speed but the important thing was to distract the French light horsemen and it worked. Our thundering hooves attracted their attention and they turned. Perhaps they thought that a solitary squadron could not deal with more than five times their number. They were wrong for the 11th was a different regiment now. Success breeds success and we had just destroyed a troop of French Dragoons and, riding boot to boot, we tore into them.

Once again, I was at the fore and that was thanks to Donna. The Hussar who rode at me had a curved sword and an elaborate moustache. Both showed him to be a peacock but, as his sword was shorter than mine there was but one outcome. His sabre meant he had to sweep at me whilst my straight blade meant I could lunge. He died before he could sweep his sabre around and as I pulled out my sword he fell to the ground. The second man in any line is rarely ready to fight. Part of it is an assumption that his comrade ahead will win, and another aspect is that he cannot see his opponent properly. As the first Hussar fell to the ground, I pulled back my arm and instead of using the tip swept the sword into the middle of the Hussar who was trying a flamboyant slash, my longer blade reached him before his weapon could get close to me. By now the squadron was driving deep into the enemy brigade and I wondered if I had put the troopers into unnecessary danger and then, as I looked across to the German Dragoon Guards, I saw the second square broken. As the French fled so the Hussars and Chasseurs realised that three regiments of heavy cavalry were about to turn their attention to them, and they ran.

Behind me, I heard General Anson sound the pursuit. The 12th, 14th and 16th Light Dragoons had been held in reserve and it was they who charged after the fleeing horsemen. We followed at a more sedate pace on blown horses; we would chase the infantry. The French had been beaten. Sadly for some of the King's German Legion, it had come a day late, but it was a massive victory and we began the chase which lasted all day. Those who could, surrendered and troopers were assigned to escort them back to our lines. Others fought on or tried to fight on. That only worked if you had numbers and the French were running in groups made up of tent mates. Their loyalty to France was gone and it was down to their loyalty to brothers in arms. Some fought while others, watching my regiment bear down on them decided that surrender was the best option. I am not sure how far east we might have got for so many surrendered that we had not enough men to pursue.

As darkness fell, we headed back to Garcia Hernandez. I rode back with Sergeant Sharp and Major Austen. The Major could not believe our success. "In two days, we have broken three squares, Major! Has that feat ever been achieved before?"

I shook my head, "Not to my knowledge but the 11th achieved something too. You charged and dispersed a strong brigade with a squadron of cavalry. The 12th were not there. I believe that, when I make my report, your commission will be confirmed, and it will have been well deserved."

He nodded, "And yet, sir, I do not feel that I am fit to even clean your boots and we are the same rank. That does not seem right."

"This war takes many different kinds of officers and we are just two. Fear not, Percy, I am content."

When we reached the village, it was dark. Colonel Cummings had organised food and shelter as well as celebratory wine. It was he gave us the numbers of dead. The Heavy Cavalry had lost just one hundred and twenty-seven men killed and wounded out of a total of seven hundred. The French had lost, in just forty minutes, one thousand one hundred men. The prisoners we had taken were five times that number. By any measure, we had a victory.

"Viscount Wellington intends us to follow the French and you, Major Matthews, are to wait here for the rest of the army. I fear we are losing you."

I smiled, "Colonel, this will be temporary. Soon Sir Arthur will have other aides that he can use." I am not sure I believed it, but I hoped it was true for I enjoyed being with the regiment.

In fact, Sir Arthur stayed with the cavalry and allowed the rest of his army to gather behind him. He summoned his generals and Marshal Beresford to give them his plan. While Captain Dunbar took notes, I guarded the door of the farmhouse he was using and so heard his plans.

"General Clausel has taken the remnants of his army north. I intend to pursue them with the cavalry and the Spanish. We will leave Valladolid in Spanish hands once more. Then, gentlemen, we will take Madrid!"

Even I was a little taken aback by that. I knew that there had been talk of recapturing the Spanish capital but until Marmont and his army were destroyed that was impossible. And so I stayed with the 11th as we chased survivors north. More prisoners were captured but the French did not attempt to hold us up. When we reached Valladolid, we discovered that the French were heading for another of their fortresses, Burgos. Badajoz was still a raw wound and Sir Arthur did not relish another siege and so, after garrisoning the town with our Spanish allies, we turned and, during the hot days of August, headed south and east, through Segovia towards Madrid. Viscount Wellington had the measure of King Joseph. The King had sent thirteen thousand men to aid Marshal Marmont, but they had been sent too late and ended up, rather like the Duke of York in the Low Countries, marching back to Madrid having arrived too late for the battle. They brought the King the news of the disaster and were already beaten before we even reached the city. The King fled north and east leaving Madrid to a victorious Viscount Wellington.

We stayed in the capital of Spain for just three weeks. That was enough time for the Spanish to occupy it and for some of our wounded to recover and then we began the long march north. When we eventually departed, Viscount Wellington left half of the army in Madrid under the command of Major General Hill for he was not convinced that the Spanish would be able to keep Marshal Soult from retaking it! The army surprised the Viscount by behaving well in Madrid and we had few incidents of drunkenness and debauchery. So it turned out that I had little to do for Madrid did not require my military prowess. I spent time in the city buying presents for Emily. Our manoeuvring and the battles had meant I had had no mail since Lisbon, and I guessed there would be a backlog waiting for me there. I decided to make up for it by spending some of my money. In this, I was aided by Captain Dunbar. Although not married he knew the sorts of things ladies liked. I knew nothing of that world and with Lieutenant Hogg and Sergeant Sharp, we spent each sunny day wandering the markets and shops and enjoying good food and wine.

It was as we were heading north to Segovia that Colonel Cummings came to speak to me as we rode on a dusty, baking road. "Jack Jones has asked if he can retire. This campaign has been one too many and, between the two of us, I think he wished he had gone when Colonel Fenton did. I am telling you, Major, because I know you are fond of the Sergeant Major."

"Thank you, sir. I think it is for the best."

"When we reach Segovia, I intend to let him go along with the others who are deemed unfit to travel to Burgos. They will spend the winter in Ciudad Rodrigo, and the Sergeant Major can carry on to Lisbon." I nodded for I knew there was more. "The thing is, Major, I am not happy about the old soldier making his way through the Portuguese highlands. I wondered if you could have Sergeant Sharp escort him. They are friends and Sergeant Sharp knows the language."

I beamed, "A capital idea and Sharp can take my purchases to the house I use in Lisbon." It was a perfect plan and I saw that the Colonel was relieved. I did not say that Sergeant Sharp would be even more delighted as it would allow him to spend time with Maria and Juan. When we made camp in Segovia the regiment held a party for the retiring Sergeant Major. He would be replaced by Joe Seymour who was, in my view, the right choice. We all drank too much, and Jack sat with me and Sergeant Sharp towards the end of the evening reminiscing and planning for the future.

"You know, sir, you came at just the right time for the Colonel. The de Veres of this world were trying to take the 11th and if that had happened, well, they would not have done as well as they did. I shall be glad to go home but I will miss you, sir."

"And where is home, Jack?"

"Not far from the home depot, Bury St Edmunds."

"Then I shall be able to see you again for I now live close to the Tottenham Court. After the long distances we have travelled over here that practically makes us neighbours."

That made him happy, "I should like that, sir."

"And if you cannot get a berth on a ship straight away then Sergeant Sharp will have you looked after."

Alan grinned, "Aye, Jack, you will like the house. A fine Portuguese lady left it to the Major. There are servants and everything. You shall live like a lord!"

Jack shook his head, "I am a simple man, Alan, a roof, a glass of something and my pipe are all that I need."

They left the next day. Jack was given a chit for his back pay and the Colonel and the rest of the officers made a collection. Jack would be relatively well off and we all knew that Colonel Fenton would make arrangements too. It was both a sad and a happy moment as we turned north to head for Burgos.

It turned into a depressing day when Spanish riders brought us the unwelcome news that the French, under General Clausel, had retaken Valladolid. Our brief holiday was over, and we were going back to war. While we gathered our four divisions at Arevalo, I was sent forward, on my own, to scout out the enemy positions. I reached the southern side of Valladolid and found the French arrayed for battle. I estimated that they had something like thirty thousand men but as I couldn't see into the city that may have been an underestimation. We had five thousand more men than the French and when I reported to Viscount Wellington, he seemed eager to bring the French to battle. We reached the city on the sixth of September but the French retreated. Viscount Wellington had his Heavy Brigade but had only retained one regiment of Light Horse, the 11th. It meant that Colonel Cummings commanded the only unit which could keep in touch with the French.

General Clausel had had the weight of the French expectations dropped on to his shoulders but he acquitted himself well. As we hurried north, towards Burgos, he sprang a trap and the 11th paid the price for their isolation. I was caught out every bit as much as Colonel Cummings. We saw the rearguard a mile up the road and we kept that same distance. It was as we passed through a wooded area to the west of the road that two regiments of Dragoons suddenly opened fire. Had the range been any closer then at least a quarter of the regiment would have been hit. As it was, saddles were emptied before the loaded carbines could be fired. I lifted my Baker and fired at the green uniforms just as Colonel Cummings shouted, "Fire!" and a ragged volley enveloped the trees in smoke. He then shouted, "Dunne, sound the retreat!"

I was the last one to ride down the road. Had the Dragoons bothered to chase us then they could have killed a few more but they had achieved their aim. General Clausel could now move north without us snapping at his heels. The ambush unnerved Sir Arthur and we moved north at a slower pace after that. We reached Burgos on the nineteenth of September. The 1st Division and Pack's Brigade of Portuguese sealed off the town which we took without a shot being fired. The castle, however, was another matter for it was an ancient fortress which had been strengthened by the French. As we had learned at Badajoz and Ciudad Rodrigo, the French knew how to defend.

Viscount Wellington sent back the 11th to Ciudad Rodrigo. The ambush had thinned their ranks and they were not needed. He was keenly aware that grazing would soon be a problem and so I said farewell to my old regiment. Without Sharp and the regiment, I felt lonely and I did not relish a siege. While the few siege guns we had were brought into position to attack the small fort of San Miguel, which guarded one side to the castle, we surrounded the town. Sir Richard Fletcher was still recovering from his wound and was back in England. Viscount Wellington needed him. Sir Arthur's aides had little to do except watch, as the Portuguese who would attack prepared their ladders and other equipment.

Captain Dunbar had learned a great deal in this campaign. "You know, Major, the men who know how to attack a fortress, the ones who stormed Ciudad Rodrigo and Badajoz are not here."

I nodded, gloomily, "I know."

Lieutenant Hogg asked, "What difference does that make? The 1st is a good division!"

"It is the experience of storming breaches, Lieutenant, which they lack. The ones who stormed Badajoz learned how to do it under fire. I fear that the ones who attack now will have to learn those lessons and they cost soldiers."

The start of the attack was a disaster. For some reason, Sir Arthur did not bother with artillery and when the Portuguese attacked the fort of San Miguel, they were cut down in great numbers. When they reached the walls, their ladders were too short! As I recalled that had been true at Badajoz too where Major Ridge had died. As the main attack failed and men fled, the French garrison turned their guns on them. It would have been a total disaster if it had not been for the Portuguese light companies who found an unguarded door and managed to break in driving the garrison from them. We had taken the fort but it had cost us four hundred and twenty-one men killed and wounded. The sixty prisoners and one hundred and ninety men we had killed or wounded did not compensate for it. Before our siege guns could be placed in the fort, we lost even more men and, once more, we missed Sir Richard Fletcher!

While the work on the batteries continued, Viscount Wellington tried an attack on the south-west wall. He had discovered that men could get within sixty feet of the walls undetected. This time the attack was a total failure with nothing to mitigate the losses. We learned from the prisoners we had taken when we had captured Fort Miguel that the commander of the garrison was Brigadier General Dubreton, and we were learning that he was every bit as good as General Phillipon had been. Although there were only twenty-nine casualties, morale was plummeting.

I sat, after the officers who had led the attack reported to him, with Sir Arthur. "Am I losing my touch, Matthews?" I knew it was a rhetorical question and I did not answer. "I hate these damned sieges and yet I cannot leave this castle across my line of retreat."

"My Lord, if you are thinking of retreating then why not do so now?"

He gave me a hawk-like look, "Do you not know me at all, Matthews? Until I am faced by overwhelmingly superior numbers then we will fight on. I will revert to the normal methods of conducting a siege. We will dig trenches and try a mine. When the guns reduce the walls then we shall see." He leaned back, "However, if we have not done so by November then I may well have to return to Ciudad Rodrigo with my tail between my legs!" This was not the same man who had tossed a chicken leg over his shoulder and raced across a battlefield to give orders!

The first mine failed because the miners underestimated the distance they had to dig, and the mine exploded short of the target. When the men attacked, they were easily defeated and so, a few days later, a second mine began. By the fourth of October, we had the men ready for an attack and the mine was detonated bringing down one hundred feet of the wall. My old friends, the 24th Foot made the attack and we took the outer walls. The mood in our camp rose when that happened. The next day Viscount Wellington went with his aides to inspect the work which was beginning on the first sap on the inner wall.

It was five in the afternoon when we went to inspect the works. I had learned how engineers worked. My time with Sir Richard Fletcher had not been wasted and although Viscount Wellington appeared disappointed, I could see that the miners and engineers had worked hard. The troops who had laboured were preparing to leave the works. After Badajoz and Ciudad Rodrigo, we had learned our lessons and no tools were left at the works overnight. Each man would take his own tools to and from the earthworks. It was then that the French launched a sortie. The French General had observed the work for the last two days and the British Army was predictable. The French Light infantry poured out and they opened fire. Miners, engineers and soldiers were struck but then the French spied us and, seeing Sir Arthur, made straight for us. We were almost totally isolated.

I reacted first, "Lieutenant Hogg, get Sir Arthur to safety!" Even as he tried to do so Lieutenant Hogg slipped and fell. He had hurt something. "Captain Dunbar, get the General out of here! I will get Lieutenant Hogg."

"Come on, my Lord." Sir Arthur had his sword drawn but he nodded his agreement.

"Lieutenant, draw your pistol!" I was glad now that I had given my pistols to the Lieutenant. I drew my own pistol and sword. I saw the muzzle flash and felt the musket ball hit my shoulder, but I still managed to fire my pistol before it dropped from my hand. I could not feel my fingers. A bayonet came towards me and then I saw the flash from Lieutenant Hogg's pistol and the musket ball drove into the man's skull. He fired a second and I put my right arm down to help him to his feet.

"Look out, sir!"

The bayonet sliced into the fleshy part of my leg. The pain was excruciating. I whirled around with my sword and it bit into the nose and skull of the light infantryman. It was obvious I could not help the Lieutenant. "Lieutenant, pull yourself clear and I will try to buy you some time. From the angle of his leg, he had broken his ankle and would not be able to walk. I realised that the French had cleared most of the miners and soldiers away and many were taking discarded picks and shovels. My wounded leg meant that I would only be able to move back slowly. All the French needed to do was aim their muskets and fire and I was a dead man. Luckily for me most had fired their Charleville muskets and not reloaded. Instead, they came at me with their bayonets. I could not use my left arm nor my left leg. Although I could not feel my fingers, I could swing my left arm and I swung it, clumsily at one bayonet while I riposted a second. The bayonet on my left sliced through my jacket and scored a bloody line along my arm. I remembered the brave Captain Mackay who had endured twenty-two bayonet wounds and survived. So far, I had a mere two. After riposting the bayonet, I lunged, and it sank into the light infantryman's side. As his fellow pulled back his arm for the coup de grace, I swung my heavy sword and the edge sliced through his tunic and arm to grate along his upper arm. He dropped the musket and seeing that Lieutenant Hogg had crawled twenty yards from me I tried to step back. It was not easy as there was spoil from the earthworks which threatened to trip me.

I heard a shout and a bugle from behind me and knew that help was on its way, but a handful of light infantrymen seemed intent on ending the life of the solitary officer who appeared to be able to withstand any number of wounds. Then they did what I would have done in the same circumstances. The five of them all ran at me at once. I would die but at least I would take some with me. The earthworks came to my aid and one stumbled, leaving one isolated and I lunged at him. His bayonet almost deflected my blade, but my father had trained me well and my sword slid over the barrel and sliced through his fingers severing two of them. A bayonet slid towards my left side and I could do nothing about it except try to move my hips out of the way. I almost succeeded but the bayonet grated off my hip bone and I felt the most agonising pain. Then there was a crack from behind me as Lieutenant Hogg, sitting on a barrel fired his pistol and killed the man who was trying to end my life. Then four of the 24th Foot came hurtling past me and they hacked and chopped into the light infantrymen with their bayonets. It was just in time for the puddling blood at my feet told me that I had been hurt.

I turned and said, "Thank you, Lieutenant. That was a fine shot, but I don't..." That was as far as I got for all went black.

Epilogue

When I woke, I was looking up at a doctor, a medical orderly and Captain Dunbar. John looked relieved. "You had us worried, Major. It has been two days since you were brought in."

An orderly poured some tea down my throat, "Get that down your throat before you try to talk sir."

The hot sweet tea tasted delicious and I drank it in one. He poured me another while Captain Dunbar looked on anxiously. "How is Lieutenant Hogg?"

John shook his head, "You are close to death and you ask about the Lieutenant! He is as well as can be expected. He was sent back to Ciudad with a broken ankle and he will be walking again in a couple of months. He will enjoy the rest and reflect that he should watch where he walks in future!"

I nodded, "And me, doctor, will I be on my feet in a month or two?"

"I am afraid it is back to England for you. The musket ball drove some fibres into your shoulder, and we had to remove some flesh to prevent infection. You were lucky with the bayonet wounds, but they grated into bones and I am not certain of the effect; you may or may not be able to walk again but the time being you will be carried everywhere. Viscount Wellington is also concerned, and you are to be taken to Lisbon and thence to England. A friend of his is a surgeon and I have a letter for you to take to him. The Viscount wishes you to be examined. You are off to England. If you are fit for service, then it will not be this year. We have an ambulance waiting to take you back." He smiled, "Ironically, it is one we captured from the French at Salamanca. You will travel in comfort and Jackson here will accompany you."

I closed my eyes. I would see Emily again, but would she have to live with a cripple?

The next day Sir Arthur and Captain Dunbar came to see me before I left. I had insisted that Donna return with me and she was tied to the ambulance by Private Jackson. Viscount Wellington said, "You may not need that again, Major, but I hope that you do. I am now left with just Dunbar here who will have to do the work of four men!"

John smiled, "And your boots are hard enough to fill as it is, Major."

I nodded, "Thank you for the letter of introduction, my Lord."

"It was the least I could do. Damn sieges. You might have been right, Matthews. Perhaps I should have walked away but we shall throw the dice one more time. Take care but get back here as soon as you can. Come along, Captain Dunbar, let us see how the miners are progressing.

Despite the efforts of Jackson and the ambulance they had found for me the journey to Ciudad Rodrigo was agony and I wondered how I would manage all the way to Lisbon. Jackson had some laudanum which helped but I did not want to become dependent upon it. It was at Ciudad Rodrigo that Sergeant Sharp caught up with me and the relief that brought was immeasurable. He and Jackson got on immediately and Sharp and he managed to make the ambulance a little more comfortable at the fortress. Before we left, he managed to acquire some brandy and some port. They numbed my pain by frequent doses. In my few moments of lucidity, when I was not in great pain, he told me of his journey. "Jack is still in the house sir. There are no transports to be had. This letter from Sir Arthur will guarantee us a berth but not the Sergeant Major."

I nodded, "Then we recruit him as another nurse for me. He can be Jackson's assistant on the voyage home."

Sharp looked sheepishly at me, "Sir, we need berths for two more passengers too." I was a little groggy as Jackson had just given me my daily dose of laudanum. I gave Sharp a blank look. "Maria, sir, and Juan." He smiled, "The last couple of days in Lisbon we became, well close, if you catch my drift. She said she would marry me and I can't leave her here, can I sir?"

I smiled, "Congratulations and I am sure that there will be a place for her at Matthew's Farm!"

The relief was obvious as he gushed forth on his plans for the future. I wondered how long Alan would remain a soldier. Was this fate? Were my wounds enough to keep me from the battlefield?

And so, we reached Lisbon and picked up Jones and the presents I had bought for my wife. We left our horses in the capable hands of the Portuguese horse master and went to the port and took Maria and Juan with us. The English harbourmaster employed by the Navy was apologetic but pointed out that no ships were sailing for England. He gestured towards the harbour which was filled with the ships of the Mediterranean and the solitary sloop, "That mail packet, *'Black Prince'* is the only one and even the Viscount's letter won't get you a berth on her!"

Sergeant Sharp grinned and said, "Would you like a one-pound wager on that, sir?"

The harbourmaster said, "Aye, and here is my coin!" Jackson was looking bemusedly when Sharp happily matched the bet. He strode off and the harbourmaster shook his head, "I am sorry Major, but this is the easiest pound I have ever earned. I would love to be wrong, however, others have tried to get a berth on that one, but the captain is a law unto himself!"

At that moment I saw Sharp returning, not only with Jonathan Teer but also four of his crew. He shook his head and said, "What you are doing over here letting the French make a pincushion of you when you have a lovely wife at home is beyond me! Come on, let us see if we can break the record for getting to London and this doctor."

Scooping up the coins Sharp said, "I told you!"

The harbourmaster laughed, "Well, it is a good cause. Good luck to you, Major."

Carried aboard by his crew I felt relief and, as we left on the next tide, I knew that I would get home. The question on my mind was, could the doctor help me, for the pain in my hip was becoming worse? We left Lisbon with dark seas and skies and they matched my mood. All the euphoria of Salamanca and Garcia Hernandez had gone for I knew that without Sir Richard, Viscount Wellington would not take Burgos and that meant a retreat back to Portugal. All that we had won we would soon lose and I would have to return to help Sir Arthur, for I owed it to the dead!

The End

Glossary

Fictional characters are in italics

Cesar Alpini- Robbie's cousin and the head of the Sicilian branch of the family
Sergeant Alan Sharp- Robbie's servant
Caçadores - Portuguese light infantry
Major Robbie (Macgregor) Matthews-illegitimate son of the *Count of Breteuil*
Colonel James Selkirk- War department and spymaster to Sir Arthur
Colpack-fur hat worn by the guards and elite companies
Crack- from the Irish 'craich', good fun, enjoyable
Crows' feet- metal spikes like a caltrop
Fascines- bundles of wood used to shore up trenches and earthworks
Gabions- barrels filled with earth
Joe Seymour- Corporal and then Sergeant 11th Light Dragoons
Joseph Fouché- Napoleon's Chief of Police and Spy catcher
Lieutenant Commander Jonathan Teer- Commander of the Black Prince
Old moustache- French slang for a veteran
Middy- Midshipman (slang)
musketoon- Cavalry musket
Paget Carbine- Light Cavalry weapon
pichet- a small jug for wine in France
Pompey- naval slang for Portsmouth
Prefeito – Portuguese official
Roast Beef- French slang for British soldiers
Rooking- cheating a customer
Snotty- naval slang for a raw lieutenant
Tarleton Helmet- Headgear worn by light cavalry until 1812
Windage- the gap between the ball and the wall of the cannon which means the ball does not fire true.

Historical note

The 11th Light Dragoons were a real regiment. However, I have used them in a fictitious manner. They act and fight as real Light Dragoons. The battles in which they fight were real battles with real Light Dragoons present- just not the 11th.

The deaths of Black Bob, General Marchant and the others occurred exactly as I wrote it. Captain Mackay, Major Ridge and the others, both French and English, mentioned in the sieges, as well as the battles, existed, and I have tried to accurately report their actions. The chicken leg incident and the words to General Alava are, allegedly, true. The regiments, the 11th apart, fought as I have described.

The year which began with Ciudad Rodrigo and ended with the failed siege of Burgos is almost unbelievable. There are so many what-ifs. Had the Spanish held the bridge over the Tormes then Clausel, who was a very able general, could have been captured and would not have been able to defend Burgos. The incident where Wellington was charged by the 12th Dragoons is also true and came from a mistaken order from a staff officer. The battles of Salamanca happened the way I wrote them. The French divisions were over extended and General Le Marchant's heavy cavalry destroyed three squares- a rare feat. A couple of eagles were also taken in this battle.

I realise that it is confusing to my reader to have German cavalry fighting on both sides but that was the reality of the Peninsula War.

I have used Robbie Matthews to represent a number of real people. Wellington famously used officers riding good horses to scout out the French and to outrun them. I have combined them in Robbie to make a better narrative. The guerrillas played a major part in the war. Despatch riders were intercepted and despatches read.

The books I used for reference were:
- Badajoz 1812 -Fletcher and Younghusband
- Bussaco 1810-Chartrand and Courcelle
- Fuentes de Oñoro 1811-Chartrand and Courcelle
- Napoleon's Line Chasseurs- Bukhari/MacBride
- Napoleon's War in Spain- Lachouque, Tranie, Carmigniani
- The Napoleonic Source Book- Philip Haythornthwaite,
- Wellington's Military Machine- Philip J Haythornthwaite
- The Peninsular War- Roger Parkinson

- Military Dress of the Peninsular War 1808-1814
- The History of the Napoleonic Wars-Richard Holmes
- The Lines of Torre Vedras 1809-1811-Fletcher and Younghusband
- The Greenhill Napoleonic Wars Data book- Digby Smith,
- The Napoleonic Wars Vol 1 & 2- Liliane and Fred Funcken
- The Napoleonic Wars- Michael Glover
- Napoleonic Heavy Cavalry and Dragoon tactics-Haythornthwaite and Hook
- Talavera 1809-Chartrand and Turner
- Salamanca 1812- Fletcher and Younghusband
- Wellington's Regiments- Ian Fletcher.
- Wellington's Light Cavalry- Bryan Fosten
- Wellington's Heavy Cavalry- Bryan Fosten
- Wellington as Military Commander- Michael Glover

Bloody Badajoz

Other books by Griff Hosker

If you enjoyed reading this book, then why not read another one by the author?

Ancient History

The Sword of Cartimandua Series
(Germania and Britannia 50 A.D. – 128 A.D.)
Ulpius Felix- Roman Warrior (prequel)
The Sword of Cartimandua
The Horse Warriors
Invasion Caledonia
Roman Retreat
Revolt of the Red Witch
Druid's Gold
Trajan's Hunters
The Last Frontier
Hero of Rome
Roman Hawk
Roman Treachery
Roman Wall
Roman Courage

The Wolf Warrior series
(Britain in the late 6th Century)
Saxon Dawn
Saxon Revenge
Saxon England
Saxon Blood
Saxon Slayer
Saxon Slaughter
Saxon Bane
Saxon Fall: Rise of the Warlord
Saxon Throne
Saxon Sword

Medieval History

The Dragon Heart Series

Bloody Badajoz

Viking Slave
Viking Warrior
Viking Jarl
Viking Kingdom
Viking Wolf
Viking War
Viking Sword
Viking Wrath
Viking Raid
Viking Legend
Viking Vengeance
Viking Dragon
Viking Treasure
Viking Enemy
Viking Witch
Viking Blood
Viking Weregeld
Viking Storm
Viking Warband
Viking Shadow
Viking Legacy
Viking Clan
Viking Bravery

The Norman Genesis Series
Hrolf the Viking
Horseman
The Battle for a Home
Revenge of the Franks
The Land of the Northmen
Ragnvald Hrolfsson
Brothers in Blood
Lord of Rouen
Drekar in the Seine
Duke of Normandy
The Duke and the King

New World Series
Blood on the Blade
Across the Seas
The Savage Wilderness
The Bear and the Wolf

The Reconquista Chronicles
Castilian Knight
El Campeador

The Aelfraed Series
(Britain and Byzantium 1050 A.D. - 1085 A.D.)
Housecarl
Outlaw
Varangian

**The Anarchy Series England
1120-1180**
English Knight
Knight of the Empress
Northern Knight
Baron of the North
Earl
King Henry's Champion
The King is Dead
Warlord of the North
Enemy at the Gate
The Fallen Crown
Warlord's War
Kingmaker
Henry II
Crusader
The Welsh Marches
Irish War
Poisonous Plots
The Princes' Revolt
Earl Marshal

**Border Knight
1182-1300**
Sword for Hire
Return of the Knight
Baron's War
Magna Carta
Welsh Wars
Henry III
The Bloody Border

Bloody Badajoz

Baron's Crusade
Sentinel of the North

Lord Edward's Archer
Lord Edward's Archer
King in Waiting

**Struggle for a Crown
1360- 1485**
Blood on the Crown
To Murder A King
The Throne
King Henry IV
The Road to Agincourt

Short stories

Tales of the Sword

Modern History

The Napoleonic Horseman Series
Chasseur a Cheval
Napoleon's Guard
British Light Dragoon
Soldier Spy
1808: The Road to Coruña
Talavera
The Lines of Torres Vedras
Bloody Badajoz

The Lucky Jack American Civil War series
Rebel Raiders
Confederate Rangers
The Road to Gettysburg

The British Ace Series
1914
1915 Fokker Scourge
1916 Angels over the Somme
1917 Eagles Fall

Bloody Badajoz

1918 We will remember them
From Arctic Snow to Desert Sand
Wings over Persia

Combined Operations series
1940-1945
Commando
Raider
Behind Enemy Lines
Dieppe
Toehold in Europe
Sword Beach
Breakout
The Battle for Antwerp
King Tiger
Beyond the Rhine
Korea
Korean Winter

Other Books
Great Granny's Ghost (Aimed at 9-14-year-old young people)

For more information on all of the books then please visit the author's web site at www.griffhosker.com where there is a link to contact him or visit his Facebook page: GriffHosker at Sword Books

204